THE
LAUGHING
POLICEMAN

MAJ SJÖWALL • PER WAHLÖÖ

Translated from the Swedish
by Alan Blair

VINTAGE BOOKS
A Division of Random House
New York

Library of Congress Cataloging in Publication Data

Sjöwall, Maj, 1935-
   The laughing policeman.

   Translation of Den skrattande polisen.
   I.   Wahlöö, Per, 1926-1975, joint author.   II.   Title.
[PZ4.S61953Lau6]   [PT9876.29.J63]   839.7'3'74   76-43000
ISBN 0-394-72341-4

1

On the evening of the thirteenth of November it was pouring in Stockholm. Martin Beck and Kollberg sat over a game of chess in the latter's apartment not far from the subway station of Skärmarbrink in the southern suburbs. Both were off duty insomuch as nothing special had happened during the last few days.

Martin Beck was very bad at chess but played all the same. Kollberg had a daughter who was just over two months old. On this particular evening he was forced to baby-sit, and Martin Beck on the other hand had no wish to go home before it was absolutely necessary. The weather was abominable. Driving curtains of rain swept over the rooftops, pattering against the windows, and the streets lay almost deserted; the few people to be seen evidently had urgent reasons to be out on such a night.

Outside the American embassy on Strandvägen and along the streets leading to it, 412 policemen were struggling with about twice as many demonstrators. The police were equipped with tear gas bombs, pistols, whips, batons, cars, motorcycles, shortwave radios, battery megaphones, riot dogs and hysterical horses. The demonstrators were armed with a letter and cardboard signs, which grew more and more sodden in the pelting rain. It was difficult to regard them as a homogeneous group, for the crowd comprised every possible kind of person, from thirteen-year-old schoolgirls in jeans and duffel coats and dead-serious political students to agitators and professional troublemakers, and at least one eighty-five-year-old woman artist with a beret and a blue silk umbrella. Some strong common motive had induced them to defy both the rain and whatever else was in store. The police, on the other hand, by no means comprised the force's élite. They had been mustered from every available precinct in town, but every policeman who knew a doctor or was good at dodging had managed to escape this unpleasant assignment. There remained those who knew what they were doing and liked it, and those who were considered cocky and who were far too young and inexperienced to try and get out of it; besides, they hadn't a clue as to what they were doing or why they were doing it. The horses reared up, chewing their bits, and the police fingered their holsters and made charge after charge with their batons. A small girl was bearing a sign with the memorable text: DO YOUR DUTY! KEEP FUCKING AND MAKE MORE POLICE! Three 190-pound patrolmen flung themselves at her, tore the sign to pieces and dragged her into a squad car, where they twisted her arms and pawed her breasts. She had turned thirteen on this very day and had not yet developed any.

Altogether more than fifty persons were seized. Many were bleeding. Some were celebrities, who were not above writing to the papers or complaining on the radio and television. At the sight of them, the sergeants on duty at the local police stations had a fit of the shivers and showed them the door with apologetic smiles and stiff bows. Others were less well treated during the inevitable questioning. A mounted policeman had been hit on the head by an empty bottle and someone must have thrown it.

The operation was in the charge of a high-ranking police officer trained at a military school. He was considered an expert on keeping order and he regarded with satisfaction the utter chaos he had managed to achieve.

In the apartment at Skärmarbrink, Kollberg gathered up the chessmen, jumbled them into the wooden box and shut the sliding lid with a smack. His wife had come home from her evening course and gone straight to bed.

"You'll never learn this," Kollberg said plaintively.

"They say you need a special gift for it," Martin Beck replied gloomily. "Chess sense I think it's called."

Kollberg changed the subject.

"I bet there's a helluva to-do at Strandvägen this evening," he said.

"I expect so. What's it all about?"

"They were going to hand a letter over to the ambassador," Kollberg said. "A letter. Why don't they send it by mail?"

"It wouldn't cause so much fuss."

"No, but all the same, it's so stupid it makes you ashamed."

"Yes," Martin Beck agreed.

He had put on his hat and coat and was about to go. Kollberg got up quickly.

"I'll come with you," he said.

"Whatever for?"

"Oh, to stroll around a little."

"In this weather?"

"I like rain," Kollberg said, climbing into his dark-blue poplin coat.

"Isn't it enough for me to have a cold?" Martin Beck said.

Martin Beck and Kollberg were policemen. They belonged to the homicide squad. For the moment they had nothing special to do and could, with relatively clear consciences, consider themselves free.

Downtown no policemen were to be seen in the streets. The old lady outside the central station waited in vain for a patrolman to come up to her, salute, and smilingly help her across the street. A person who had just smashed the glass of a showcase with a brick had no need to worry that the rising and falling wail from a patrol car would suddenly interrupt his doings.

The police were busy.

A week earlier the police commissioner had said in a public statement that many of the regular duties of the police would have to be neglected because they were obliged to protect the American ambassador against letters and other things from people who disliked Lyndon Johnson and the war in Vietnam.

Detective Inspector Lennart Kollberg didn't like Lyndon Johnson and the war in Vietnam either, but he did like strolling about the city when it was raining.

At eleven o'clock in the evening it was still raining and the demonstration could be regarded as broken up.

At the same time eight murders and one attempted murder were committed in Stockholm.

2

Rain, he thought, looking out of the window dejectedly. November darkness and rain, cold and pelting. A forerunner of the approaching winter. Soon it would start to snow.

Nothing in town was very attractive just now, especially not this street with its bare trees and large, shabby apartment houses. A bleak esplanade, misdirected and wrongly planned from the outset. It led nowhere in particular and never had, it was just there, a dreary reminder of some grandiose city plan, begun long ago but never finished. There were no lighted shop windows and no people on the sidewalks. Only big, leafless trees and street lamps, whose cold white light was reflected by puddles and wet car roofs.

He had trudged about so long in the rain that his hair and the legs of his pants were sopping wet, and now he felt the moisture along his shins and right down his neck to the shoulder blades, cold and trickling.

He undid the two top buttons of his raincoat, stuck his right hand inside his jacket and fingered the butt of the pistol. It, too, felt cold and clammy.

At the touch, an involuntary shudder passed through the man in the dark-blue poplin raincoat and he tried to think of something else. For instance of the hotel balcony at Andraitz, where he had spent his vacation five months earlier. Of the heavy, motionless heat and of the bright sunshine over the quayside and the fishing boats and of the limitless, deep-blue sky above the mountain ridge on the other side of the bay.

Then he thought that it was probably raining there too at this time of year and that there was no central heating in the houses, only open fireplaces.

And that he was no longer in the same street as before and would soon be forced out into the rain again.

4

He heard someone behind him on the stairs and knew that it was the person who had got on outside Ahléns department store on Klarabergsgatan in the center of the city twelve stops before.

Rain, he thought. I don't like it. In fact I hate it. I wonder when I'll be promoted. What am I doing here anyway and why aren't I at home in bed with . . .

And that was the last he thought.

The bus was a red doubledecker with cream-colored top and gray roof. It was of the type Leyland Atlantean and built in England, but constructed for the Swedish right-hand traffic, introduced two months before. On this particular evening it was plying on route 47 in Stockholm, between Bellmansro at Djurgården and Karlberg, and vice versa. Now it was heading northwest and approaching the terminus on Norra Stationsgatan, situated only a few yards from the city limits between Stockholm and Solna.

Solna is a suburb of Stockholm and functions as an independent municipal administrative unit, even if the boundary between the two cities can only be seen as a dotted line on the map.

It was big, this red bus; over 36 feet long and nearly 15 feet high. It weighed more than 15 tons. The headlights were on and it looked warm and cozy with its misty windows, as it droned along deserted Karlbergsvägen between the lines of leafless trees. Then it turned right into Norrbackagatan and the sound of the engine was fainter on the long slope down to Norra Stationsgatan. The rain beat against the roof and windows, and the wheels flung up hissing cascades of water as it glided downward, heavily and implacably.

The hill ended where the street did. The bus was to turn at an angle of 30 degrees, onto Norra Stationsgatan, and then it had only some 300 yards left to the end of the line.

The only person to observe the vehicle at this moment was a man who stood flattened against a house wall over 150 yards farther up Norrbackagatan. He was a burglar who was about to smash a window. He noticed the bus because he wanted it out of the way and had waited for it to pass.

He saw it slow down at the corner and begin to turn left with its side lights blinking. Then it was out of sight. The rain pelted down harder than ever. The man raised his hand and smashed the pane.

What he did not see was that the turn was never completed.

The red doubledecker bus seemed to stop for a moment in the middle of the turn. Then it drove straight across the street, climbed the sidewalk and burrowed halfway through the wire fence separating Norra Stationsgatan from the desolate freight yard on the other side.

Then it pulled up.

The engine died but the headlights were still on, and so was the lighting inside.

The misty windows went on gleaming cozily in the dark and cold.

And the rain lashed against the metal roof.

The time was three minutes past eleven on the evening of the thirteenth of November, 1967.

In Stockholm.

3

Kristiansson and Kvant were radio patrol policemen in Solna.

During their not-very-eventful careers they had picked up thousands of drunks and dozens of thieves, and once they had presumably saved the life of a six-year-old girl by seizing a notorious sex maniac who was just about to assault and murder her. This had happened less than five months ago, and although it was a fluke it constituted a feat which they intended to live on for a long time.

On this particular evening they had not picked up anything at all, apart from a glass of beer each; as this was perhaps against the rules, it had better be ignored.

Just before ten thirty they got a call on the radio and drove to an address at Kapellgatan in the suburb of Huvudsta, where someone had found a lifeless figure lying on the front steps. It took them only three minutes to drive there.

Sure enough, sprawling in front of the street door lay a human being in frayed black pants, down-at-heel shoes and a shabby pepper-and-salt overcoat. In the lighted hallway inside stood an elderly woman in slippers and dressing gown. She was evidently the one who had complained. She gesticulated at them through the glass door, then opened it a few inches, stuck her arm through the crack and pointed demandingly to the motionless form.

"A-ha, and what's all this?" Kristiansson said.

Kvant bent down and sniffed.

"Out cold," he said with deeply-felt distaste. "Give us a hand, Kalle."

"Wait a second," Kristiansson said.

"Eh?"

"Do you know this man, madam?" Kristiansson asked more or less politely.

"I should say I do."

"Where does he live?"

The woman pointed to a door three yards farther inside the hall.

"There," she said. "He fell asleep while he was trying to unlock the door."

"Oh yes, he has the keys in his hand," Kristiansson said, scratching his head. "Does he live alone?"

"Who could live with an old bastard like that?" the lady said.

"What are you going to do?" Kvant asked suspiciously.

Kristiansson didn't answer. Bending down, he took the keys from the sleeper's hand. Then he jerked the drunk to his feet with a grip that denoted many years' practice, pushed open the front door with his knee and dragged the man toward the apartment. The woman stood on one side and Kvant remained on the outer steps. Both watched the scene with passive disapproval.

Kristiansson unlocked the door, switched on the light in the room and pulled off the man's wet overcoat. The drunk lurched, collapsed on to the bed and said, "Thanksh, Miss."

Then he turned over on his side and fell asleep. Kristiansson laid the keys on a kitchen chair beside the bed, put out the light, shut the door and went back to the car.

"Good night, madam," he said.

The woman stared at him with pursed lips, tossed her head and disappeared.

Kristiansson did not act like this from love of his fellow humans, but because he was lazy.

None knew this better than Kvant. While they were still serving as ordinary patrolmen on the beat in Malmö, he had many a time seen Kristiansson lead drunks along the street and even across bridges in order to get them into the next precinct.

Kvant sat at the wheel. He switched on the ignition and said sourly, "Siv oftentimes says I'm lazy. She should see you."

Siv was Kvant's wife and also his dearest and often sole subject of conversation.

"Why should I get puked on for nothing?" Kristiansson said philosophically.

Kristiansson and Kvant were similar in build and appearance. Both were 6 feet 1 inch tall, fair, broad-shouldered and blue-eyed. But they had widely different temperaments and didn't always see eye to eye. This was one of the questions upon which they were not agreed.

Kvant was incorruptible. He never compromised over things he saw, but on the other hand he was an expert at seeing as little as possible.

He drove slowly, in glum silence, following a twisting route from Huvudsta that led past the Police Training College, then through an area of communal garden plots, past the railroad museum, the National Bacteriological Laboratory, the School for the Blind, and then zigzag through the extensive university district with its various institutions, finally emerging via the railroad administration buildings on to Tomtebodavägen.

It was a brilliantly thought-out course, leading through areas which were almost guaranteed empty of people. They met not a single car the whole way and saw only two living creatures, first a cat and then another cat.

When they reached the end of Tomtebodavägen, Kvant stopped the car with the radiator one yard from the Stockholm city limit and let the engine idle while he considered how to arrange the rest of their shift.

I wonder if you've got the cheek to turn around and drive back the same way, Kristiansson thought. Aloud he said, "Can you lend me 10 kronor?"

Kvant nodded, took his wallet out of his breast pocket and handed the note to his colleague without even a glance at him. At the same instant he made a quick decision. If he crossed the city limits and followed Norra Stationsgatan for some five hundred yards in a north-easterly direction they would only need to be in Stockholm for two minutes. Then he could turn in to Eugeniavägen, drive across the hospital area and continue through Haga Park and along by the Northern Cemetery, finishing up finally at police headquarters. By that time their shift would be over and the chance of seeing anyone on the way should be infinitesimal.

The car drove into Stockholm and turned left onto Norra Stationsgatan.

Kristiansson tucked the 10 kronor into his pocket and yawned. Then he peered out into the pouring rain and said, "Over there, running this way's a bastard."

Kristiansson and Kvant were from Skåne, in the far South, and their sense of word order left much to be desired.

"He has a dog, too," Kristiansson said. "And he's waving at us."

"It's not my table," Kvant said.

The man with the dog, an absurdly small dog which he practically dragged after him through the puddles, rushed out into the road and planted himself right in front of the car.

"God damn!" Kvant swore, jamming on the brakes.

He wound the side window down and roared, "What do you mean by running out into the road like that?"

"There's . . . there's a bus over there," the man gasped out, pointing along the street.

"So what?" Kvant said rudely. "And how can you treat the dog like that? A poor dumb animal?"

"There's . . . there's been an accident."

"All right, we'll look into it," Kvant said impatiently. "Move aside."

He drove on.

"And don't do that again!" he shouted over his shoulder.

Kristiansson stared through the rain.

"Yes," he said resignedly. "A bus has driven off the road. One of those doubledeckers."

"And the lights are on," Kvant said. "And the door in front is open. Hop out and take a look, Kalle."

He pulled up at an angle behind the bus. Kristiansson opened the door, straightened his shoulder belt automatically and said to himself, "A-ha, and what's all this?"

Like Kvant, he was dressed in boots and leather jacket with shiny buttons and carried a baton and pistol at his belt.

Kvant remained sitting in the car, watching Kristiansson, who moved leisurely toward the open front door of the bus.

Kvant saw him grasp the rail and lazily heave himself up onto the step to peer into the bus. Then he gave a start and crouched down quickly, while his right hand flew to the pistol holster.

Kvant reacted swiftly. It took him only a second to switch on the red lamps, the searchlight and the orange-colored flashing light of the patrol car.

Kristiansson was still crouching down beside the bus when Kvant flung open the car door and rushed out into the downpour. All the same, Kvant had drawn and cocked his 7.65 mm. Walther and had even cast a glance at his watch.

It showed exactly thirteen minutes past eleven.

4

The first senior policeman to arrive at Norra Stationsgatan was Gunvald Larsson.

He had been sitting at his desk at police headquarters at Kungsholmen, thumbing through a dull and wordy report, very listlessly and for about the umpteenth time, while he wondered why on earth people didn't go home.

In the category of "people" he included the police commissioner, a deputy commissioner and several different superintendents and inspectors who, on account of the happily concluded riots, were trotting about the staircases and corridors. As soon as these persons thought fit to call it a day and take themselves off, he would do so himself, as fast as possible.

The phone rang. He grunted and picked up the receiver.

"Hello. Larsson."

"Radio Central here. A Solna radio patrol has found a whole bus full of dead bodies on Norra Stationsgatan."

Gunvald Larsson glanced at the electric wall clock, which showed eighteen minutes past eleven, and said, "How can a Solna radio patrol find a bus full of dead bodies in Stockholm?"

Gunvald Larsson was a detective inspector in the Stockholm homicide squad. He had a rigid disposition and was not one of the most popular members of the force.

But he never wasted any time and so he was the first one there.

He braked the car, turned up his coat collar and stepped out into the rain. He saw a red doubledecker bus standing right across the sidewalk; the front part had broken through a high wire fence. He also saw a black Plymouth with white fenders and the word POLICE in white block letters across the doors. It had its emergency lights on and in the cone of the searchlight stood two uniformed patrolmen with pistols in their hands. Both looked unnaturally pale. One of them had vomited down the front of his leather jacket and was wiping himself in embarrassment with a sodden handkerchief.

"What's the trouble?" Gunvald Larsson asked.

"There . . . there are a lot of corpses in there," said one of the policemen.

"Yes," said the other. "Yes, that's right. There are. And a lot of cartridges."

"And a man who shows signs of life."

"And a policeman."

"A policeman?" Gunvald Larsson asked.

"Yes. A C.I.D. man."

"We recognize him. He works at Västberga. On the homicide squad."

"But we don't know his name. He has a blue raincoat. And he's dead."

The two radio police both talked at once, uncertainly and quietly.

They were anything but small, but beside Gunvald Larsson they did not look very impressive.

Gunvald Larsson was 6 feet 5 inches tall and weighed nearly 220 pounds. His shoulders were as broad as those of a professional heavyweight boxer and he had huge, hairy hands. His fair hair, brushed backward, was already dripping wet.

The sound of many wailing sirens cut through the splashing of the rain. They seemed to be coming from all directions. Gunvald Larsson pricked up his ears and said, "Is this Solna?"

"Right on the city limits," Kvant replied slyly.

Gunvald Larsson cast an expressionless blue glance from Kristiansson to Kvant. Then he strode over to the bus.

"It looks like . . . like a shambles in there," Kristiansson said.

Gunvald Larsson didn't touch the bus. He stuck his head in through the open door and looked around.

"Yes," he said calmly. "So it does."

5

Martin Beck stopped in the doorway of his apartment in Bagarmossen. He took off his raincoat and shook the water off it on the landing before hanging it up and closing the door.

It was dark in the hall but he didn't bother to switch on the light. He saw a ray of light under the door of his daughter's room and he heard the radio or record player going inside. He knocked and went in.

The girl's name was Ingrid and she was sixteen. She had matured somewhat of late, and Martin Beck got on with her much better than before. She was calm, matter-of-fact and fairly intelligent, and he liked talking to her. She was in the last grade of the comprehensive school and had no difficulty with her schoolwork, without on that account being what in his day had been called a grind.

She was lying on her back in bed, reading. The record player on the bedside table was going. Not pop music but something classical, Beethoven, he guessed.

"Hello," he said. "Not asleep yet?"

He stopped, almost paralyzed by the utter futility of his words. For a moment he thought of all the trivialities that had been spoken between these walls during the last ten years.

Ingrid put down her book and shut off the record player.

"Hi, Dad. What did you say?"

He shook his head.

"Lord, how wet your legs are," the girl said. "Is it raining so hard?"

"Cats and dogs. Are Mom and Rolf asleep?"

"I think so. Mom bundled Rolf off to bed right after dinner. She said he had a cold."

Martin Beck sat down on the bed.

"Didn't he have?"

"Well, *I* thought he looked well enough. But he went to bed without any fuss. Probably in order to get off school tomorrow."

"You seem to be hard at work, anyway. What are you studying?"

"French. We've a test tomorrow. Like to quiz me?"

"Wouldn't be much use. French isn't my strong point. Go to sleep now instead."

He stood up and the girl snuggled down obediently under the quilt. He tucked her in and before he shut the door behind him he heard her whisper, "Keep your fingers crossed tomorrow."

"Good night."

He went into the kitchen in the dark and stood for a while by the window. The rain seemed to be less heavy now, but it may have been because the kitchen window was sheltered from the wind. Martin Beck wondered what had happened during the demonstration against the American embassy and whether the papers tomorrow would describe the police's behavior as clumsy and inept or as brutal and provocative. In any case the opinions would be critical. Since he was loyal to the force and had been so for as long as he could remember, Martin Beck admitted only to himself that the criticism was often justified, even if it were a bit one-sided. He thought of what Ingrid had said one evening a few weeks ago. Many of her schoolmates were politically active, taking part in meetings and demonstrations, and most of them strongly disliked the police. As a child, she had said, she could boast and be proud of the fact that her father was a policeman, but now she preferred to keep quiet about it. Not that she was ashamed, but she was often drawn into discussions in which she was expected to stand up for the entire police force. Silly, of course, but there it was.

Martin Beck went into the living room, listened at the door of his wife's bedroom and heard her light snoring. Cautiously he let down the sofa bed, switched on the wall lamp and drew the curtains. He had bought the sofa recently and moved out of the common bedroom, on the pretext that he didn't want to disturb his wife when he came home late at night. She had protested, pointing out that sometimes he worked all night and therefore must sleep in the daytime, and she didn't want him lying there making a mess of the living room. He had promised on these occasions to lie and make a mess in the bedroom; she wasn't in there much in the daytime anyway. Now he had been sleeping in the living room for the past month and liked it.

His wife's name was Inga.

Contact between them had worsened with the years, and it was a relief not to have to share a bed with her. This feeling sometimes gave him a bad conscience, but after seventeen years of marriage there didn't seem to be much he could do about it, and he had long since given up worrying over whose fault it might be.

Martin Beck stifled a coughing attack, took off his wet pants and hung them over a chair near the radiator. As he sat on the sofa pulling off his socks it crossed his mind that Kollberg's nocturnal walks in the rain might be due to the fact that his marriage, too, was slipping into boredom and routine.

Already? Kollberg had only been married for eighteen months.

Before the first sock was off he had dismissed the thought. Lennart and Gun were happy together, not a doubt of that. Besides, what business was it of his?

He got up and walked naked across the room to the bookshelf. He looked over the books for a long time before choosing one. It was written by the old English diplomat Sir Eugene Millington-Drake and was about the *Graf Spee* and the Battle of La Plata. He had bought it secondhand about a year ago but hadn't yet taken the time to read it. He crawled down into bed, coughed guiltily, opened the book and found he had no cigarettes. One of the advantages of the sofa bed was that he could now smoke in bed without complications.

He got up again, fetched a damp and flattened pack of Floridas out of his raincoat pocket, laid out the cigarettes to dry on the bedside table and lighted the one that seemed most likely to burn. He had the cigarette between his teeth and one leg in bed when the telephone rang.

The telephone was out in the hall. Six months ago he had ordered an extra jack to be installed in the living room, but knowing the normal working speed of the Telephone Service, he imagined he'd be lucky if he had to wait only another six months before the jack was installed.

He strode quickly across the floor and lifted the receiver before the second ring had finished.

"Beck."

"Superintendent Beck?"

He didn't recognize the voice at the other end.

"Yes, speaking."

"This is Radio Central. Several passengers have been found shot dead in a bus on route 47 near the end of the line on Norra Stationsgatan. You're asked to go there at once."

Martin Beck's first thought was that he was a victim of a practical joke or that some antagonist was trying to trick him to go out into the rain just to give him trouble.

"Who gave you the message?" he asked.

"Hansson from the Fifth. Superintendent Hammar has already been notified."

"How many dead?"

"They're not sure yet. Six at least."

"Anyone arrested?"

"Not as far as I know."

Martin Beck thought: I'll pick up Kollberg on the way. Hope there's a taxi. And said, "O.K. I'll come at once."

"Oh, Superintendent . . ."

"Yes?"

"One of the dead . . . he seems to be one of your men."

Martin Beck gripped the receiver hard.

"Who?"

"I don't know. They didn't say a name."

Martin Beck flung down the receiver and leaned his head against the wall. Lennart! It must be him. What the hell was he doing out in the rain? What the hell was he doing on a 47 bus? No, not Kollberg, it must be a mistake.

He picked up the phone and dialed Kollberg's number.

He heard a ring at the other end. Two. Three. Four. Five.

"Kollberg."

It was Gun's sleepy voice. Martin Beck tried to sound calm and natural.

"Hello. Is Lennart there?"

He thought he heard the bed creak as she sat up, and it was an eternity before she answered.

"No, not in bed at any rate. I thought he was with you. Or rather that you were here."

"He left when I did. To take a walk. Are you sure he's not at home?"

"He may be in the kitchen. Hang on and I'll have a look."

It was another eternity before she came back.

"No, Martin, he's not at home."

Now her voice was anxious.

"Wherever can he be?" she said. "In this weather?"

"I expect he's just out getting a breath of air. I just got home, so he can't have been out long. Don't worry."

"Shall I ask him to call you when he comes?"

She sounded reassured.

"No, it's not important. Sleep well. So long."

He put down the receiver. Suddenly he felt so cold that his teeth were chattering. He picked up the receiver again and stood with it in his hand, thinking that he must call up someone and find out exactly what had happened. Then he decided that the best way was to get to the place himself as fast as he could. He dialed the direct number of the nearest taxi stand and got a reply immediately.

Martin Beck had been a policeman for twenty-three years. During that time several of his colleagues had been killed in the course of duty. It had hit him hard every time it happened, and somewhere at the back of his mind was also the realization that police work was getting more and more risky and that next time it might be his own turn. But when it came to Kollberg, his feelings were not merely those of a colleague. Over the years they had become more and more dependent on each other in their work. They were a good complement to one another and they had learned to understand each other's thoughts and feelings without wasting words. When Kollberg got married eighteen months ago and moved to Skärmarbrink they had also come closer together geographically and had taken to meeting in their spare time.

Quite recently Kollberg had said, in one of his rare moments of depression, "If you weren't there, God only knows whether I'd stay on the force."

Martin Beck thought of this as he pulled on his wet raincoat and ran down the stairs to the waiting taxi.

6

Despite the rain and the late hour a cluster of people had collected outside the cordon toward Karlbergsvägen. They stared curiously at Martin Beck as he got out of the taxi. A young patrolman in a black raincape made a violent movement to check him, but another policeman grabbed his arm and saluted.

A small man in a light-colored trench coat and cap placed himself in Martin Beck's way and said, "My condolences, Superintendent. I just heard a rumor that one of your—"

Martin Beck gave the man a look that made him swallow the rest of the sentence.

He knew the man in the cap only too well and disliked him intensely. The man was a free-lance journalist and called himself a crime reporter. His specialty was reporting murders and his accounts were full of sensational, repulsive and usually erroneous details. In fact only the very worst weeklies published them.

The man slunk off and Martin Beck swung his legs over the rope. He saw that a similar cordon had been made a little farther up toward Torsplan. The roped-off area was swarming with black-and-white cars and unidentifiable figures in shiny raincoats. The ground around the red doubledecker was loose and squelchy.

18

The bus was lit up inside and the headlights were on, but the cones of light did not reach far in the heavy rain. The ambulance from the State Forensic Laboratory stood at the rear of the bus with its radiator pointing to Karlbergsvägen. The medico-legal expert's car was also on the scene. Behind the broken wire fence some men were busy setting up floodlights. All these details showed that something far out of the ordinary had happened.

Martin Beck glanced up at the dismal apartment houses on the other side of the street. Figures were silhouetted in several of the lighted windows, and behind rain-streaked panes, like blurred white patches, he saw faces pressed against the glass. A bare-legged woman in boots and with a raincoat over her nightgown came out of an entrance obliquely opposite the scene of the accident. She got half-way across the street before being stopped by a policeman, who took her by the arm and led her back to the doorway. The patrolman strode along and she half ran beside him while the wet white nightgown twisted itself around her legs.

Martin Beck could not see the doors of the bus but he saw people moving about inside, and presumed that men from the forensic laboratory were already at work. He couldn't see any of his colleagues from the homicide squad, either, but guessed that they were somewhere on the other side of the vehicle.

Involuntarily he slowed his steps. He thought of what he was soon to see and clenched his hands in his coat pockets as he gave the forensic technicians' gray vehicle a wide berth.

In the glow from the doubledecker's open middle doors stood Hammar, who had been his boss for many years and was now a chief superintendent. He was talking to someone who was evidently inside the bus. He broke off and turned to Martin Beck.

"There you are. I was beginning to think they'd forgotten to call you."

Martin Beck made no answer but went over to the doors and looked in.

He felt his stomach muscles knotting. It was worse than he had expected.

The cold bright light made every detail stand out with the sharpness of an etching. The whole bus seemed to be full of twisted, lifeless bodies covered with blood.

He would like to have turned and walked away and not had to look, but his face did not betray his feelings. Instead, he forced himself to make a systematic mental note of all the details. The men from the laboratory were working silently and methodically. One of them looked at Martin Beck and slowly shook his head.

Martin Beck regarded the bodies one by one. He didn't recognize any of them. At least not in their present state.

"The one up there," he said suddenly, "has he . . ."

He turned to Hammar and broke off short.

Behind Hammar, Kollberg appeared out of the dark, bare-headed and with his hair stuck to his forehead.

Martin Beck stared at him.

"Hi," said Kollberg. "I was beginning to wonder what had happened to you. I was about to tell them to call you again."

He stopped in front of Martin Beck and gave him a searching look.

Then he gave a swift, nauseated glance at the interior of the bus and went on, "You need a cup of coffee. I'll get one for you."

Martin Beck shook his head.

"Yes," Kollberg said.

He squished off. Martin Beck stared after him, then went over to the front doors and looked in. Hammar followed with heavy steps.

The bus driver lay slumped over the wheel. He had evidently been shot through the head. Martin Beck regarded what had been the man's face and was vaguely surprised that he didn't feel any nausea. He turned to Hammar, who was staring expressionlessly out into the rain.

"What on earth was he doing here?" Hammar said tonelessly. "On this bus?"

And at that instant Martin Beck knew to whom the man on the phone had been referring.

Nearest the window behind the stairs leading to the top deck sat Åke Stenström, detective sub-inspector on the homicide squad and one of Martin Beck's youngest colleagues.

"Sat" was perhaps not the right word. Stenström's dark-blue poplin raincoat was soaked with blood and he sprawled in his seat, his right shoulder against the back of a young woman who was sitting next to him, bent double.

He was dead. Like the young woman and the six other people in the bus.

In his right hand he held his service pistol.

7

The rain kept on all night and although the sun, according to the almanac, rose at twenty minutes to eight the time was nearer nine before it was strong enough to penetrate the clouds and disseminate an uncertain, hazy light.

Across the sidewalk on Norra Stationsgatan stood the red doubledecker bus just as it had stopped ten hours previously.

But that was the only thing that was the same. By now about fifty men were inside the extensive cordons, and outside them the crowd of curious onlookers got bigger and bigger. Many had been standing there ever since midnight, and all they had seen was police and ambulance men and wailing emergency vehicles of every conceivable kind. It had been a night of sirens, with a constant stream of cars roaring along the wet streets, apparently going nowhere and for no reason.

Nobody knew anything for sure, but there were two words that were whispered from person to person and soon spread in concentric circles through the crowd and the surrounding houses and city, finally taking more def-inite shape and being flung out across the country as a whole. By now the words had reached far beyond the frontiers.

Mass murder.

Mass murder in Stockholm.

Mass murder in a bus in Stockholm.

Everybody thought they knew this much at least.

Very little more was known at police headquarters on Kungsholmsgatan. It wasn't even known for certain who was in charge of the investigation. The confusion was complete. Telephones rang incessantly, people came and went, floors were dirtied and the men who dirtied them were irritable and clammy with sweat and rain.

"Who's working on the list of names?" Martin Beck asked.

"Rönn, I should think," said Kollberg without turning round. He was busy taping a plan to the wall. The sketch was over 3 yards long and more than ½ yard wide and was awkward to handle.

"Can't someone give me a hand?" he said.

"Sure," said Melander calmly, putting down his pipe and standing up.

Fredrik Melander was a tall, lean man of grave appearance and methodical disposition. He was forty-eight years old and a detective inspector on the homicide squad. Kollberg had worked together with him for many years. He had forgotten how many. Melander, on the other hand, had not. He was known never to forget anything.

Two telephones rang.

"Hello. This is Superintendent Beck. Who? No, he's not here. Shall I ask him to call? Oh, I see."

He put the phone down and reached for the other one. An almost white-haired man of about fifty opened the door cautiously and stopped doubtfully on the threshold.

"Well, Ek, what do you want?" Martin Beck asked as he lifted the receiver.

"About the bus . . . ," the white-haired man said.

"When will I be home? I haven't the vaguest idea," said Martin Beck into the telephone.

"Hell," Kollberg exclaimed as the strip of tape got tangled up between his fat fingers.

"Take it easy," Melander said.

22

Martin Beck turned back to the man in the doorway.

"Well, what about the bus?"

Ek shut the door behind him and studied his notes.

"It's built by the Leyland factories in England," he said. "The type's called Atlantean, but here it's called Type H35. It holds seventy-five seated passengers. The odd thing is—"

The door was flung open. Gunvald Larsson stared incredulously into his untidy office. His light raincoat was sopping wet, like his pants and his fair hair. His shoes were muddy.

"What a helluva mess in here," he grumbled.

"What was the odd thing about the bus?" Melander asked.

"Well, that particular type isn't used on route 47."

"Isn't it?"

"Not as a rule, I mean. They usually put German buses on, made by Büssing. They're also doubledeckers. This was just an exception."

"A brilliant clue," Gunvald Larsson said. "The madman who did this only murders people in English buses. Is that what you mean?"

Ek looked at him resignedly. Gunvald Larsson shook himself and said, "By the way, what's the horde of apes doing down in the vestibule? Who are they?"

"Journalists," Ek said. "Someone ought to talk to them."

"Not me," Kollberg said promptly.

"Isn't Hammar or the Commissioner or the Attorney General or some other higher-up going to issue a communiqué?" Gunvald Larsson said.

"It probably hasn't been worded yet," said Martin Beck. "Ek is right. Someone ought to talk to them."

"Not me," Kollberg repeated.

Then he wheeled round, almost triumphantly, as if he had had a brainwave.

"Gunvald," he said. "You were the one who got there first. You can hold the press conference."

Gunvald Larsson stared into the room and pushed a wet tuft of hair off his forehead with the back of his big hairy right hand. Martin Beck said nothing, not even bothering to look toward the door.

"Okay," Gunvald Larsson said. "Get them herded in somewhere. I'll talk to them. There's just one thing I must know first."

"What?" Martin Beck asked.

"Has anyone told Stenström's mother?"

Dead silence fell, as though the words had robbed everyone in the room of the power of speech, including Gunvald Larsson himself. The man on the threshold looked from one to the other.

At last Melander turned his head and said, "Yes. She's been told."

"Good," Gunvald Larsson said, and banged the door.

"Good," said Martin Beck to himself, drumming the top of the desk with his fingertips.

"Was that wise?" Kollberg asked.

"What?"

"Letting Gunvald . . . Don't you think we'll get bawled out enough in the press as it is?"

Martin Beck looked at him but said nothing. Kollberg shrugged.

"Oh well," he said. "It doesn't matter."

Melander went back to the desk, picked up his pipe and lighted it.

"No," he said. "It couldn't matter less."

He and Kollberg had got the sketch up now. An enlarged drawing of the lower deck of the bus. Some figures were sketched in. They were numbered from one to nine.

"Where's Rönn with that list?" Martin Beck mumbled.

"Another thing about the bus—" Ek said obstinately.

And the telephones rang.

8

The office where the first improvised confrontation with the press took place was decidedly ill-suited to the purpose. It contained nothing but a table, a few cupboards and four chairs, and when Gunvald Larsson entered the room, it was already stuffy with cigarette smoke and the smell of wet overcoats.

He stopped just inside the door, looked round at the assembled journalists and photographers and said tonelessly, "Well, what do you want to know?"

They all began to talk at once. Gunvald Larsson held up his hand and said, "One at a time, please. You, there, can start. Then we'll go from left to right."

Thereafter the press conference proceeded as follows:

QUESTION: When was the bus found?
ANSWER: About ten minutes past eleven last night.
Q: By whom?
A: A man in the street who then stopped a radio patrol car.
Q: How many persons were in the bus?
A: Eight.
Q: Were they all dead?
A: Yes.
Q: How had those persons died?
A: It's too soon yet to say.
Q: Was their death caused by external violence?
A: Probably.
Q: What do you mean by probably?
A: Exactly what I say.
Q: Were there any signs of shooting?
A: Yes.
Q: So all these people had been shot dead?
A: Probably.
Q: So it's really a question of mass murder?
A: Yes.
Q: Have you found the murder weapon?
A: No.
Q: Have the police detained anyone yet?
A: No.
Q: Are there any traces or clues that point to one particular person?
A: No.
Q: Were the murders committed by one and the same person?

A: Don't know.

Q: Is there anything to indicate that more than one person killed these eight people?

A: No.

Q: How could one single person kill eight people in a bus before anyone had time to resist?

A: Don't know.

Q: Were the shots fired by someone inside the bus or did they come from outside?

A: They did not come from outside.

Q: How do you know?

A: The windowpanes that were damaged had been fired at from inside.

Q: What kind of weapon had the murderer used?

A: Don't know.

Q: It must surely have been a machine gun or a submachine gun?

A: No comments.

Q: Was the bus standing still when the murders were committed or was it moving?

A: Don't know.

Q: Doesn't the position in which the bus was found indicate that the shooting took place while it was in movement and that it then drove up on the sidewalk?

A: Yes.

Q: Did the police dogs get a scent?

A: It was raining.

Q: It was a doubledecker bus, wasn't it?

A: Yes.

Q: Where were the bodies found? On the upper or lower deck?

A: On the lower one.

Q: All eight?

A: Yes.

Q: Have the victims been identified?

A: No.

Q: Has any of them been identified?

A: Yes.

Q: Who? The driver?

A: No. A policeman.

Q: A policeman? Can we have his name?

A: Yes. Detective Sub-inspector Åke Stenström.
Q: Stenström? From the homicide squad?
A: Yes.

A couple of the reporters tried to push toward the door, but Gunvald Larsson again put up his hand.

"No running back and forth, if you don't mind," he said. "Any more questions?"

Q: Was Inspector Stenström one of the passengers in the bus?
A: He wasn't driving at any rate.
Q: Do you consider he was there just by chance?
A: Don't know.
Q: The question was put to you personally. Do you consider it a mere chance that one of the victims is a man from the C.I.D.?
A: I have not come here to answer personal questions.
Q: Was Inspector Stenström working on any special investigation when this happened?
A: Don't know.
Q: Was he on duty last night?
A: No.
Q: He was off duty?
A: Yes.
Q: Then he must have been there by chance. Can you name any of the other victims?
A: No.
Q: This is the first time a real mass murder has occurred in Sweden. On the other hand there have been several similar crimes abroad of recent years. Do you think that this maniacal act was inspired by what has happened in America, for instance?
A: Don't know.
Q: Is it the opinion of the police that the murderer is a madman who wants to draw sensational attention to himself?
A: That is one theory.
Q: Yes, but it doesn't answer my question. Are the police working on the lines of that theory?
A: All clues and suggestions are being followed.

27

Q: How many of the victims are women?
A: Two.
Q: So six of the victims are men?
A: Yes.
Q: Including the bus driver and Inspector Stenström?
A: Yes.
Q: Just a minute, now. We've been told that one of the persons in the bus survived and was taken away in one of the ambulances that arrived on the scene before the police had had time to cordon off the area.
A: Oh?
Q: Is this true?
A: Next question.
Q: Apparently you were one of the first policemen to arrive on the scene?
A: Yes.
Q: What time did you get there?
A: At 11:25.
Q: What did it look like inside the bus just then?
A: What do you think?
Q: Can you say it was the most ghastly sight you've ever seen in your life?

Gunvald Larsson stared vacantly at the questioner, who was quite a young man with round, steelrimmed glasses and a somewhat unkempt red beard. At last he said, "No. I can't."

The reply caused some bewilderment. One of the women journalists frowned and said lamely and incredulously, "What do you mean by that?"

"Exactly what I say."

Before joining the police force Gunvald Larsson had been a regular seaman in the navy. In August, 1943, he had been one of those to go through the submarine *Ulven,* which had struck a mine and had been salvaged after having lain on the seabed for three months. Several of the thirty-three killed had been in the same courses with him. After the war, one of his duties had been to help with the extradition of the Baltic collaborators from the camp at Ränneslätt. He had also seen the arrival of thousands of victims who had been repatriated from the German concentration camps. Most of these had been women and many of them had not survived.

However, he saw no reason to explain himself to this youthful assembly but said laconically, "Any more questions?"

"Have the police been in touch with any witnesses of the actual event?"

"No."

"In other words, a mass murder has been committed in the middle of Stockholm. Eight persons have been killed, and that's all the police have to say?"

"Yes."

With that, the press conference was concluded.

9

It was some time before anyone noticed that Rönn had come in with the list. Martin Beck, Kollberg, Melander and Gunvald Larsson stood leaning over one of the tables, which was littered with photographs from the scene of the crime, when Rönn stood next to them and said, "It's ready now, the list."

He was born and raised in Arjeplog and although he had lived in Stockholm for more than twenty years he had still kept his north-Swedish dialect.

He laid the list on a corner of the table, drew up a chair and sat down.

"Don't go around frightening people," Kollberg said.

It had been silent in the room for so long that he had started at the sound of Rönn's voice.

"Well, let's see," Gunvald Larsson said impatiently, reaching for the list.

He looked at it for a while. Then he handed it back to Rönn.

"That's about the most cramped writing I've ever seen.

Can you really read that yourself? Haven't you typed out any copies?"

"Yes," Rönn replied. "I have. You'll get them in a minute."

"O.K.," said Kollberg. "Let's hear."

Rönn put on his glasses and cleared his throat. He glanced through his notes.

"Of the eight dead, four lived in the vicinity of the terminus," he began. "The survivor also lived there."

"Take them in order if you can," Martin Beck said.

"Well, first of all there's the driver. He was hit by two shots in the back of the neck and one in the back of the head and must have been killed outright."

Martin Beck had no need to look at the photograph that Rönn extracted from the pile on the table. He remembered all too well how the man in the driver's seat had looked.

"The driver's name was Gustav Bengtsson. He was forty-eight, married, two children, lived at Inedalsgatan 5. His family has been notified. It was his last run for the day and when he had let off the passengers at the last stop he would have driven the bus to the Hornsberg depot at Lindhagensgatan. The money in his fare purse was untouched and in his wallet he had 120 kronor."

He glanced at the others over his glasses.

"There's no more about him for the moment."

"Go on," Melander said.

"I'll take them in the same order as on the sketch. The next is Åke Stenström. Five shots in the back. One in the right shoulder from the side, might have been a ricochet. He was twenty-nine and lived—"

Gunvald Larsson interrupted him.

"You can skip that. We know where he lived."

"I didn't," Rönn said.

"Go on," said Melander.

Rönn cleared his throat.

"He lived on Tjärhovsgatan together with his fiancée . . ."

Gunvald Larsson interrupted him again.

"They were not engaged. I asked him not long ago."

Martin Beck cast an irritated glance at Gunvald Larsson and nodded to Rönn to continue.

"Together with Åsa Torell, twenty-four. She works at a travel agency."

He gave Gunvald Larsson a quick look and said, "In sin. I don't know whether she's been told."

Melander took his pipe out of his mouth and said, "She has been told."

None of the five men around the table looked at the pictures of Stenström's mutilated body. They had already seen them and preferred not to see them again.

"In his right hand he held his service pistol. It was cocked but he had not fired a shot. In his pockets he had a wallet containing 37 kronor, identification card, a snapshot of Åsa Torell, a letter from his mother and some receipts. Also, driving license, notebook, pens and bunch of keys. It will all be sent up to us when the boys at the lab are through with it. Can I go on?"

"Yes, please," said Kollberg.

"The girl in the seat next to Stenström was called Britt Danielsson. She was twenty-eight, unmarried and worked at Sabbatsberg Hospital. She was a registered nurse."

"I wonder whether they were together," Gunvald Larsson said. "Perhaps he was having a bit of fun on the side."

Rönn looked at him disapprovingly.

"We'd better find out," Kollberg said.

"She shared a room at Karlbergsvägen 87 with another nurse from Sabbatsberg. According to her roommate, Monika Granholm by name, Britt Danielsson was coming straight from the hospital. She was hit by one shot. In the temple. She was the only one in the bus to be struck by only one bullet. She had thirty-eight different things in her handbag. Shall I enumerate them?"

"Christ, no," said Gunvald Larsson.

"Number four on the list and on the sketch is Alfons Schwerin, the survivor. He was lying on his back on the floor between the two longitudinal seats at the rear. You already know his injuries. He was hit in the abdomen and one bullet lodged in the region of the heart. He lives alone at Norra Stationsgatan 117. He is forty-three and employed by the highway department of the city council. How is he, by the way?"

"Still in a coma," Martin Beck said. "The doctors say there's just a chance he'll regain consciousness. But if he does they don't know whether he'll be able to talk or even to remember anything."

"Can't you talk with a bullet in your belly?" Gunvald Larsson asked.

"Shock," said Martin Beck.

He pushed back his chair and stretched himself. Then he lighted a cigarette and stood in front of the sketch.

"What about this one in the corner?" he said. "Number five?"

He pointed to the seat at the very back of the bus in the right-hand corner. Rönn consulted his notes.

"He got eight bullets in him. In the chest and abdomen. He was an Arab and his name was Mohammed Boussie, Algerian subject, thirty-six, no relations in Sweden. He lived at a kind of boarding house on Norra Stationsgatan. Was obviously on his way home from work at the Zig-Zag, that grill restaurant on Vasagatan. There's nothing more to say about him at the moment."

"Arabia," said Gunvald Larsson. "Isn't that where there's usually such a helluva lot of shooting?"

"Your political knowledge is devastating," Kollberg said. "You should apply for a transfer to Sepo."

"Its correct name is the Security Department of the National Police Board," said Gunvald Larsson.

Rönn got up, fished one or two pictures out of the pile and lined them up on the table.

"This guy we haven't been able to identify," he said. "Number six. He was sitting on the outside seat immediately behind the middle doors and was hit by six shots. In his pockets he had the striking surface of a matchbox, a packet of Bill cigarettes, a bus ticket and 1,823 kronor in cash. That was all."

"A lot of money," Melander said thoughtfully.

They leaned over the table and studied the pictures of the unknown man. He had slithered down in the seat and lay sprawled against the back with arms hanging and his left leg stuck out in the aisle. The front of his coat was soaked in blood. He had no face.

"Hell, it would have to be *him*," Gunvald Larsson said. "His own mother wouldn't recognize him."

Martin Beck had resumed his study of the sketch on the wall. Holding his left hand in front of his face he said, "I'm not so sure there weren't two of them after all."

The others looked at him.

"Two what?" Gunvald Larsson asked.

"Two gunmen. Look at all the passengers, they never moved from their seats. Except the one who's still alive and he might have tumbled off afterward."

"Two madmen?" Gunvald Larsson said skeptically. "At the same time?"

Kollberg went and stood beside Martin Beck.

"You mean that someone should have had time to re-act if there had been only one? Hm, maybe. But he simply mowed them down. It happened rather fast, and when you think they were all caught napping . . ."

"Shall we go on with the list? We'll find that out as soon as we know whether there was one weapon or two."

"Sure," said Martin Beck. "Go on, Einar."

"Number seven is a foreman called Johan Källström. He was sitting beside the man who has not yet been identified. He was fifty-two, married and lived at Karlbergs-vägen 89. According to his wife he was coming from the workshop on Sibyllegatan, where he'd been working over-time. Nothing startling about him."

"Nothing except that he got a bellyful of lead on the way home from work," said Gunvald Larsson.

"By the window immediately in front of the middle doors we have Gösta Assarsson, number eight. Forty-two. Half his head was shot away. He lived at Tegnér-gatan 40, where he also had his office and his business, an export and import firm that he ran together with his brother. His wife didn't know why he was on the bus. According to her, he should have been at a club meeting on Narvavägen."

"A-ha," said Gunvald Larsson. "Out carousing."

"Yes, there are signs that point to that. In his briefcase he had a bottle of whisky. Johnnie Walker, Black Label."

"A-ah," said Kollberg, who was an epicure.

33

"In addition he was well supplied with condoms," said Rönn. "He had seven in an inside pocket. Plus a checkbook and over 800 kronor in cash."

"Why seven?" Gunvald Larsson asked.

The door opened and Ek stuck his head in.

"Hammar says you're all to be in his office in fifteen minutes. Briefing. Quarter to eleven, that's to say."

He disappeared.

"O.K., let's go on," Martin Beck said.

"Where were we?"

"The guy with the seven rubbers," said Gunvald Larsson.

"Is there anything more to be said about him?" Martin Beck asked.

Rönn glanced at the sheet of paper covered with his scribbling.

"I don't think so."

"Go on, then," said Martin Beck, sitting down at Gunvald Larsson's desk.

"Two seats in front of Assarsson sat number nine, Mrs. Hildur Johansson, sixty-eight, widow, living at Norra Stationsgatan 119. Shot in the shoulder and through the neck. She has a married daughter on Västmannagatan and was on her way home from there after baby-sitting."

Rönn folded the piece of paper and tucked it into his jacket pocket.

"That's the lot," he said.

Gunvald Larsson sighed and arranged the pictures in nine neat stacks.

Melander put his pipe down, mumbled something and went out to the toilet.

Kollberg tilted his chair and said, "And what do we learn from all this? That on quite an ordinary evening on quite an ordinary bus, nine quite ordinary people get mowed down with a submachine gun for no apparent reason. Apart from this guy who hasn't been identified, I can't see anything odd about any of these people."

"Yes, one," Martin Beck said. "Stenström. What was he doing on that bus?"

Nobody answered.

An hour later Hammar put exactly the same question to Martin Beck.

Hammar had summoned the special investigation group that from now on was to work entirely on the bus murders. The group consisted of seventeen experienced C.I.D. men, with Hammar in charge. Martin Beck and Kollberg also led the investigation.

All available facts had been studied, the situation had been analyzed and assignments allotted. When the briefing was over and all except Martin Beck and Kollberg had left the room, Hammar said, "What was Stenström doing on that bus?"

"Don't know," Martin Beck replied.

"And nobody seems to know what he was working on of late. Do either of you know?"

Kollberg threw up his hands and shrugged.

"Haven't the vaguest idea. Over and above daily routine, that is. Presumably nothing."

"We haven't had so much recently," Martin Beck said. "So he has had quite a bit of time off. He had put in an enormous amount of overtime before, so it was only fair."

Hammar drummed his fingers against the edge of the desk and wrinkled his brows in thought. Then he said, "Who was it that informed his fiancée?"

"Melander," said Kollberg.

"I think someone ought to have a talk with her as soon as possible," Hammar said. "She must at all events know what he was up to."

He paused, then added, "Unless he . . ."

He fell silent.

"What?" Martin Beck asked.

"Unless he was going with that nurse on the bus, you mean," Kollberg said.

Hammar said nothing.

"Or was out on another similar errand," Kollberg said.

Hammar nodded.

"Find out," he said.

10

Outside police headquarters on Kungsholmsgatan stood two persons who definitely wished they had been somewhere else. They were dressed in police caps and leather jackets with gilded buttons, they had shoulder belts diagonally across their chests and carried pistols and batons at their waists. Their names were Kristiansson and Kvant.

A well-dressed, elderly woman came up to them and asked, "Excuse me, but how do I get to Hjärnegatan?"

"I don't know, madam," Kvant said. "Ask a policeman. There's one standing over there."

The woman gaped at him.

"We're strangers here ourselves," Kristiansson put in quickly, by way of explanation.

The woman was still staring after them as they mounted the steps.

"What do you think they want us for?" Kristiansson asked anxiously.

"To give evidence, of course," Kvant replied. "We made the discovery, didn't we?"

"Yes," Kristiansson said. "We did, but—"

"No 'buts,' now, Kalle. Into the elevator with you."

On the third floor they met Kollberg. He nodded to them, gloomily and absently. Then he opened a door and said, "Gunvald, those two guys from Solna are here now."

"Tell them to wait," said a voice from inside the office.

"Wait," Kollberg said, and disappeared.

When they had waited for twenty minutes Kvant shook himself and said, "What the hell's the idea. We're supposed to be off duty, and I've promised Siv to mind the kids while she goes to the doctor."

"So you said," Kristiansson said dejectedly.

"She says she feels something funny in her cu—"

"Yeah, you said that too," Kristiansson murmured.

"Now she'll probably be in a terrible temper again," Kvant said. "I can't make the woman out these days. And she's starting to look such a fright. Has Kerstin also got broad in the beam like that?"

Kristiansson didn't answer.

Kerstin was his wife and he disliked discussing her.

Kvant didn't seem to care.

Five minutes later Gunvald Larsson opened the door and said curtly, "Come in."

They went in and sat down. Gunvald Larsson eyed them critically.

"Sit down, by all means."

"We have already," Kristiansson said fatuously.

Kvant silenced him with an impatient gesture. He began to scent trouble.

Gunvald Larsson stood silent for a moment. Then he placed himself behind the desk, sighed heavily and said, "How long have you both been on the force?"

"Eight years," said Kvant.

Gunvald Larsson picked up a sheet of paper from the desk and studied it.

"Can you read?" he asked.

"Oh yes," said Kristiansson, before Kvant could stop him.

"Read, then."

Gunvald Larsson pushed the sheet across the desk.

"Do you understand what's written there? Or do I have to explain it?"

Kristiansson shook his head.

"I'll explain gladly," Gunvald Larsson said. "That is a preliminary report from the investigation at the scene of the crime. It shows that two persons with size eleven shoes have left behind them about one hundred footprints all over that goddam bus, both on the upper and lower deck. Who do you think these two persons can be?"

No answer.

"To explain further, I can add that I spoke to an expert at the lab not long ago, and he said that the scene of the crime looked as if a herd of hippopotamuses had been trotting about there for hours. This expert considers it incredible that a herd of human beings, consisting of only

37

two individuals, should be able to wipe out almost every trace so completely and in such a short time."

Kvant began to lose his temper, and stared stonily at the man behind the desk.

"Now it so happens that hippopotamuses and other animals don't usually go about armed," Gunvald Larsson went on in honeyed tones. "Nevertheless, someone fired a shot inside the bus with a 7.65 mm. Walther—to be exact, up through the front stairs. The bullet ricocheted against the roof and was found embedded in the padding of one of the seats on the upper deck. Who do you think can have fired that shot?"

. "We did," Kristiansson said. "That's to say, I did."

"Oh, really? And what were you firing at?"

Kristiansson scratched his neck unhappily.

"Nothing," he said.

"It was a warning shot," Kvant said.

"Intended for whom?"

"We thought the murderer might still be in the bus and was hiding on the top deck," Kristiansson said.

"And was he?"

"No," said Kvant.

"How do you know? What did you do after that cannonade?"

"We went up and had a look," Kristiansson said.

"There was nobody there," said Kvant.

Gunvald Larsson glared at them for at least half a minute. Then he slammed the flat of his hand on the desk and roared, "So both of you went up! How the hell could you be so goddam stupid?"

"We each went up a different way," Kvant said defensively. "I went up the back stairs and Kalle took the front stairs."

"So that whoever was up there couldn't escape," said Kristiansson, trying to make things better.

"But Jesus Christ there wasn't anyone up there! All you managed to do was to ruin every single footprint there was in the whole goddam bus! To say nothing of outside! And why did you go tramping about among the bodies? Was it to make even more of a gory mess inside there?"

"To see if anyone was still alive," Kristiansson said.

He turned pale and swallowed.

"Now don't start throwing up again, Kalle," Kvant said reprovingly.

The door opened and Martin Beck came in. Kristiansson stood up at once, and after a moment Kvant followed his example.

Martin Beck nodded to them and looked inquiringly at Gunvald Larsson.

"Are you the one who is shouting? It doesn't help much, bawling out these boys."

"Yes it does," Gunvald Larsson retorted. "It's constructive."

"Constructive?"

"Exactly. These two idiots . . ."

He broke off and reconsidered his vocabulary.

"These two colleagues are the only witnesses we have. Listen now, you two! What time did you arrive on the scene?"

"Thirteen minutes past eleven," Kvant said. "I took the time on my chronograph."

"And I sat in exactly the same spot where I'm sitting now," Gunvald Larsson said. "I received the call at eighteen minutes past eleven. If we allow a wide margin and say that you fumbled with the radio for half a minute and that it took fifteen seconds for the Radio Central to contact me, that still leaves more than four minutes. What were you doing during that time?"

"Well . . . ," said Kvant.

"You ran about like poisoned rats, tromping in blood and brains and moving bodies and doing God knows what. For four minutes."

"I really can't see what's constructive—" Martin Beck began, but Gunvald Larsson cut him off.

"Wait a minute. Apart from the fact that these nitwits spent four minutes ruining the scene of the crime, they did get there at thirteen minutes past eleven. And they didn't go of their own accord but were told by the man who first discovered the bus. Is that right?"

"Yes," said Kvant.

"The old boy with the dog," said Kristiansson.

"Exactly. They were notified by a person whose name

they didn't even bother to find out and whom we probably would never have identified if he hadn't been nice enough to come here today. When did you first catch sight of this man with the dog?"

"Well . . . ," said Kvant.

"About two minutes before we got to the bus," said Kristiansson, looking down at his boots.

"Exactly. Because according to his statement they wasted at least a minute sitting in the car and shouting at him rudely. About dogs and things. Am I right?"

"Yes," mumbled Kristiansson.

"When you received the information the time was therefore approximately ten or eleven minutes past. How far from the bus was this man when he stopped you?"

"About three hundred yards," said Kvant.

"That's a fact, that's a fact," said Gunvald Larsson. "And since this man was seventy years old and also had a sick dachshund to drag along . . ."

"Sick?" said Kvant in surprise.

"Exactly," Gunvald Larsson replied. "The goddam dog had a slipped disk and was almost lame in the hind legs."

"I'm at last beginning to see what you mean," said Martin Beck.

"Mm-m. I had the man do a trial run on the same stretch today. Dog and all. Made him do it three times, then the dog gave up."

"But that's cruelty to animals," Kvant said indignantly.

Martin Beck cast a surprised and interested glance at him.

"At any rate the outfit couldn't cover the distance in under three minutes, however hard it tried. Which means that the man must have caught sight of the stationary bus at seven minutes past eleven at the latest. And we know almost for sure that the massacre took place between three and four minutes earlier."

"How do you know that?" Kristiansson and Kvant said in chorus.

"None of your business," Gunvald Larsson retorted.

"Inspector Stenström's watch," said Martin Beck. "One of the bullets passed straight through his chest and landed up in his right wrist. It broke off the stem of his wrist watch, an Omega Speedmaster, which according to the expert made the watch stop at the same instant. The hands showed three minutes and thirty-seven seconds past eleven."

Gunvald Larsson glowered at him.

"We knew Inspector Stenström, and he was meticulous about time," Martin Beck said sadly. "He was what watchmakers sometimes call a second hunter. That is, his watch always showed the exact time. Go on, Gunvald."

"This man with the dog came walking along Norrbackagatan from the direction of Karlbergsvägen. He was in fact overtaken by the bus just where the street begins. It took him about five minutes to trudge down Norrbackagatan. The bus did the same stretch in about forty-five seconds. He met nobody on the way. When he got to the corner he saw the bus standing on the other side of the street."

"So what," said Kvant.

"Shut up," said Gunvald Larsson.

Kvant made a violent movement and opened his mouth, but glanced at Martin Beck and shut it again.

"He did not see that the windows had been shattered, which, by the way, these two wonderboys didn't notice either when they eventually managed to crawl along. But he did see that the front door was open. He thought there had been an accident and hurried to get help. Calculating, quite correctly, that it would be quicker for him to reach the last bus stop than to go back up the hill along Norrbackagatan, he started off along Norra Stationsgatan in a southwesterly direction."

"Why?" said Martin Beck.

"Because he thought there'd be another bus waiting at the end of the line. As it happened, there wasn't. Instead, unfortunately, he met a police patrol car."

Gunvald Larsson cast an annihilating china-blue glance at Kristiansson and Kvant.

"A patrol car from Solna that came creeping out of its district like something that comes out when you lift up a rock. Well, how long had you been skulking with the engine idling and the front wheels on the city limits?"

"Three minutes," said Kvant.

41

"Four or five, more like it," said Kristiansson.

Kvant gave him a withering look.

"And did you see anyone coming that way?"

"No," said Kristiansson. "Not until that man with the dog."

"Which proves that the murderer cannot have made off to the southwest along Norra Stationsgatan, nor south up Norrbackagatan. If we take it that he did not hop over into the freight yard, there's only one possibility left. Norra Stationsgatan in the opposite direction."

"How do . . . we know that he didn't head into the station yard?" Kristiansson asked.

"Because that was the only spot where you two hadn't trampled down everything in sight. You forgot to climb over the fence and mess around there, too."

"O.K., Gunvald, you've made your point, now," Martin Beck said. "Good. But as usual it took a helluva time to get down to brass tacks."

This remark encouraged Kristiansson and Kvant to exchange a look of relief and secret understanding. But Gunvald Larsson cracked out, "If you two had had any sense in your thick skulls you would have got into the car, caught the murderer and nabbed him."

"Or have been butchered ourselves," Kristiansson retorted misanthropically.

"When I grab that guy I'm damn well going to shove you two in front of me," Gunvald Larsson said savagely.

Kvant stole a glance at the wall clock and said, "Can we go now? My wife—"

"Yes," said Gunvald Larsson. "You can go to hell!"

Avoiding Martin Beck's reproachful look, he said, "Why didn't they think?"

"Some people need longer than others to develop their train of thought," Martin Beck said amiably. "Not only detectives."

11

"Now we must think," Gunvald Larsson said briskly, banging the door. "There's a briefing with Hammar at three o'clock sharp. In ten minutes."

Martin Beck, sitting with the telephone receiver to his ear, threw him an irritated glance, and Kollberg looked up from his papers and muttered gloomily, "As if we didn't know. Try thinking yourself on an empty stomach and see how easy it is."

Having to go without a meal was one of the few things that could put Kollberg in a bad mood. By this time he had gone without at least three meals and was therefore particularly glum. Moreover, he thought he could tell from Gunvald Larsson's satisfied expression that the latter had just been out and had something to eat, and the thought didn't make him any happier.

"Where have you been?" he asked suspiciously.

Gunvald Larsson didn't answer. Kollberg followed him with his eyes as he went over and sat down behind his desk.

Martin Beck put down the phone.

"What's biting you?" he said.

Then he got up, took his notes and went over to Kollberg.

"It was from the lab," he said. "They've counted sixty-eight fired cases."

"What caliber?" Kollberg asked.

"As we thought. Nine millimeters. Nothing to say that sixty-seven of them didn't come from the same weapon."

"And the sixty-eighth?"

"Walther 7.65."

"The shot fired at the roof by that Kristiansson," Kollberg declared.

"Yes."

43

"It means there was probably only one madman after all," Gunvald Larsson said.

"Yes," said Martin Beck.

Going over to the sketch, he drew an X inside the widest of the middle doors.

"Yes," Kollberg said. "That's where he must have stood."

"Which would explain . . ."

"What?" Gunvald Larsson asked.

Martin Beck didn't answer.

"What were you going to say?" Kollberg asked. "Which would explain . . . ?"

"Why Stenström didn't have time to shoot," Martin Beck said.

The others looked at him wonderingly.

"Hungh-h," said Gunvald Larsson.

"Yes, yes, you're right, both of you," Martin Beck said doubtfully and massaged the root of his nose between the thumb and forefinger of his right hand.

Hammar flung open the door and entered the room, followed by Ek and a man from the office of the public prosecutor.

"Reconstruction," he said abruptly. "Stop all telephone calls. Are you ready?"

Martin Beck looked at him mournfully. It had been Stenström's habit to enter the room in exactly the same way, unexpectedly and without knocking. Almost always. It had been extremely irritating.

"What have you got there?" Gunvald Larsson asked. "The evening papers?"

"Yes," Hammar replied. "Very encouraging."

He held the papers up and gave them a hostile glare. The headlines were big and black but the text contained very little information.

"I quote," Hammar said. " 'This is the crime of the century,' says tough C.I.D. man Gunvald Larsson of the Stockholm homicide squad, and goes on: 'It was the most ghastly sight I've ever seen in my life.' Two exclamation marks."

Gunvald Larsson heaved himself back in the chair and frowned.

44

"You're in good company," said Hammar. "The minister of justice has also excelled himself. 'The tidal wave of lawlessness and the mentality of violence must be stopped. The police have cast in all resources of men and materials in order to apprehend the culprit without delay.'"

He looked around him and said, "So these are the resources."

Martin Beck blew his nose.

"'The direct investigation force already comprises more than a hundred of the country's most skilled criminal experts,'" Hammar went on. "'The biggest squad ever known in this country's history of crime.'"

Kollberg sighed and scratched his head.

"Politicians," Hammar mumbled to himself.

Tossing the newspapers on to the desk, he said, "Where's Melander?"

"Talking to the psychologists," Kollberg said.

"And Rönn?"

"At the hospital."

"Any news from there yet?"

Martin Beck shook his head.

"They're still operating," he said.

"Well," Hammar said. "The reconstruction."

Kollberg looked through his papers.

"The bus left Bellmansro about ten o'clock," he said.

"About?"

"Yes. The whole timetable had been thrown off by the commotion on Strandvägen. The buses were stuck in traffic jams or police cordons, and as there were already big delays the drivers had been told to ignore the departure times and turn straight round at the last stops."

"By radio?"

"Yes. This instruction had already been sent out to the drivers on route 47 by shortly after nine o'clock. On Stockholm Transport's own wavelength."

"Go on."

"We assume that there are people who rode part of the way on the bus on this particular run. But so far we haven't traced any such witnesses."

"They'll turn up," said Hammar.

He pointed to the newspapers and added, "After this."

"Stenström's watch had stopped at eleven, three and thirty-seven," Kollberg went on in a monotone. "There is reason to presume that the shots were fired at precisely that time."

"The first or the last?" Hammar asked.

"The first," Martin Beck said.

Turning to the sketch on the wall, he put his right forefinger on the X he had just drawn.

"We assume that the gunman stood just here," he said. "In the open space by the exit doors."

"On what do you base that assumption?"

"The trajectories. The position of the fired cases in relation to the bodies."

"Right. Go on."

"We also assume that the murderer fired three bursts. The first forward, from left to right, thereby shooting all persons sitting in the front of the bus—those marked here on the sketch as numbers one, two, three, eight and nine. Number one stands for the driver and number two for Stenström."

"And then?"

"Then he turned around, probably to the right, and fired the next burst at the four persons at the rear of the bus, still from left to right, killing numbers five, six and seven. And wounding number four—Schwerin, that is. Schwerin was lying on his back at the rear of the aisle. We take this to mean that he had been sitting on the longitudinal seat on the left side of the bus and that he had time to stand up. He would therefore have been hit last."

"And the third burst?"

"Was fired forward," Martin Beck said. "This time from right to left."

"And the weapon must be a submachine gun?"

"Yes," Kollberg replied. "In all probability. If it's the ordinary army type—"

"One moment," Hammar interrupted. "How long should this have taken? To shoot forward, swing right around, shoot backward, point the weapon forward again and empty the magazine?"

"As we still don't know what kind of weapon he

used—" Kollberg began, but Gunvald Larsson cut him off.

"About ten seconds."

"How did he get out of the bus?" Hammar asked.

Martin Beck nodded to Ek and said, "Your department."

Ek passed his fingers through his silvery hair, cleared his throat and said, "The door that was open was the rear entrance door. In all likelihood the murderer left the bus that way. In order to open it he must first move straight forward along the aisle to the driver's seat, then stretch his arm over or past the driver and push a switch."

He took out his glasses, polished them with his handkerchief and went over to the wall.

"I've had two instruction sketches blown up here," he said. "One showing the instrument panel in its entirety, the other showing the actual lever for the front doors. On the first sketch the switch for the door circuits is marked with number 15 and the door lever with number 18. The lever is therefore to the left of the wheel, in front of and obliquely below the side window. The lever itself, as you see from the second sketch, has five different positions."

"Who could make head or tail out of all this?" Gunvald Larsson said.

"In the horizontal position, or position one, both doors are shut," Ek went on unperturbed. "In position two, one step upward, the rear entrance door is opened, in position three, two steps upward, both doors are opened. The lever also has two positions downward—numbers four and five. In the first of these, the front entrance door is opened, in the second, both doors are opened."

"Sum up," said Hammar.

"To sum up," Ek said, "the person in question must have moved from his presumed position by the exit doors straight forward along the aisle to the driver's seat. He has leaned over the driver, who lay slumped over the wheel, and turned the lever to position two, thereby opening the rear entrance door. That is to say, the one that was still open when the first police car got there."

Martin Beck picked up the thread at once.

"Actually there are signs showing that the last shots of

all were fired while the gunman was moving forward along the aisle. To the left. One of them seems to have hit Stenström."

"Pure trench warfare tactics," said Gunvald Larsson.

"Gunvald made a very pertinent comment just now," Hammar said drily. "That he didn't understand a thing. All this shows that the murderer was quite at home in the bus and knew how to work the instrument panel."

"At least how to work the doors," Ek said pedantically.

There was silence in the room. Hammar frowned. At last he said, "Do you mean to say that someone suddenly went and stood in the middle of the bus, shot everyone there and then simply went on his way? Without anyone having time to react? Without the driver seeing anything in his mirror?"

"No," Kollberg said. "Not exactly."

"What *do* you mean then?"

"That someone came down the rear stairs from the top deck with the submachine gun at the ready," Martin Beck said.

"Someone who had been sitting up there alone for a while," Kollberg said. "Someone who had taken his time to wait for the most suitable moment."

"How does the bus driver know if there's anyone on the top deck?" Hammar asked.

They all looked expectantly at Ek, who again cleared his throat and said, "There are photoelectric cells on the stairs. These in their turn send impulses to a counter on the instrument panel. For each passenger who goes up the front stairs the counter adds a one. The driver can therefore keep a check the whole time on how many are up there."

"And when the bus was found the counter showed zero?"

"Yes."

Hammar stood in silence for a few seconds. Then he said, "No. It doesn't hold water."

"What doesn't?" Martin Beck asked.

"The reconstruction."

"Why not?" said Kollberg.

"It seems far too well thought out. A mentally deranged mass murderer doesn't act with such careful planning."

"Oh, I dunno," said Gunvald Larsson. "That madman in America who shot over thirty persons from a tower last summer, he had planned as carefully as hell. He even had food with him."

"Yes," Hammar said. "But there was one thing he hadn't figured out."

"What?"

It was Martin Beck who answered: "How he was to get away."

12

Seven hours later the time was ten o'clock in the evening and Martin Beck and Kollberg were still at police headquarters on Kungsholmsgatan.

Outside it was dark and the rain had stopped.

Nothing special had occurred. The official word was that the state of the investigation was unchanged.

The dying man at Karolinska Hospital was still dying.

In the course of the afternoon, twenty helpful witnesses had come forward. Nineteen of them turned out to have ridden on other buses.

The only remaining witness was a girl of eighteen who had got on at Nybroplan and gone three stops to Sergels torg, where she had changed to the subway. She said that several passengers had got off at the same time as she, which seemed likely. She managed to recognize the driver, but that was all.

Kollberg paced restlessly up and down, eyeing the door repeatedly as if expecting someone to throw it open and rush into the room.

Martin Beck stood in front of the sketches on the wall. He had clasped his hands behind him and rocked slowly to and fro from sole to heel and back, an irritating habit he had acquired during his years as a patrolman on the beat long ago and which he had never been able to get rid of since.

They had hung their jackets over the chairbacks and rolled up their shirtsleeves. Kollberg's tie lay on the desk where he had tossed it, and although the room was not particularly warm he was perspiring in the face and under the arms. Martin Beck was seized with a long, racking cough, then he put his hand thoughtfully to his chin and went on studying the sketches.

Kollberg stopped his pacing, looked at him critically and declared, "You sound goddam awful."

"And you get more and more like Inga every day."

And just then Hammar threw open the door and marched in.

"Where are Larsson and Melander?"

"Gone home."

"And Rönn?"

"At the hospital."

"Oh yes, of course. Heard anything from there?"

Kollberg shook his head.

"You'll be up to full strength tomorrow."

"Full strength?"

"Reinforcements. From outside."

Hammar made a short pause. Then he added ambiguously, "It's considered necessary."

Martin Beck blew his nose with great care.

"Who is it?" Kollberg asked. "Or shall I say who are they?"

"A man called Månsson is coming up from Malmö tomorrow. Do you know him?"

"I've met him," Martin Beck replied without the faintest trace of enthusiasm.

"So have I," said Kollberg.

"And they're trying to get Gunnar Ahlberg free from Motala."

"He's O.K.," Kollberg said listlessly.

"That's all I know," Hammar said. "Someone from Sundsvall, too, I think. Don't know who."

"I see," said Martin Beck.

"Unless you solve it before then, of course," Hammar said bleakly.

"Of course," Kollberg agreed.

"Facts seem to point to . . ."

Hammar broke off and gave Martin Beck a searching look.

"What's wrong with you?"

"I've got a cold."

Hammar went on staring at him. Kollberg followed his look and said, by way of diverting his attention, "All we know is that someone shot nine people in a bus last night. And that he followed the internationally familiar pattern of sensational mass murderers by not leaving any traces and by not getting caught. He can, of course, have committed suicide, but in that case we know nothing about it. We have two substantial clues. The bullets and the fired cases, which may possibly lead us to the weapon, and the man in the hospital, who might regain consciousness and tell us who fired the shots. As he was sitting at the rear of the bus he must have seen the murderer."

"Hunh," Hammar grunted.

"It's not very much, I grant you," said Kollberg. "Especially if this Schwerin dies or turns out to have lost his memory—he's seriously injured. We've no motive, for instance. And no witnesses that are any use."

"They may turn up," Hammar said. "And the motive needn't be any problem. Mass murderers are psychopaths and the reasons for their actions are often an element in the pathological picture."

"Oh," Kollberg said. "Melander's looking after the scientific relations. I expect he'll be along with a memorandum one of these days."

"Our best chance . . ." Hammar said, looking at the clock.

"Is the inside investigation," Kollberg added.

"Exactly. In nine cases out of ten it leads to the murderer. Don't stay on here too long to no purpose. Better for you to be rested tomorrow. Good night."

He left the room, and there was silence. After a few seconds Kollberg sighed and said, "What *is* wrong with you?"

Martin Beck didn't answer.

"Stenström?"

Kollberg nodded to himself and said philosophically, "To think how I've bawled that kid out. Over the years. And then he goes and gets murdered."

"This Månsson," Martin Beck said. "Do you remember him?"

Kollberg nodded.

"The guy with the toothpicks. I don't believe in roping in every available man like this. It would be far better if they let us get on with this by ourselves. You and I and Melander."

"Well, Ahlberg's O.K., at any rate."

"Sure," Kollberg replied. "But how many murder investigations has he had down there in Motala during the last ten years?"

"One."

"Exactly. Besides, I don't care for Hammar's habit of standing there and slinging clichés and truisms in our faces. 'Psychopaths,' 'an element in the pathological picture,' 'up to full strength.' Yuk."

Another silence. Then Martin Beck looked at Kollberg and said, "Well?"

"Well what?"

"What was Stenström doing on that bus?"

"That's just it," said Kollberg. "What the devil was he doing there? That girl, maybe. The nurse."

"Would he go about armed if he was out with a girl?"

"He might. So as to seem tough."

"He wasn't that kind," Martin Beck said. "You know that as well as I do."

"Well, in any case, he often had his pistol on him. More often than you. And a helluva sight more often than I."

"Yes—when he was on duty."

"I only met him when he was on duty," Kollberg said drily.

"So did I. But it's a fact that he was one of the first to die in that horrible bus. Even so, he had time to undo two buttons of his overcoat and get out his pistol."

"Which means that he had already unbuttoned his coat," Kollberg said thoughtfully. "One more thing."

"Yes?"

"Hammar said something today at the reconstruction."

"Yes," Martin Beck murmured. "He said something to this effect: 'It doesn't hold water. A mentally deranged mass murderer doesn't plan so carefully.' "

"Do you think he was right?"

"Yes, in principle."

"Which would mean?"

"That the man who did the shooting is no mentally deranged mass murderer. Or rather that he didn't do it merely to cause a sensation."

Kollberg wiped the sweat off his brow with a folded handkerchief, regarded it thoughtfully and said, "Mr. Larsson said—"

"Gunvald?"

"He and no other. Before going home to spray his armpits he said from the loftiness of his wisdom that he didn't understand a thing. He didn't understand, for instance, why the madman didn't take his own life or stay there to be arrested."

"I think you underestimate Gunvald," Martin Beck said.

"Do you?"

Kollberg gave an irritated shrug.

"Aingh. The whole thing is just nonsense. There's no doubt whatever that this is a mass murder. And that the murderer is mad. For all we know he may be sitting at home at this very moment in front of the TV, enjoying the effect. Or else he might very well have committed suicide. The fact that Stenström was armed means nothing at all, since we don't know his habits. Presumably he was together with that nurse. Or he was on his way to a whore. Or to a pal of his. He may even have quarreled with his girl or been bawled out by his mother and sat sulking on a bus because it was too late to go to the movies and he had nowhere else to go."

"We can find that out, anyway," Martin Beck said.

"Yes. Tomorrow. But there's one thing we can do this very moment. Before anyone else does it."

"Go through his desk out at Västberga," Martin Beck said.

"Your power of deduction is admirable," Kollberg declared.

He stuffed his tie into his pants pocket and started climbing into his jacket.

The air was raw and misty, and the night frost lay like a shroud over trees and streets and rooftops. Kollberg had difficulty in seeing through the windshield and muttered dismal curses when the car skidded on the bends. All the way out to the southern police headquarters they spoke only once.

"Do mass murderers usually have a hereditary criminal streak?" Kollberg wondered.

And Martin Beck answered, "Yes, usually. But by no means always."

The building out at Västberga was silent and deserted. They crossed the vestibule and went up the stairs, pressed the buttons of the numerical code on the round dial beside the glass doors on the third floor, and went on into Stenström's office.

Kollberg hesitated a moment, then sat down at the desk and tried the drawers. They were not locked.

The room was neat and tidy but quite impersonal. Stenström had not even had a photograph of his fiancée on the desk.

On the other hand, two photos of himself lay on the pen tray. Martin Beck knew why. For the first time in several years Stenström had been lucky enough to be off duty over Christmas and New Year. He had already booked seats on a charter plane to the Canary Islands. He had had the pictures taken because he had to get a new passport.

Lucky.

Thought Martin Beck, looking at the photos, which were very recent and better than those published on the front pages of the evening papers.

Stenström looked, if anything, younger than his twenty-nine years. He had a bright, frank expression and dark-brown hair, combed back. Here, as it usually did, it looked rather unruly.

At first he had been considered naïve and mediocre by

54

a number of colleagues, including Kollberg, whose sarcastic remarks and often condescending manner had been a continuous trial. But that was in the past. Martin Beck remembered that once, while they were still housed in the old police premises out at Kristineberg, he had discussed this with Kollberg. He had said, "Why are you always nagging at the kid?"

And Kollberg had answered, "In order to break down his put-on self-confidence. To give him a chance to build it up new. To help turn him into a good policeman one day. To teach him to knock at doors."

It was conceivable that Kollberg had been right. At any rate, Stenström had improved with the years. And although he had never learned to knock at doors, he had developed into a good policeman—capable, hard-working and reasonably discerning. Outwardly, he had been an adornment to the force: a pleasant appearance, a winning manner, physically fit and a good athlete. He could almost have been used in recruiting advertisements, which was more than could be said of certain others. For instance, of Kollberg, with his arrogance and flabbiness and tendency to run to fat. Of the stoical Melander, whose appearance in no way challenged the hypothesis that the worst bores often made the best policemen. Or of the red-nosed and in all respects equally mediocre Rönn. Or of Gunvald Larsson, who could frighten anyone at all out of his wits with his colossal body and staring eyes and who was proud of it, what is more.

Or of himself either, for that matter, the snuffling Martin Beck. He had looked in the mirror as recently as the evening before and seen a tall, sinister figure with a lean face, wide forehead, heavy jaws and mournful gray-blue eyes.

In addition, Stenström had had certain specialties which had been of great use to them all.

Martin Beck thought of all this while he regarded the objects that Kollberg systematically took out of the drawers and placed on the desk.

But now he was coldly appraising what he knew of the man whose name had been Ake Stenström. The feelings that had threatened to overwhelm him not long ago, while

55

Hammar stood scattering truisms about him in the office at Kungsholmsgatan, were gone. The moment was past and would never recur.

Ever since Stenström had put his cap on the hatrack and sold his uniform to an old classmate from the police school, he had worked under Martin Beck. First at Kristineberg, at the then national homicide squad which had belonged to the municipal police and functioned chiefly as a kind of emergency corps, intended to assist hard-pressed local police in the provinces.

Later, at the turn of the year 1964–65, the police in its entirety had been nationalized, and by degrees they had moved out here to Västberga.

In the course of the years Kollberg had been given various assignments, and Melander had been transferred at his own request, but Stenström had been there all the time. Martin Beck had known him for more than five years, and they had worked together with innumerable investigations. During this time Stenström had learned what he knew about practical police work, and that was not a little. He had also matured, overcome most of his uncertainty and shyness, left home and in time moved in with a young woman, together with whom he said he wanted to spend the rest of his life. Shortly before this, his father had died and his mother had moved back to Västmanland.

Martin Beck should, therefore, know most of what there was to know about him.

Oddly enough, he didn't know very much. True, he had all the important data and a general idea, presumably well-founded, of Stenström's character, his merits and failings as a policeman, but over and above this there was little to add.

A nice guy. Ambitious, persevering, smart, ready to learn. On the other hand rather shy, still a trifle childish, anything but witty, not much sense of humor on the whole. But who had?

Perhaps he'd had a complex.

Because of Kollberg, who used to excel in literary quotations and complicated sophisms. Because of Gunvald Larsson, who once, in fifteen seconds, had kicked in a locked door and knocked a maniac ax-murderer senseless while Stenström stood two yards away wondering what ought to be done. Because of Melander, whose face never gave anything away ánd who never forgot anything he had once seen, read or heard.

Well, who wouldn't get a complex from that sort of thing?

Why did he know so little? Because he had not been sufficiently observant? Or because there was nothing to know?

Martin Beck massaged his scalp with his fingertips and studied what Kollberg had laid on the desk.

There had been a pedantic trait in Stenström, for instance this fad that his watch must show the correct time to the very second, and it was also reflected in the meticulous tidiness on and in his desk.

Papers, papers and more papers. Copies of reports, notes, minutes of court proceedings, stenciled instructions and reprints of legal texts. All in neatly arranged bundles.

The most personal things were a box of matches and an unopened pack of chewing gum. Since Stenström neither smoked nor was addicted to excessive chewing, he had presumably had these objects so that he could offer some form of service to people who came there to be questioned or perhaps just to sit and chat.

Kollberg sighed deeply and said, "If I had been the one sitting in that bus, you and Stenström would have been rummaging through my drawers just now. It would have given you a helluva sight more trouble than this. You'd probably have made finds that would have blackened my memory."

Martin Beck could well imagine what Kollberg's drawers looked like but refrained from comment.

"This couldn't blacken anyone's memory," Kollberg said.

Again Martin Beck made no reply. They went through the papers in silence, quickly and thoroughly. There was nothing that they could not immediately identify or place in its natural context. All notes and all documents were connected with investigations that Stenström had been working on and that they knew all about.

At last there was only one thing left. A brown envelope in quarto size. It was sealed and rather fat.

"What do you think this can be?" Kollberg said.

"Open it and see."

Kollberg turned the envelope all ways.

"He seems to have sealed it up very carefully. Look at these strips of tape."

He shrugged, took the paper knife from the pen tray and resolutely slit open the envelope.

"Hm-m," Kollberg said. "I didn't know that Stenström was a photographer."

He glanced through the bunch of photographs and then spread them out in front of him.

"And I would never have thought he had interests like this."

"It's his fiancée," said Martin Beck tonelessly.

"Yes, but all the same, I would never have dreamed he had such far-out tastes."

Martin Beck looked at the photographs, dutifully and with the unpleasant feeling he always had when he was more or less forced to intrude on anything to do with other people's private lives. This reaction was spontaneous and innate, and not even after twenty-three years as a policeman had he learned to master it.

Kollberg was not troubled by any such scruples. Moreover, he was a sensualist.

"By God, she's quite a dish," he said appreciatively and with great emphasis.

He went on studying the pictures.

"She can stand on her hands too," he said. "I wouldn't have imagined that she looked like that."

"But you've seen her before."

"Yes, dressed. This is an entirely different matter."

Kollberg was right, but Martin Beck preferred to say no more.

His only comment was, "And tomorrow you'll be seeing her again."

"Yes," Kollberg replied. "And I'm not looking forward to it."

Gathering up the photographs, he put them back into

58

the envelope. Then he said, "We'd better be getting home. I'll give you a lift."

They put out the light and left. In the car Martin Beck said, "By the way, how did you come to be at Norra Stationsgatan last night? Gun didn't know where you were when I called up and you were on the scene long before I was."

"It was pure chance. After leaving you I walked toward town. On Skanstull Bridge two guys in a patrol car recognized me. They had just got the alarm on the radio and they drove me straight in. I was one of the first there."

They sat in silence for a long time. Then Kollberg said in a puzzled tone, "What do you think he wanted those pictures for?"

"To look at," Martin Beck replied.

"Of course. But still . . ."

13

Before Martin Beck left the apartment on Wednesday morning he called up Kollberg. Their conversation was brief and to the point.

"Kollberg."

"Hi. It's Martin. I'm leaving now."

"O.K."

When the train glided into the subway station at Skärmarbrink, Kollberg was waiting on the platform. They had made it a habit always to get into the last car and in this way they often had each other's company into town even when they hadn't arranged it.

They got off at Medborgarplatsen and came up onto Folkungagatan. The time was twenty minutes past nine and a watery sun filtered through the gray sky. They turned up their coat collars against the icy wind and started walking east along Folkungagatan.

As they turned the corner onto Östgötagatan Kollberg

said, "Have you heard how the wounded man is? Schwerin?"

"Yes, I called up the hospital this morning. The operations have succeeded insomuch as he's alive. But he's still unconscious and the doctors can't say anything about the outcome until he wakes up."

"Is he going to wake up?"

Martin Beck shrugged.

"They don't know. I certainly hope so."

"I wonder how long it will be before the newspapers nose him out."

"At Karolinska they promised to keep their mouths shut," Martin Beck said.

"Yes, but you know what journalists are. Like leeches."

They turned onto Tjärhovsgatan and walked along to number 18.

They found the name TORELL on the list of tenants in the entrance, but above the door plate two flights up was a white card with the name ÅKE STENSTRÖM drawn in India ink.

The girl who opened the door was small; automatically Martin Beck estimated her height at 5 feet 3 inches.

"Come in and take your coats off," she said, closing the door behind them.

The voice was low and rather hoarse.

Åsa Torell was dressed in narrow black slacks and a cornflower-blue rib-knitted polo sweater. On her feet she had thick gray skiing socks which were several sizes too large and had presumably been Stenström's. She had brown eyes and dark hair cut very short. Her face was angular and could be called neither sweet nor pretty; if anything, quaint and piquant. She was slight of build, with slim shoulders and hips and small breasts.

She stood quiet and expectant while Martin Beck and Kollberg put their hats beside Stenström's old cap on the rack and took off their overcoats. Then she led the way into the apartment.

The living room, which had two windows onto the street, had a pleasant, cozy atmosphere. Against one wall stood a huge bookcase with carved sides and top piece. Apart from it and a wing chair upholstered in leather, the furniture looked fairly new. A bright-red rya rug covered most of the floor, and the thin woolen curtains had exactly the same shade of red.

The room was irregular in shape, and from the far corner, a short passage led out into the kitchen. Through an open door in the corridor one could see into the other rooms. The kitchen and bedroom faced the courtyard at the back.

Åsa Torell sat in the leather armchair and tucked her feet under her. She pointed to two safari chairs, and Martin Beck and Kollberg sat down. The ashtray on the low table between them and the young woman was filled to overflowing with cigarette butts.

"I do hope you realize how sorry we are that we have to intrude like this," Martin Beck said. "But it was essential to talk to you as soon as possible."

Åsa Torell did not answer at once. She picked up the cigarette that lay burning on the edge of the ashtray and drew at it deeply. Her hand was inclined to shake and she had dark rings under her eyes.

"Of course I do," she said. "It was just as well you came. I've been sitting in this chair ever since . . . well, since I heard that . . . I've been sitting here trying to realize that it's true."

"Miss Torell," Kollberg said. "Haven't you anyone who can come here and be with you?"

She shook her head.

"No. And anyway, I don't want anyone here."

"Your parents?"

Again she shook her head.

"Mom died last year. And Dad has been dead for twenty years."

Martin Beck leaned forward and gave her a searching look.

"Have you slept at all?" he asked.

"I don't know. The ones that were here yesterday gave me a couple of pills, so I expect I did sleep for a while. It doesn't matter. I'll be all right."

Stubbing out the cigarette, she murmured, her eyes lowered, "I'll just have to try and get used to the fact that he's dead. It may take time."

Neither Martin Beck nor Kollberg could think of anything to say. Martin Beck suddenly noticed that the room was stuffy and the air thick with cigarette smoke. An oppressive silence weighed on them all. At last Kollberg cleared his throat and said gravely, "Miss Torell, do you mind if we ask you one or two things about Stenstr—about Åke?"

Åsa Torell raised her eyes slowly. Suddenly they twinkled and she smiled.

"You surely don't mean me to call you Superintendent Beck and Inspector Kollberg? You must call me Åsa, because I'm going to say Martin and Lennart to you. You see, I know you both quite well in a way."

She gave them a mischievous look and added, "Through Åke. He and I saw quite a lot of each other. We've lived here for several years."

Messrs. Kollberg and Beck, undertakers, thought Martin Beck. Pull your socks up. The girl's O.K.

"We've heard about you, too," Kollberg said in a lighter tone.

Åsa went over and opened a window. Then she took the ashtray out into the kitchen. Her smile was gone and her face had a set look. She came back with a new ashtray and curled up again in the chair.

"Would you mind telling me just what happened," she said. "I wasn't told much yesterday and I'm not going to read the papers."

Martin Beck lighted a Florida.

"O.K.," he said.

She sat quite still, never taking her eyes off him while he related the course of events as far as they had been able to reconstruct it. Only certain details did he omit. When he had finished Åsa said, "Where was Åke going? Why was he on that bus at all?"

Kollberg glanced at Martin Beck and said, "That's what we were hoping you would be able to tell us."

Åsa Torell shook her head.

"I've no idea."

"Do you know what he was doing earlier in the day?" Martin Beck asked.

She looked at him in surprise.

"Don't *you* know? He was working all day. Surely you ought to know what he was doing?"

Martin Beck hesitated a moment. Then he said, "The last time I saw him alive was on Friday. He was up for a while in the morning."

She got up and paced about. Then she turned around.

"But he was working both on Saturday and on Monday. We left here together on Monday morning. Didn't *you* see Åke on Monday?" She stared at Kollberg, who shook his head.

"Did he say he was going out to Västberga?" Kollberg asked. "Or to Kungsholmsgatan?"

Åsa thought for a moment.

"No, he didn't say where he was going. That probably explains it. He must have been working on something in town."

"Did you say he worked on Saturday, too?" Martin Beck asked.

She nodded.

"Yes, but not all day. We left here together in the morning, and I finished at one and came straight home. Åke got home not long after. He had done the shopping. On Sunday he was free. We spent the whole day together."

She went back to the armchair and sat down, clasped her hands round her drawn-up knees and bit her underlip.

"Didn't he tell you what he was working on?" Kollberg asked.

Åsa shook her head.

"Didn't he usually tell you?" Martin Beck asked.

"Oh, yes. We told each other everything. But not lately. He said nothing about this last job. I thought it was funny he didn't talk to me about it. He always used to discuss the different cases, especially when it was something tricky and difficult. But perhaps he wasn't allowed—"

She broke off and raised her voice.

"Anyway, why are you asking me? You were his superiors. If you're trying to find out whether he told me any police secrets, then I can assure you he didn't. He didn't say one word about his job during the last three weeks."

"Perhaps it was because he didn't have anything special to tell you about," Kollberg said soothingly. "The last three weeks have been unusually uneventful and we've had very little to do."

Åsa looked hard at him.

"How can you say that? Åke, at any rate, had a lot to do. He was working practically night and day."

14

Rönn looked at his watch and yawned.

He glanced at the wheeled stretcher and the person who lay there, bandaged beyond description. Then he regarded the complex apparatus that was apparently necessary to keep the injured man alive, and the snooty middle-aged nurse who checked that everything was functioning as it should. At the moment she was deftly changing one of the rigged-up dropping bottles. Her actions were quick and precise; they showed many years' training and admirable economy of movement.

Rönn sighed and yawned again behind the mask.

The nurse spotted it at once and gave him a swift, disapproving glance.

He had spent far too many hours in this antiseptic isolation ward with its cold light and bare white walls, or roaming about the corridor outside the operating theater.

Moreover, for most of the time he had been in the company of a man called Ullholm, whom he had never seen before but who nevertheless turned out to be a plainclothes detective.

Rönn was not one of the shining lights of the age and he didn't pretend to be particularly well informed. He was quite content with himself and with life in general, and thought that things were pretty good as they were. It was these qualities, in fact, that made him a useful and capable policeman. He had a simple, straightforward attitude to things and had no talent for creating problems and difficulties which did not exist.

He liked most people and most people liked him.

But even to someone with Rönn's uncomplicated outlook, this Ullholm stood out as a monster of nagging tedium and reactionary stupidity.

Ullholm was dissatisfied with everything, from his salary grade, which not surprisingly was too low, to the police commissioner, who hadn't the sense to take strong measures.

He was indignant that children were not taught manners at school and that discipline was too slack within the police force.

He was particularly virulent about three categories of citizens who had never caused Rönn any headaches or worry: foreigners, teenagers and socialists.

Ullholm thought it was a scandal that police patrolmen were allowed to have beards.

"A mustache at the very most," he said. "But even that is extremely questionable. You see what I mean, don't you?"

He considered that there had been no law and order in society since the thirties.

He put the greatly increasing crime and brutality down to the fact that the police were not given proper military training and no longer wore sabers.

The introduction of right-hand traffic was a scandalous blunder that had made the situation much worse in a community that was already undisciplined and morally corrupt.

"Furthermore, it increases promiscuity," he said. "You see what I mean, don't you?"

"Huh," said Rönn.

"Promiscuity. All these turn-around areas and parking facilities along the main highways. You see what I mean, don't you?"

He was a man who knew most things and understood everything. Only on one occasion did he consider himself forced to ask Rönn for information. He began by saying, "When you see all this laxity you long to get back to nature. I'd make for the mountains if it weren't that the whole of Lapland is lousy with Lapps. You see what I mean, don't you?"

"I'm married to a Lapp girl," Rönn said.

Ullholm looked at him with a peculiar mixture of distaste and curiosity. Lowering his voice, he said, "How interesting and extraordinary. Is it true that Lapp women have it crosswise?"

"No," Rönn replied wearily. "It is not true. It's just a wrong idea that many people have."

Rönn wondered why the man hadn't long ago been transferred to the lost-and-found office.

Ullholm droned on incessantly and concluded every declaration of principle with the words, "You see what I mean, don't you?"

Rönn saw only two things.

First: what had actually happened at investigation headquarters when he had asked the innocent question, "Who's on duty at the hospital?"

Kollberg had rooted indifferently among his papers and said, "Someone called Ullholm."

The only one to recognize the name was Gunvald Larsson, who exclaimed, "What! Who?"

"Ullholm," Kollberg repeated.

"It must be stopped! We'll have to send along someone to look after him. Someone more or less sane."

Rönn had turned out to be this more or less sane person. Still just as innocently, he had asked, "Am I to relieve him?"

"Relieve him? No, that's impossible. He'll think then that he's been slighted. Will write hundreds of petitions. Report the national police board to the civil ombudsman. Call up the minister of justice."

And as Rönn was on the way out, Gunvald Larsson had given him a last instruction: "Einar!"

"Yes?"

"And don't let him say one word to the witness until you've seen the death certificate."

Second: that he must in some way dam up the spate of words. At last he did find a theoretical solution. Put into practice, it worked as follows:

Ullholm wound up a long declaration by saying, "It goes quite without saying that as a private person and a conservative, a citizen in a free democratic country, I

66

don't make the slightest discrimination among people on account of color, race or opinions. But *you* just imagine a police force swarming with Jews and communists. You see what I mean, don't you?"

Whereupon Rönn cleared his throat modestly behind his mask and said, "Yes. But as a matter of fact, I myself am one of those socialists, so . . ."

"A communist!?"

"Yes. A communist."

Ullholm wrapped himself in sepulchral silence and went over to the window.

He had been standing there now for two hours, grimly staring out at the treacherous world surrounding him.

Schwerin had been operated on three times; both the bullets had been removed from his body but none of the doctors looked particularly cheerful and the only answers Rönn had received to his discreet questions had been shrugs.

But about a quarter of an hour ago one of the surgeons had come into the isolation ward and said, "If he is going to regain consciousness at all, it should be within the next half-hour."

"Will he pull through?"

The doctor gave Rönn a long look and said, "It seems unlikely. He has a good physique, of course, and his general condition is fairly satisfactory."

Rönn looked down at the patient dejectedly, wondering just how a person should look before his general condition could be regarded as not so good or just plain bad.

He had carefully thought out two questions, which for safety's sake he had written down in his notebook.

The first one was:

Who did the shooting?

And the second:

What did he look like?

He had also made one or two other preparations: set up his portable transistor tape recorder on a chair at the head of the bed, plugged in the microphone and hung it over the chairback. Ullholm had not taken part in these, contenting himself with an occasional critical glance at Rönn from his place over by the window.

The clock showed twenty-six minutes past two when the nurse suddenly bent over the injured man and beckoned the two policemen with a swift, impatient gesture, at the same time putting out her other hand and pressing the bell.

Rönn hurried over and seized the microphone.

"I think he's waking up," the nurse said.

The injured man's face seemed to undergo some sort of change. A quiver passed through his eyelids and nostrils.

"Yes," the nurse said. "Now."

Rönn held out the microphone.

"Who did the shooting?" he asked.

No reaction. After a moment Rönn repeated the question.

"Who did the shooting?"

Now the man's lips moved and he said something. Rönn waited only two seconds before saying, "What did he look like?"

The injured man reacted again and this time the answer was more articulated.

A doctor entered the room.

Rönn had just opened his mouth to repeat question number two when the man in the bed turned his head to the left. The lower jaw slipped down and a slimy, blood-streaked pulp welled out of his mouth.

Rönn looked up at the doctor, who consulted his instruments and nodded gravely.

Ullholm came up to Rönn and snapped, "Is that really all you can get out of this questioning?"

Then he said in a loud, bullying voice, "Now listen to me, my good man, this is Detective Inspector Ullholm speaking—"

"He's dead," Rönn said quietly.

Ullholm stared at him and uttered one word: "Bungler."

Rönn pulled out the microphone plug and took the tape recorder over to the window. Turned the spool back cautiously with his forefinger and pressed the playback button.

"Who did the shooting?"

"Dnrk."

"What did he look like?"

"Koleson."

"What do you make of this?" he asked.

Ullholm glared at Rönn for at least ten seconds. Then he said, "Make of it? I'm going to report you for breach of duty. It can't be helped. You see what I mean, don't you?"

He turned on his heel and strode energetically from the room. Rönn looked sadly after him.

15

An icy gust of wind whipped a shower of needle-sharp grains of snow against Martin Beck as he opened the main door of police headquarters, making him gasp for breath. He lowered his head to the wind and hurriedly buttoned his overcoat. The same morning he had at last capitulated to Inga's nagging, to the freezing temperature and to his cold, and put on his winter coat. Pulling the woolen scarf higher round his neck, he started walking toward the center of town.

When he had crossed Agnegatan he stopped, at a loss, trying to figure out what bus to take. He had not yet learned all the new routes since the trolleys had been taken off in conjunction with the change-over to right-hand traffic in September.

A car pulled up beside him. Gunvald Larsson wound the side window down and called, "Jump in."

Martin Beck gratefully settled himself into the front seat.

"Ugh, what horrible weather. You hardly have time to notice there's been a summer when the winter starts all over again. Where are you off to?"

"Västmannagatan," Gunvald Larsson replied. "I'm going up to have a talk with that daughter of the old girl in the bus."

"Good," said Martin Beck. "You can let me off outside Sabbatsberg Hospital."

They drove across Kungsbron and past the old market hall. Minute grains of snow swirled up against the windshield.

"This sort of snow is utterly useless," Gunvald Larsson said. "It doesn't even lie. Just flies about blocking the view."

Unlike Martin Beck, Gunvald Larsson liked cars and was considered a very good driver.

They followed Vasagatan to Norra Bantorget and outside Norra Latin secondary school they overtook a double-decker bus on route 47.

"Ugh!" Martin Beck exclaimed. "From now on we'll feel ill at the very sight of one of those buses."

Gunvald Larsson cast a quick glance at it.

"Not the same kind," he said. "That one's a German bus. Büssing."

After a minute or so he said, "Are you coming with me to see Assarsson's wife? The guy with the condoms. I'm to be there at three o'clock."

"I don't know," Martin Beck said.

"I thought as you're in the vicinity. It's only one block away from Sabbatsberg. Then I can drive you back afterward."

"Perhaps. It depends when I finish with that nurse."

At the corner of Dalagatan and Tegnérgatan they were stopped by a man in a yellow protective helmet and with a red flag in his hand. Inside the grounds of Sabbatsberg Hospital work was going on with the extensive rebuilding; the old buildings were to be torn down and new ones were already shooting up. At present they were blasting away the high rocks toward Dalagatan. As the noise of the explosion was still echoing between the housewalls, Gunvald Larsson said, "Why don't they blow the whole of Stockholm to bits in one go instead of doing it piecemeal? They ought to do what Ronald Reagan or whatever-his-name-is said about Vietnam: Asphalt it and paint on yellow stripes and make parking lots of the goddam thing. It could hardly be worse than when the town planners get their way."

Martin Beck got out of the car in front of the entrance

to the part of the hospital nearest the Eastman Institute and containing the maternity ward and the women's clinic.

The turn-around area in front of the doors was empty, but as he came nearer he saw a woman in a sheepskin coat peering out at him through the glass doors. She came out and said, "Superintendent Beck? I'm Monika Granholm."

She seized his hand in an iron grip and squeezed it passionately. He almost seemed to hear the bones of his hand crunch and he hoped that she didn't exert the same strength when handling the newborn babies.

She was almost as tall as Martin Beck and considerably larger. Her complexion was fresh and rosy, her teeth white and strong, the light-brown hair was thick and wavy and the irises in her big beautiful eyes had the same color as her hair. Everything about her radiated health and strength.

The dead girl in the bus had been small and delicate and must have looked very fragile beside this roommate.

They went out toward Dalagatan.

"Do you mind if we go to the Wasahof just across the street?" Monika Granholm asked. "I must have something inside me before I can talk."

The lunch hour was over and there were several vacant tables in the restaurant. Martin Beck chose a window table, but Monika Granholm preferred to sit farther inside.

"I don't want anyone from the hospital to see us," she said. "You've no idea how they gossip."

She confirmed this by regaling Martin Beck with choice tidbits of the gossip while she set to work heartily on a mountainous helping of meat balls and mashed potatoes. Martin Beck watched her enviously under lowered lids. As usual he was not hungry, only slightly sick, and he drank coffee in order to make his condition a little worse. He let her finish eating and was about to lead the conversation around to her dead colleague when she pushed her plate away and said, "That's better. Now you can fire away with your questions, and I'll try to answer as well as I can. May I just ask one question first?"

"Of course," Martin Beck replied, offering her a Florida from the pack.

She shook her head.

"I don't smoke, thanks. Have you caught that madman yet?"

"No," Martin Beck said. "Not yet."

"People are awfully het up, you know. One of the girls from the maternity ward doesn't dare take the bus to work any more. She's afraid the maniac will suddenly be standing there with his submachine gun. She's taken a taxi to and from the hospital ever since it happened. You must see that you catch him."

She looked exhortingly at Martin Beck.

"We're doing our best," he said.

She nodded.

"Good," she said.

"Thank you," Martin Beck replied gravely.

"What is it you want to know about Britt?"

"How well did you know her? How long had you two been sharing an apartment?"

"I knew her better than anyone, I should think. We've been roommates for three years, ever since she started here at Sabb. She was the world's best pal and a very capable nurse. Although she was delicate she worked hard. The perfect nurse. Never spared herself."

She took the coffee pot and filled Martin Beck's cup.

"Thank you," he said. "Didn't she have a boyfriend?"

"Oh yes, an awfully nice fellow. I don't think they were formally engaged, but she had already given me to understand she'd soon be moving. I've an idea they were going to get married in the new year. He already has an apartment."

"Had they known each other long?"

She bit her thumbnail and thought hard.

"Ten months at least. He's a doctor. Well, they say girls take up nursing just for the chance of marrying doctors, but it wasn't so with Britt anyway. She was awfully shy, and scared of men, if anything. Then she went on the sicklist last winter, she was anemic and generally rundown, and she had to go for a checkup pretty often. That's

72

how she met Bertil. It was love at first sight. She used to say it was his love that made her well, not his treatment."

Martin Beck sighed resignedly.

"What's wrong with that?" she asked suspiciously.

"Nothing at all. Did she know many men?"

Monika Granholm smiled and shook her head.

"Only the ones she met at the hospital. She was very reserved. I don't think she'd ever been with a man until she met this Bertil."

She drew patterns on the table with her finger. Then she frowned and looked at Martin Beck.

"Is it her love life you're interested in? What's that got to do with it?"

Martin Beck took his wallet out of his breast pocket and laid it in front of him on the table.

"Beside Britt Danielsson in the bus sat a man. That man was a policeman and his name was Åke Stenström. We have reason to suspect that he and Miss Danielsson knew one another and were together on the bus. What we're interested to know is this: Did Miss Danielsson ever mention the name of Åke Stenström?"

He took Stenström's photograph out of the wallet and put it in front of Monika Granholm.

"Have you ever seen this man?"

She looked at the photo and shook her head. Then she picked it up and studied it more closely.

"Yes," she said. "In the papers. Though this picture's better."

Handing back the photograph she said, "Britt didn't know the man. I can almost swear to that. And it's quite out of the question that she would have allowed anyone but her fiancé to see her home. She just wasn't that type."

Martin Beck put the wallet back in his pocket.

"They may have been friends and—"

She shook her head vigorously.

"Britt was very correct, very shy and, as I said, almost afraid of men. Besides, she was head over heels in love with Bertil and would never have looked at another fellow. Neither as a friend nor anything else. What's more, I was the only person on earth she confided in, except

Bertil of course. She told me everything. I'm sorry, Superintendent, but this must be a mistake."

Opening her handbag, she took out her purse.

"I must get back to my babies. I have seventeen at the
moment."

She started poking in her purse but Martin Beck put
out his hand and checked her.

"This is on the national government," he said.

When they were standing outside the hospital gates
Monika Granholm said, "It *is* possible they might have
known each other, been childhood playmates or schoolmates and met by chance. But that's all I can think of.
Britt lived in Eslöv until she was twenty. Where did this
policeman come from?"

"Hallstahammar," Martin Beck replied. "What is this
doctor's name besides Bertil?"

"Persson."

"And where does he live?"

"Gillerbacken 22, Bandhagen."

He held out his hand with some hesitation and for
safety's sake kept his glove on.

"My regards to the national government and thanks
for the lunch," Monika Granholm said, and strode off
briskly down the slope.

16

Gunvald Larsson's car was parked outside Tegnérgatan 40. Martin Beck looked at his watch and pushed
open the street door.

The time was twenty minutes past three, which meant
that Gunvald Larsson, who was always punctual, had already been with Mrs. Assarsson for twenty minutes. By
this time he had probably found out the main events of
her husband's life ever since he started school; Gunvald

Larsson's interrogation technique was to begin at the beginning and uncover everything step by step. While the method could be effective, often it was merely tiresome and wasted time.

The door of the apartment was opened by a middle-aged man wearing a dark suit with a silver-white tie. Martin Beck introduced himself and showed his official badge. The man held out his hand.

"I'm Ture Assarsson, brother of the . . . of the dead man. Please come in, your colleague is already here."

He waited while Martin Beck hung up his overcoat and then led the way through a pair of tall double doors.

"Märta, my dear, this is Superintendent Beck," he said.

The living room was large and rather dark. In a low, oat-colored sofa, which was over three yards long, sat a lean woman in a black jersey coat and skirt, with a glass in her hand. Putting the glass down on a black marble table in front of the sofa, she held out her hand with gracefully bent wrist, as though expecting him to kiss it. Martin Beck took her dangling fingers clumsily and mumbled, "My condolences, Mrs. Assarsson."

On the other side of the marble table stood a group of three low, pink easychairs, and in one of them sat Gunvald Larsson, looking peculiar. Only when Martin Beck, after a condescending gesture from Mrs. Assarsson, sat down himself did he realize Gunvald Larsson's problem.

As the construction of the chair really permitted only an outstretched horizontal position, and it would look odd with a reclining interrogator, Gunvald Larsson had more or less folded himself double. He was red in the face from the discomfort and glared at Martin Beck between his knees, which stuck up like two alpine peaks in front of him.

Martin Beck twisted his legs first to the left, then to the right, then he tried to cross them and wedge them under the chair, but it was too low. At last he adopted the same position as Gunvald Larsson.

Meanwhile the widow had drained her glass and held it out to her brother-in-law to be refilled. He gave her a searching look and then went and fetched a carafe and a clean glass from a sideboard.

"You'll have a glass of sherry, won't you, Superintendent," he said.

And before Martin Beck had time to protest the man had filled the glass and placed it on the table in front of him.

"I was just asking Mrs. Assarsson if she knew why her husband was on that bus on Monday night," Gunvald Larsson said.

"And I gave the same reply to you as I did to the person who had the bad taste to question me about my husband only seconds after I had been informed of his death. That I don't know."

She raised her glass to Martin Beck and drained it in one gulp. Martin Beck made an attempt to reach his sherry glass but missed by about a foot and fell back into the chair.

"Do you know where your husband was earlier in the evening?" he asked.

Putting down her glass, she took an orange-colored cigarette with a gold tip out of a green glass box on the table. She fumbled with the cigarette and tapped it several times on the lid of the box before allowing her brother-in-law to light it for her. Martin Beck noticed that she was not quite sober.

"Yes, I do," she said. "He was at a meeting. We had dinner at six o'clock, then he changed and went out about seven."

Gunvald Larsson took a piece of paper and a ball-point pen out of his breast pocket and asked, as he dug at his ear with the pen, "A meeting? Where and with whom?"

Assarsson looked at his sister-in-law and when she didn't answer he said, "It was an organization of old school friends. They called themselves the Camels. It consisted of nine members, who had kept in touch ever since they were at the naval cadet school together. They used to meet at the home of a businessman called Sjöberg on Narvavägen."

"The Camels?" Gunvald Larsson exclaimed incredulously.

"Yes," Assarsson replied. "They used to greet each

other by saying: 'Hi, old camel,' so they took to calling themselves the Camels."

The widow looked critically at her brother-in-law.

"It's an idealistic association," she said. "It does a lot for charity."

"Oh?" Gunvald Larsson said. "As for instance?"

"It's secret," Mrs. Assarsson replied. "Not even we wives were allowed to know. Some societies do that. Work *sub rosa*, so to say."

Feeling Gunvald Larsson's eyes on him, Martin Beck said, "Mrs. Assarsson, do you know when your husband left Narvavägen?"

"Well, I couldn't get to sleep, so I got up about two o'clock in the morning to take a little nightcap, and when I saw that Gösta hadn't come home I called up the Screw —that's what they call Mr. Sjöberg—and the Screw said that Gösta had left about half-past ten."

She stubbed out her cigarette.

"Where do you *think* he was going with the 47 bus?" Martin Beck asked.

Assarsson gave him an anxious look.

"He was on his way to some business acquaintance, of course. My husband was very energetic and worked very hard with his firm—that's to say, Ture here is also part-owner, of course—and it wasn't at all unusual for him to have business dealings at night. For instance, when people came up from the provinces and were only in Stockholm overnight and then, er . . ."

She seemed to lose the thread. She picked up her empty glass and twiddled it between her fingers.

Gunvald Larsson was busy writing on his scrap of paper. Martin Beck stretched one leg and massaged his knee.

"Have you any children, Mrs. Assarsson?" he asked.

Mrs. Assarsson put her glass in front of her brother-in-law to be refilled, but he immediately took it to the side-board without looking at her. She gave him a resentful look, stood up with an effort and brushed some cigarette ash off her skirt.

"No, Superintendent Peck, I haven't. Unfortunately my husband couldn't give me any children."

She stared vacantly at a point beyond Martin Beck's left ear. He could see now that she was pretty well stewed. She blinked slowly a couple of times and then looked at him.

"Are your parents American, Superintendent Peck?" she asked.

"No," Martin Beck replied.

Gunvald Larsson was still scribbling. Martin Beck craned his neck and looked at the piece of paper. It was covered with camels.

"If Superintendents Peck and Larsson will excuse me, I must retire," Mrs. Assarsson said, walking unsteadily toward the door.

"Good-bye, it's been *so* nice," she said vaguely, and closed the door behind her.

Gunvald Larsson put away his pen and the paper with the camels and struggled out of the chair.

"Whom did he sleep with?" he asked, without looking at Assarsson.

Assarsson glanced at the closed door.

"Eivor Olsson," he replied. "A girl at the office."

17

There was little to be said in favor of this repulsive Wednesday.

Not surprisingly, the evening papers had ferreted out the story of Schwerin, splashing it across the front pages and larding it with details and sarcastic gibes at the police.

The investigation was already at a deadlock. The police had smuggled away the only important witness. The police had lied to the press and the public.

If the press and the Great Detective the General Public were not given correct information, how could the police count on help?

The only thing the papers didn't say was that Schwerin

had died, but that was probably only because they had been so early going to press.

They had also managed somehow to nose out the dismal truth about the state in which the forensic laboratory technicians had found the scene of the crime.

Valuable time had been lost.

Unhappily, too, the mass murder had coincided with a raid—decided on several weeks earlier—on kiosks and tobacco shops in an attempt to confiscate pornographic literature.

One of the newspapers was kind enough to point out in a prominent place that a maniac mass murderer was running amok in town and that the public was panic-stricken.

And, it went on, while the scent grew cold a whole army of Swedish style Keystone Cops were plodding about looking at porno pictures, scratching their heads and trying to make out the ministry of justice's hazy instructions as to what could be considered offensive to public decency.

When Kollberg arrived at Kungsholmsgatan at about four o'clock in the afternoon, he had ice crystals in his hair and eyebrows, a grim expression on his face and the evening papers under his arm.

"If we had as many stoolies as local rags, we'd never have to lift a finger," he said.

"It's a question of money," Melander said.

"I know that. Does that make it any better?"

"No," Melander said. "But it's as simple as that."

He knocked out his pipe and returned to his papers.

"Have you finished talking to the psychologists?" Kollberg asked sourly.

"Yes," Melander replied without looking up. "The compendium is being typed out."

A new face was to be seen at investigation headquarters. One third of the promised reinforcements had arrived. Månsson from Malmö.

Månsson was almost as big as Gunvald Larsson but he showed a much more peaceable front to the world. He had driven up from Skåne during the night in his own car. Not in order to be able to collect the paltry mileage allowance for gasoline, but because he correctly considered it might be an advantage to have at his disposal a car with an m license from the Malmö area.

He was standing now by the window, gazing out and chewing at a toothpick.

"Is there anything I can do?" he asked.

"Yes. There are one or two we haven't had time to interrogate yet. Here, for instance. Mrs. Esther Källström. She is the widow of one of the victims."

"Johan Källström, the foreman?"

"Precisely. Karlbergsvägen 89."

"Where's Karlbergsvägen?"

"There's a map on the wall over there," Kollberg said wearily.

Månsson laid the chewed toothpick in Melander's ashtray, took a new one out of his breast pocket and looked at it apathetically. He studied the map for a while, then put on his overcoat. In the doorway he turned and looked at Kollberg.

"Say . . ."

"Yes, what is it?"

"Do you know of any shop where you can buy flavored toothpicks?"

"No, I really don't."

"Oh," Månsson said dejectedly.

Then he added informatively, "I'm told they do exist. I'm trying to give up smoking."

When the door had closed behind him Kollberg looked at Melander and said, "I've only met that guy once before. In Malmö in the summer of last year. And he said exactly the same thing then."

"About the toothpicks?"

"Yes."

"Extraordinary."

"What?"

"Not being able to find out about them after more than a year."

"Oh, you're hopeless," Kollberg exclaimed.

"Are you in a bad mood?"

"What the hell do you expect?" Kollberg snapped.

"There's no point in losing your temper. It only makes things worse."

"I like that, coming from you. You haven't any temper to lose."

Melander didn't reply to this, and the conversation came to an end.

Despite all statements to the contrary, the Great Detective the General Public was hard at work during the afternoon.

Several hundred people called up or looked in personally to say they thought they had ridden on that very bus.

All these statements had to be ground through the investigation mill and for once this tedious work turned out to be not entirely wasted.

A man who had boarded a doubledecker bus at Djurgårdsbron about ten o'clock on Monday evening said he was willing to swear that he had seen Stenström. He said this on the telephone and he was passed along to Melander, who immediately asked him to come up.

The man was about fifty. He seemed quite sure.

"So you saw Detective Inspector Stenström?"

"Yes."

"Where?"

"When I got on at Djurgårdsbron. He was sitting on the left near the stairs behind the driver."

Melander nodded to himself. No details had as yet leaked out to the press about how the victims had been sitting in relation to each other.

"Are you sure it was Stenström?"

"Yes."

"How do you know?"

"I recognized him. I've been a night watchman."

"Yes," Melander said. "A couple of years ago you sat in the vestibule of the old police headquarters on Agnegatan. I remember you."

"Why, so I did," the man said in astonishment. "But I don't recognize you."

"I only saw you twice," Melander replied. "And we didn't speak to each other."

"But I remember Stenström very well, because . . ."

He hesitated.

"Yes?" Melander prompted in a friendly tone. "Because . . . ?"

"Well, he looked so young, and he was wearing jeans and a sportshirt, so I thought he didn't belong there. I asked him to prove his identity. And . . ."

"Yes?"

"About a week later I made the same mistake. Very annoying."

"Oh, well, it easily happens. When you saw him the night before last, did he recognize you?"

"No, definitely not."

"Was anyone sitting beside him?"

"No, the seat was empty. I remember particularly, because I thought I'd say hello to him and sit there. But then I felt sort of awkward."

"Pity," Melander said. "And you got off at Sergels torg?"

"Yes, I changed to the subway."

"Was Stenström still there?"

"I think so. I hadn't seen him get off at any rate. Though of course I was sitting upstairs."

"Would you like a cup of coffee?"

"Well, I don't mind if I do," the man said.

"Would you be good enough to look at some pictures?" Melander asked. "But I'm afraid they're not very pleasant."

"No, I suppose not," the man mumbled.

He looked through the pictures, turning pale and swallowing once or twice. But the only person he recognized was Stenström.

Not long afterward Martin Beck, Gunvald Larsson and Rönn arrived practically at the same time.

"What?" said Kollberg. "Has Schwerin . . . ?"

"Yes," Rönn said. "He's dead."

"And?"

"He said something."

"What?"

"Don't know," Rönn replied, placing the tape recorder on the desk.

They stood around the desk listening.

"Who did the shooting?"

"Dnrk."

"What did he look like?"

"Koleson."

"Is that really all you can get out of this questioning?"

"Now listen to me, my good man, this is Detective Inspector Ullholm speaking—"

"He's dead."

"Jesus Christ," Gunvald Larsson exclaimed. "The very sound of that voice makes me want to throw up. He once reported me for breach of duty."

"What had you done?" Rönn asked.

"Said 'cunt' in the guardroom at Klara police station. A couple of the boys came in dragging a naked whore. She was loaded to the gills and was howling and had torn all her clothes off in the car. I tried to make them see that they should at least cover up her—well, wrap a blanket around her or something before carting her off to headquarters. Ullholm made out that I had caused mental injury to a girl who was not yet of age by using coarse and offensive language. He was the officer on duty. Then he applied for a transfer to Solna, to get closer to nature."

"Nature?"

"Yes, his wife, I presume."

Martin Beck played back the tape.

"Who did the shooting?"

"Dnrk."

"What did he look like?"

"Koleson."

"Are the questions your own idea?" Gunvald Larsson asked.

"Yes," Rönn replied modestly.

"Fantastic."

"He was only conscious for half a minute," Rönn said in a hurt tone. "Then he died."

Martin Beck played back the tape once more.

They listened over and over again.

"What on earth does he say?" Kollberg said.

He had not had time to shave and scratched at his stubble thoughtfully.

Martin Beck turned to Rönn.

"What do you think?" he said. "You were there."

"Well," Rönn said, "I think he understands the questions and is trying to answer."

"And?"

"That he answers the first question in the negative, for instance 'I don't know.' "

"How the hell do you make that out of 'Dnrk'?" Gunvald Larsson asked in astonishment.

Rönn reddened and shifted his weight from one foot to the other.

"Yes," said Martin Beck, "how do you reach that conclusion?"

"Well, I just sort of got that impression."

"Hm," Gunvald Larsson said. "And then?"

"To the second question he answers quite plainly 'Koleson.' "

"So I hear," Kollberg said. "But what does he mean?"

Martin Beck massaged his scalp with his fingertips.

"Karlsson, perhaps," he said, thinking hard.

"He says 'Koleson,' " Rönn maintained stubbornly.

"Yes," said Kollberg. "But there's no one with that name."

"We'd better check," Melander said. "The name *might* exist. Meanwhile . . ."

"Yes?"

"Meanwhile I think we ought to send this tape to an expert for analysis. If our own boys can't get anything out of it we can contact the radio. Their sound technicians have all the facilities. They can separate the sounds on the tape and try out different speeds."

"Yes," Martin Beck said. "It's a good idea."

"But for Christ's sake wipe out Ullholm first," Gunvald Larsson growled, "or we'll be the laughingstock of all Sweden."

He looked around the room.

"Where's that joker Månsson?"

"Got lost, I expect," Kollberg said. "We'd better alert all the patrol cars."

He sighed heavily.

Ek came in, a worried look on his face as he stroked his silver hair.

"What is it?" Martin Beck asked.

"The newspapers are complaining they haven't been given a picture of that man who is still unidentified."

"You know yourself what that picture would look like," Kollberg said.

"Sure, but—"

"Wait a minute," Melander said. "We can better the description. Between thirty-five and forty, height 5 feet 7 inches, weight 152 pounds, shoe size 8½, brown eyes, dark-brown hair. Scar from an appendicitis operation. Brown hair on chest and stomach. Scar from some old injury on the ankle. Teeth . . . No, it's no good."

"I'll send it out," Ek said and left the room.

They stood in silence for a while.

"Fredrik has got hold of something," said Kollberg. "That Stenström was already sitting in the bus when it got to Djurgårdsbron. So he must have come from Djurgården."

"What the hell was he doing there?" said Gunvald Larsson. "In the evening? In that weather?"

"I've also got hold of something," said Martin Beck. "That apparently he didn't know that nurse at all."

"Are you quite sure?" Kollberg asked.

"No."

"He seems to have been alone at Djurgårdsbron," Melander said.

"Rönn has also come up with something," said Gunvald Larsson.

"What?"

"That 'Dnrk' means 'I don't know.' To say nothing of this guy Koleson."

This was as far as they got on Wednesday, the fifteenth of November.

Outside, the snow was falling in large wet blobs. Darkness had already closed in.

Of course there was no one called Koleson. At least not in Sweden.

During Thursday they didn't get anywhere.

When Kollberg got home to his apartment on Palandergatan on Thursday evening the time was already past eleven o'clock. His wife sat reading in the circle of light under the floor lamp. She was dressed in a short housecoat buttoned in front and sat curled up in the armchair with her bare legs drawn up under her.

"Hello," said Kollberg. "How is your Spanish course going?"

"To the dogs, of course. Absurd to imagine you can do anything at all when you're married to a policeman."

Kollberg made no reply to this. Instead he got undressed and went into the bathroom. Shaved and took a long shower, hoping that some stupid neighbor wouldn't call up the police to send out a radio car, complaining of the water running so late. Then, putting on his bathrobe, he went into the living room and sat down opposite his wife. Regarded her thoughtfully.

"Haven't seen you for ages," she said without raising her eyes. "How are you all getting on?"

"Badly."

"I *am* sorry. It seems odd that someone can shoot nine people dead in a bus in the middle of town just like that. And that the police can't think of anything cleverer than making a lot of ridiculous raids."

"Yes," Kollberg said. "It is odd."

"Is there anyone else besides you who hasn't been home for thirty-six hours?"

"Probably."

She went on reading. He sat in silence for some time, perhaps ten or fifteen minutes, without taking his eyes off her.

"What are you goggling at?" she asked, still without looking up but with a note of mischief in her voice.

Kollberg didn't answer, and she appeared to be more deeply engrossed in her reading than ever. She had dark hair and brown eyes, her features were regular and her eyebrows thick. She was fourteen years younger than he was and had just turned twenty-nine, and he had always thought she was very pretty. At last he said,

"Gun?"

For the first time since he came home she looked at him, with a faint smile and a glint of shameless sensuality in her eyes.

"Yes?"

86

"Stand up."

"Why, certainly."

She turned down the upper right-hand corner of the page she had just read, shut the book and laid it on the arm of the chair. Stood up and let her arms hang loosely, her bare feet wide apart. She looked at him steadily.

"Not at all nice."

"Me?"

"No. Making dog-ears."

"It's my book," she said. "Bought with my own money."

"Strip," he said.

Raising her right hand to her neckband, she undid the buttons, slowly and one by one. Still without taking her eyes off him she opened the thin cotton housecoat and let it fall to the floor behind her.

"Turn around," said Kollberg.

She turned her back to him.

"You are beautiful."

"Thank you. Am I to stand like this?"

"No. The front is better."

"O-oh."

She turned right round and looked at him with the same expression on her face as before.

"Can you stand on your hands?"

"I could, at any rate, before I met you. Since then I've had no cause to. Shall I try?"

"You needn't bother."

"I can if you like."

She walked across the room and stood on her hands, arching her body upward and putting her feet against the wall. No effort at all.

Kollberg looked at her thoughtfully.

"Do you want me to stay like this?" she asked.

"No, it's not necessary."

"I'll do it gladly if it amuses you. They say you faint after a time. Of course in that case you can cover me over with a cloth or something."

"No, come down now."

She put her feet gracefully to the floor and stood upright, looking at him over her shoulder.

"Supposing I wanted to take your photograph like that?" he said. "What would you say?"

"What do you mean by like that? Naked?"

"Yes."

"Standing on my hands?"

"Yes, that for instance."

"You don't even have a camera."

"No, but that's neither here nor there."

"Of course you can if you want to. You can do whatever you goddam like with me. I already told you that two years ago."

He didn't answer. She remained standing by the wall.

"What are you going to do with the pictures anyway?"

"That's just the question."

Turning around, she went up to him. Then she said, "And now do you mind if I ask: What the hell is this all about? If it so happens that you want to make love to me, there's a comfortable bed in there, and if you can't be bothered going so far, this rya rug is also first-rate. Nice and soft. I made it myself."

"Stenström had a bundle of pictures like that in the drawer of his desk."

"At the office?"

"Yes."

"Of whom?"

"His girl."

"Åsa?"

"Yes."

"That can't have been any great feast for the eyes."

"I wouldn't say that," Kollberg replied.

She looked at him and frowned.

"The question is, why?" he said.

"Does it matter?"

"I don't know. I can't explain it."

"Perhaps he just wanted to look at them."

"That's what Martin said."

"It seems much more sensible, of course, to go home and have a look now and again."

"Of course, Martin isn't always so bright either. He's worried about us, for instance. You can tell by the look of him."

"About us? Why?"

"Because I went out alone on Friday evening, I think."

"He has a wife, hasn't he?"

"Something doesn't add up," Kollberg said. "With Stenström and these pictures."

"Why? You know how men are. Was she attractive in the pictures?"

"Yes."

"Very?"

"Yes."

"You know what I should say now."

"Yes."

"But I'm not going to say it."

"No. I know that, too."

"So far as Stenström is concerned, he probably wanted to show them to his pals. To boast."

"It doesn't add up. He wasn't like that."

"Why are you worrying about this?"

"Don't know. I suppose because there are no other clues left."

"Do you call this a clue? Do you think someone shot Stenström because of these pictures? In that case why should he kill eight more people?"

Kollberg looked at her intently.

"Exactly. That's a good question."

Bending over, she kissed him lightly on the forehead.

"Let's go to bed," Kollberg said.

"A brilliant idea. I'll just make a bottle for Bodil first. It only takes thirty seconds. According to the directions on the package. I'll see you in bed. Or on the floor or in the bathtub or wherever you goddam like."

"The bed, thanks."

She went out into the kitchen. Kollberg got up and turned off the floor lamp.

"Lennart?"

"Yes?"

"How old is Asa?"

"Twenty-four."

"Woman's sexual activity culminates between twenty-nine and thirty-two. Kinsey says so."

"Oh? And man's?"

"At eighteen."

He heard her whisking the babyfood in the saucepan. Then she called out, "But with men it's more individual. If that's any consolation."

Kollberg watched his wife through the half-open kitchen door. She was standing naked at the counter by the sink, stirring the saucepan. His wife was a long-legged girl of normal build and sensual nature. She was exactly what he wanted, but it had taken him over twenty years to find her and another year to think it over.

At the moment her posture was impatient and she kept fidgeting with her feet.

"Thirty seconds," she muttered to herself. "Goddam liars."

Kollberg smiled in the dark. He knew that soon he would be spared the thought of Stenström and the red doubledecker bus. For the first time in three days.

Martin Beck had not spent twenty years in search of his wife. He had met her seventeen years ago, made her pregnant on the spot and married in haste.

He had indeed repented at leisure, and now she was standing at the bedroom door, a living reminder of his mistake, in a crumpled nightdress and with red marks from the pillow on her face.

"You'll wake the whole house with your coughing and snuffling."

"I'm sorry."

"And why do you lie there smoking in the middle of the night?" she went on. "Your throat's bad enough as it is."

Stubbing out the cigarette, he said, "I'm sorry if I woke you up."

"Oh, it doesn't matter. The main thing is that you don't go and get pneumonia again. You'd better stay at home tomorrow."

"I can't very well."

"Nonsense. If you're ill you shouldn't go to work. You're not the only policeman. Besides, you should be asleep and not lie reading those old reports. You'll never clear up that taxi murder anyhow. It's half-past one.

Leave that old pile of papers alone and put the light out. Good night."

"Good night," Martin Beck said mechanically to the closed bedroom door.

Frowning, he slowly put the stapled report down. It was quite wrong to call it an old pile of papers, as it was a copy of the postmortem reports handed to him just as he was going home the evening before. It was true, however, that a few months earlier he had lain awake at night going through the investigation into the murder of a taxi driver twelve years before.

He lay still for a while, staring up at the ceiling. When he heard his wife's light snoring from the bedroom, he got up swiftly and tiptoed out into the hall. Hesitated a moment with his hand on the telephone. Then he shrugged, lifted the receiver and dialed Kollberg's number.

"Kollberg," Gun said breathlessly.

"Hi. Is Lennart there?"

"Yes. Closer than you'd think."

"What is it?" Kollberg muttered.

"Am I disturbing you?"

"You might say that. What the hell is it now?"

"Do you remember last summer, just after the park murders?"

"Yes, what?"

"We had nothing special to do then and Hammar said we were to look through old unsolved cases. Remember?"

"Of course, I damn well remember. What about it?"

"I went through the taxi murder in Borås and you worked on that old boy at Östermalm who simply disappeared seven years ago."

"Yes. Are you calling up just to say that?"

"No. What was Stenström working on? He had just got back from his vacation then."

"I haven't the vaguest idea. I thought he told you."

"No, he never mentioned it to me."

"Then he must have told Hammar."

"Yes. Yes, of course. Yes, you're right. So long then. Sorry I woke you up."

"Go to hell."

Martin Beck heard him bang the receiver down. He

stood with the phone to his ear for a few seconds before putting it down and slouching back to the sofa bed.

He lay down again and put the light out. Lay there in the dark feeling he had made a fool of himself.

18

Contrary to all expectations, Friday morning brought a hopeful scrap of news.

Martin Beck received it by telephone and the others heard him say, "What! Have you? Really?"

Everyone in the room dropped what he was doing and stared at him. Putting down the receiver he said, "They're through with the ballistic investigation."

"And?"

"They think they've identified the weapon."

"Oh," Kollberg said listlessly.

"A submachine gun," Gunvald Larsson said. "The army has thousands lying about in unguarded military depots. Might just as well deal them out free to the thieves and save themselves the trouble of putting on new padlocks once a week. As soon as I have half an hour to spare I'll ride out into town and buy half a dozen."

"It's not quite what you all think," Martin Beck said, holding the slip of paper he had scribbled on. "Model 37, Suomi type."

"Really?" Melander asked.

"That old kind with the wooden butt," Gunvald Larsson said. "I haven't seen one like that since the forties."

"Made in Finland or made here under license?" Kollberg asked.

"Finnish," Martin Beck said. "The guy who called up said they were almost sure. Old ammunition too. Made at Tikkakoski sewing machine factory."

"M 37," Kollberg said. "With 70-shot ammunition drum. Who is likely to have one today?"

"Nobody," Gunvald Larsson replied. "Today it's lying at the bottom of the harbor. A hundred feet down."

"Presumably," Martin Beck said. "But who can have had one four days ago?"

"Some mad Finn," Gunvald Larsson growled. "Out with the dog wagon and round up all the crazy Finns in town. A helluva nice job."

"Shall we say anything of this to the papers?" Kollberg asked.

"No," said Martin Beck. "Not a whisper."

They relapsed into silence. This was the first clue. How long would it take them to find the next?

The door was flung open and a young man came in and looked about him in curiosity. He had a brown envelope in his hand.

"Whom are you looking for?" Kollberg asked.

"Melander," the youth said.

"Detective Inspector Melander," Kollberg said reprimandingly. "He's sitting over there."

The young man went over and put the envelope on Melander's desk. As he was about to leave the room, Kollberg added, "I didn't hear you knock."

The youth checked himself, his hand on the doorhandle, but said nothing. There was silence in the room. Then Kollberg said, slowly and distinctly, as though explaining something to a child, "Before entering a room, you knock at the door. Then you wait until you are told to come in. Then you open the door and enter. Is that clear?"

"Yes," the young man mumbled, staring at Kollberg's feet.

"Good," Kollberg said, turning his back on him.

The young man slunk out of the door, closing it silently behind him.

"Who was that?" Gunvald Larsson asked.

Kollberg shrugged.

"Reminded me of Stenström actually," Gunvald Larsson said.

Melander put down his pipe, opened the envelope and drew some typewritten sheets bound in green covers. The booklet was about half an inch thick.

"What's that?" Martin Beck asked.

Melander glanced through it.

"The psychologists' compendium," he replied. "I've had it bound."

"A-ha," Gunvald Larsson said. "And what brilliant theories have they come up with? That our poor mass murderer was once put off a bus during puberty because he couldn't pay his fare and that this experience left such deep scars in his sensitive ment—"

Martin Beck cut him short.

"That is not amusing, Gunvald," he snapped.

Kollberg gave him a surprised glance and turned to Melander. "Well, Fredrik, what have you got out of that little opus?"

Melander scratched at his pipe and emptied it onto a piece of paper, which he then folded up and threw into the wastepaper basket.

"We have no Swedish precedents," he said. "Unless we go back as far as the Nordlund massacre on the steamer *Prins Carl*. So they've had to base their research on American surveys that have been made during the last few decades."

He blew at his pipe to see if it was clear and then started to fill it as he went on. "Unlike us, the American psychologists have no lack of material to work on. The compendium here mentions the Boston strangler; Speck, who murdered eight nurses in Chicago; Whitman, who killed sixteen persons from a tower and wounded many more; Unruh, who rushed out onto a street in New Jersey and shot thirteen people dead in twelve minutes, and one or two more whom you've probably read about before."

He riffled through the compendium.

"Mass murders seem to be an American specialty," Gunvald Larsson said.

"Yes," Melander agreed. "And the compendium gives some plausible theories as to why it is so."

"The glorification of violence," said Kollberg. "The career-centered society. The sale of firearms by mail order. The ruthless war in Vietnam."

Melander sucked at his pipe to get it burning and nodded.

"Among other things," he said.

"I read somewhere that out of every thousand Americans, one or two are potential mass murderers," Kollberg said. "Though don't ask me how they arrived at that conclusion."

"Market research," Gunvald Larsson said. "It's another American specialty. They go around from house to house asking people if they could imagine themselves committing a mass murder. Two in a thousand say, 'Oh yes, that would be nice.' "

Martin Beck blew his nose and looked irritably at Gunvald Larsson with red eyes.

Melander leaned back in his chair and stretched his legs in front of him.

"What do your psychologists have to say about the mass murderer's character?" Kollberg asked.

Melander turned the pages to a certain passage and read out:

" 'He is probably under thirty, often shy and reserved but regarded by those around him as well-behaved and diligent. It is possible that he drinks liquor, but it is more usual for him to be a teetotaler. He is likely to be small of stature or afflicted with disfigurement or some other physical deformity which sets him apart from ordinary people. He plays an insignificant part in the community and has grown up in straitened circumstances. In many cases his parents have been divorced or he is an orphan and has had an emotionally starved childhood. Often he has not previously committed any serious crime.' "

Raising his eyes, he said, "This is based on a compilation of facts that have emerged from interrogations and mental examinations of American mass murderers."

"A mass murderer like this must be stark, raving mad," Gunvald Larsson said. "Can't people *see* that before he rushes out and kills a bunch of people?"

" 'A person who is a psychopath can appear quite normal until the moment when something happens to trigger off his abnormality. Psychopathy implies that one or more of this person's traits are abnormally developed, while in other respects he is quite normal—for instance as regards aptitude, working capacity, etc. And in fact, most of these people who have suddenly committed a mass murder, recklessly and apparently without any motive, are described by neighbors and friends as considerate, kind and polite, and the last people on earth one would expect to act in this manner. Several of these American cases have told that they have been aware of their disease for some time and have tried to suppress their destructive tendencies, until at last they gave way to them. A mass murderer can suffer from persecution mania or megalomania or have a morbid guilt complex. It is not unusual for him to explain his actions by saying simply that he wanted to become famous and see his name in big headlines. Almost always, a desire for revenge or self-assertion lies behind the crime. He feels belittled, misunderstood and badly treated. In almost every case he has great sexual problems.' "

When Melander finished reading there was silence in the room. Martin Beck stared out of the window. He was pale and hollow-eyed and stooped more than usual.

Kollberg sat on Gunvald Larsson's desk, linking his paper clips together into a long chain. Irritated, Gunvald Larsson pulled the box of clips toward him. Kollberg broke the silence.

"That man Whitman, who shot a lot of people from the university tower in Austin," he said. "I read a book about him yesterday, in which an Austrian psychology professor stated that Whitman's sexual problem really was that he wanted to have intercourse with his mother. Instead of boring into her with his penis, he wrote, he stuck a knife into her. I haven't Fredrik's memory, but the last sentence of the book went like this: 'Then he climbed the erect tower—a distinct phallic symbol—and discharged his deathly seed like arrows of love over Mother Earth.' "

Månsson entered the room, his everlasting toothpick in the corner of his mouth.

"What the blazes are you talking about?" he asked.

"Maybe the bus is some sort of sex symbol," Gunvald Larsson said reflectingly. "Horizontal, though."

Månsson goggled at him.

Martin Beck got up, went over to Melander and picked up the green booklet.

"I'll borrow this and read through it in peace and quiet," he said. "Without any witty comments."

He walked toward the door but was stopped by Månsson, who took his toothpick out of his mouth and said, "What am I to do now?"

"I don't know. Ask Kollberg," Martin Beck said curtly and left the room.

"You can go and talk to that Arab's landlady," Kollberg said.

He wrote the name and address on a piece of paper, which he gave to Månsson.

"What's bothering Martin?" Gunvald Larsson asked. "Why's he so sore?"

Kollberg shrugged.

"I expect he has his reasons," he said.

It took Månsson a good half hour to make his way through the Stockholm traffic to Norra Stationsgatan. As he parked the car opposite the terminus of route 47 the time was a few minutes past four and it was already dark.

There were two tenants called Karlsson in the building, but Månsson had no difficulty working out which was the right one.

On the door were eight cards, fastened with thumb tacks. Two of them were printed, the others were written in a variety of hands and all bore foreign names. The name Mohammed Boussie was not among them.

Månsson rang the bell and the door was opened by a swarthy man in wrinkled pants and white undervest.

"May I speak to Mrs. Karlsson?" Månsson said.

The man showed white teeth in a broad smile and flung out his arms.

"Mrs. Karlsson not home," he said in broken Swedish. "Back soon."

"Then I'll wait here," Månsson said, stepping into the hall.

Unbuttoning his coat he looked at the smiling man.

"Did you know Mohammed Boussie who lived here?" he asked.

The smile was wiped off the man's face.

"Yes," he said. "It goddam terrible. Awful. He be my friend, Mohammed."

"Are you an Arab too?" Månsson asked.

"No. Turk. You foreigner too?"

"No," Månsson replied. "Swedish."

"Oh, I thought you had a little accent," the Turk said.

As Månsson did have a broad Skåne accent, it was not surprising that the Turk took him for a foreigner.

"I'm a policeman," Månsson said, looking at the man sternly. "I'd like to look around if you don't mind. Is there anyone else at home?"

"No, only me. I sick."

Månsson looked about him. The hall was dark and narrow; it was furnished with a kitchen chair, a small table and an umbrella stand of metal. On the table lay a couple of newspapers and some letters with foreign stamps. In addition to the front door, there were five doors in the hall; two of these, smaller than the others, probably belonged to a toilet and a clothes closet. One of them was a double door; Månsson went over to it and opened one half.

"Mrs. Karlsson's private room," the man in the undervest cried out in alarm. "To go in, forbidden."

Månsson glanced into the room, which was cluttered with furniture and evidently served as both bedroom and living room.

The next door led to the kitchen, which was large and had been modernized.

"Forbidden to go in kitchen," said the Turk behind him.

"How many rooms are there?" Månsson asked.

"Mrs. Karlsson's and the kitchen and the room for us," said the man. "And the toilet and closet."

Månsson frowned.

"Two rooms and kitchen, that is," he said to himself.

"You look our room," the Turk said, holding open the door.

The room measured about 23 feet by 16. It had two windows on to the street with flimsy, faded curtains. Along the walls stood beds of various types and between the windows was a narrow couch with the head to the wall.

Månsson counted six beds. Three of them were unmade. The room was littered with shoes, clothes, books and newspapers. The center of the floor was occupied by a round, white-lacquered table, surrounded by five odd chairs. The remaining piece of furniture was a tall, dark-stained chest of drawers, which stood against the wall by one of the windows.

The room had two more doors. A bed was placed in front of one of them, which without doubt led to Mrs. Karlsson's room and was locked. Inside the other was a small closet, stuffed with clothes and suitcases.

"Do six of you sleep here?" Månsson asked.

"No, eight," the Turk replied.

Walking over to the bed in front of the door, he half drew out a trundle bed and pointed to one of the other beds.

"Two like this," he said. "Mohammed had that one."

"Who are the other seven?" Månsson asked. "Turks like you?"

"No, we three Turks, two—one Arab, two Spanish men, one Finnish man, and the new one, he Greek."

"Do you eat here too?"

The Turk glided swiftly across the room and moved the pillow on one of the beds. Månsson caught a glimpse of a pornographic magazine before it was hidden by the pillow.

"Excuse, please," the Turk said. "Here it is . . . it is not so tidy. Do we eat here? No, cooking forbidden. Forbidden to use kitchen, forbidden to have electric hot plate in room. We not allowed to cook, not allowed to make coffee."

"How much rent do you pay?"

"We pay 350 kronor each," said the Turk.

"A month?"

"Yes. All months 350 kronor."

He nodded and scratched himself in the thick black growth resembling horsehair on his chest, visible above the low-necked vest.

"I earn lot of money," he said. "One hundred seventy kronor a week. I am truck driver. Before, I work restaurant and not earn so good."

"Do you know whether Mohammed Boussie had any relations?" Månsson asked. "Parents or brothers and sisters?"

The Turk shook his head.

"No, I not know. We were much pals, but Mohammed not say much. He very afraid."

Månsson stood by the window looking at a knot of shivering people who stood waiting for the bus at the terminus.

He turned around.

"Afraid?"

"Not afraid. What do you say? Ah yes, shuy."

"Shy, uh-huh," Månsson said. "Do you know how long he lived here?"

The Turk sat down on the couch between the windows and shook his head.

"No, I not know. I come here last month and Mohammed—he already live here."

Månsson had broken into a sweat under his thick overcoat. The air seemed thick with the smell that had oozed from the room's eight inmates.

Månsson wished fervently that he were back in Malmö, in his nice tidy apartment.

Fishing his last toothpick out of his pocket, he asked, "When will Mrs. Karlsson be back?"

The Turk shrugged.

"I not know. Soon."

Månsson stuck the toothpick in his mouth, sat down at the round table and waited.

After half an hour he tossed the chewed remains of the toothpick into the ashtray. Two more of Mrs. Karlsson's lodgers had arrived, but there was still no sign of the landlady herself.

The newcomers were the two Spaniards, and since their knowledge of Swedish was scanty and Månsson didn't know one word of Spanish, he soon gave up trying to question them. The only information he got was that their names were Ramón and Juan and that they worked as busboys at a grill bar.

The Turk had thrown himself on the couch and was

leafing idly through a German magazine. The Spaniards talked animatedly while they changed their clothes for an evening out; their plans seemed to include a girl called Kerstin, whom they were evidently discussing.

Månsson kept looking at his watch. He had made up his mind not to wait a minute longer than half-past five.

At twenty-eight minutes past five Mrs. Karlsson returned.

She placed Månsson in her best sofa, offered him a glass of port and burst into a jeremiad concerning her trials as a landlady.

"It's not at all nice, I can tell you, for a poor lone woman to have the house full of men," she whined. "And foreigners, what's more. But what is a poor hard-up widow to do?"

Månsson made a rough estimate. The hard-up widow raked in nearly 3,000 kronor a month in rent.

"That Mohammed," she said, pursing her lips. "He owed me a month's rent. Perhaps you could arrange for me to get it? He had money in the bank all right."

To Månsson's question about her impression of Mohammed, she replied, "Well, for an Arab he was quite nice, really. They're usually so dirty and unreliable, you know. But he was nice and quiet and seemed to behave himself all right—he didn't drink and I don't think he brought girls in. But as I said, he owes me a month's rent."

She appeared to be well informed about the private lives of her lodgers; sure enough, Ramón was going with a slut called Kerstin, but she could tell him little about Mohammed.

He had a married sister in Paris, who used to send him letters, but she couldn't read them because they were written in Arabic.

Mrs. Karlsson fetched a bundle of letters and gave them to Månsson. The sister's name and address were written on the backs of the envelopes.

All Mohammed Boussie's worldly possessions had been packed into a canvas suitcase. Månsson took this with him as well.

Mrs. Karlsson reminded him once more of the unpaid rent before shutting the door after him.

"My God, what an old bitch," Månsson mumbled to himself as he went down the stairs to the street and his car.

19

Monday. Snow. Wind. Bitter cold.

"Fine track snow," Rönn said.

He was standing by the window, looking dreamily out over the street and the rooftops, which were only just visible in the floating white haze.

Gunvald Larsson glared at him suspiciously and said, "Is that meant to be a joke?"

"No. I was just thinking how it felt when I was a boy."

"Extremely constructive. You wouldn't care to do something a little more worthwhile? To help the investigation along?"

"Sure," Rönn said. "But . . ."

"But what?"

"That's just what I was going to say. But what?"

"Nine people have been murdered," Gunvald Larsson said. "And here you stand not knowing what to do with yourself. You're a detective, aren't you?"

"Yes."

"Well then, detect, for Christ's sake."

"Where?"

"I don't know. Do something."

"What are you doing yourself?"

"Can't you see? I'm sitting here reading this psychological bilge that Melander and the doctors have concocted."

"Why?"

"I don't know. How can I know everything?"

A week had passed since the bloodbath in the bus. The

state of the investigation was unchanged and the lack of constructive ideas was making itself felt. Even the spate of useless tips from the general public had begun to dry up.

The consumer society and its harassed citizens had other things to think of. Although it was over a month to Christmas, the advertising orgy had begun and the buying hysteria spread as swiftly and ruthlessly as the Black Death along the festooned shopping streets. The epidemic swept all before it and there was no escape. It ate its way into houses and apartments, poisoning and breaking down everything and everyone in its path. Children were already howling from exhaustion and fathers of families were plunged into debt until their next vacation. The gigantic legalized confidence trick claimed victims everywhere. The hospitals had a boom in cardiac infarctions, nervous breakdowns and burst stomach ulcers.

The police stations downtown had frequent visits from the outriders of the great family festival, in the shape of Santa Clauses who were dragged blind drunk out of doorways and public urinals. At Mariatorget two exhausted patrolmen dropped a drunken Father Christmas in the gutter when they tried to get him into a taxi.

During the ensuing uproar the two policemen were hard pressed by bewildered, screaming children and furious, foul-mouthed boozers. One of the patrolmen lost his temper when a lump of ice landed in his eye and he resorted to his baton. Hit out at random and struck an inquisitive old-age pensioner. It didn't look pretty and the policehaters were given grist for their mill.

"There's a latent hatred of police in all classes of society," Melander said. "And it needs only an impulse to trigger it off."

"Oh," Kollberg said, with complete lack of interest. "And what is the reason for that?"

"The reason is that the police are a necessary evil," Melander said. "Everybody knows, even professional criminals, that they may suddenly find themselves in situations in which only the police can help them. When the burglar wakes up at night and hears a rattling in his cellar, what does he do? Calls the police, of course. But so long as such situations don't crop up, most people react with either fear or contempt when the police, in one way or the other, interfere in their existence or disturb their peace of mind."

"Well, that's the last straw, if we have to regard ourselves as a necessary evil," Kollberg muttered despondently.

"The crux of the problem is, of course," Melander went on, quite unconcerned, "the paradox that the police profession in itself calls for the highest intelligence and exceptional mental, physical and moral qualities in its practicians but has nothing to attract persons who possess them."

"You're horrible," Kollberg said.

Martin Beck had heard the argument many times before and was not amused.

"Can't you carry on your sociological discussions somewhere else?" he said grumpily. "I'm trying to think."

"Of what?" Kollberg said.

And the telephone rang.

"Hello. Beck."

"Hjelm here. How's it going?"

"Between ourselves, badly."

"Have you identified that guy with no face yet?"

Martin Beck had known Hjelm for many years and had great confidence in him. He was not the only one; Hjelm was considered by many to be one of the cleverest forensic technicians in the world. If he were handled in the right way.

"No," Martin Beck said. "Nobody seems to miss him. And the door-knockers have drawn a blank."

He drew a deep breath and went on.

"You don't mean to say you've produced something new?"

Hjelm must be flattered—that was a well-known fact.

"Yes," he said smugly. "We've given him an extra look-over. Tried to build up a more detailed picture. That gives some idea of the living person. I think we've managed to give him a certain character."

Can I say: "You don't mean it?" thought Martin Beck.

"You don't mean it," he said.

"Yes, I do," Hjelm said delightedly. "The result's better than we expected."

What should he pile on now? "Fantastic"? "Splendid"? Just plain: "Fine"? Or "Terrific"? Must go into training at Inga's coffee klatsch, he thought.

"Great," he said.

"Thanks," Hjelm replied enthusiastically.

"Don't mention it. I suppose you can't tell me—"

"Oh, sure. That's why I called up. We took a look at his teeth first. Not easy. They're in bad shape. But the fillings we have found are carelessly done. I don't think they can be the work of a Swedish dentist. I won't say any more on that point."

"That in itself is a good deal."

"Then there's his clothes. We've traced his suit to one of the Hollywood shops here in Stockholm. There are three, as you may know. One on Vasagatan, one on Götgatan and one at St. Eriksplan."

"Good," Martin Beck said laconically.

He couldn't play the hypocrite any more.

"Yes," Hjelm said sourly, "that's what I think. Further, the suit was dirty. It has certainly never been dry-cleaned, and I should think he's worn it day in day out for a long time."

"How long?"

"A year, at a guess."

"Have you anything more?"

There was a pause. Hjelm had kept the best till last. This was only a rhetorical pause.

"Yes," he said at length. "In the breast pocket of the jacket we found crumbs of hashish, and some grains in the right pants pocket derived from crushed Preludin tablets. The analyses of certain tests from the autopsy confirm that the man was a junkie."

New pause. Martin Beck said nothing.

"In addition, he had gonorrhea. In an advanced stage."

Martin Beck finished making his notes, said thank you and put down the phone.

"Reeks of the underworld," Kollberg declared.

He had been standing behind the chair eavesdropping.

"Yes," Martin Beck said. "But his fingerprints are not in our files."

"Perhaps he was a foreigner."

"Quite possibly," Martin Beck agreed. "But what shall we do with this information? We can hardly let it out to the press."

"No," Melander said. "But we can let it circulate by word of mouth among stoolies and known addicts. Via the drug squad and the community relations workers in the various police districts."

"Mmm," Martin Beck murmured. "Do that then."

Not much use, he thought. But what else was to be done? During the last few days the police had made two spectacular raids on the so-called underworld. The result was exactly what they expected. Meager. The raids had been foreseen by all except those who were most broken-down and destitute. The majority of those who had been picked up by the police—about one hundred and fifty— had been in need of immediate care and could be passed on to various institutions.

The inside investigation had so far produced nothing, and the detectives who handled the contacts with the dregs of society said they were convinced the stoolies really didn't know anything.

Everything seemed to bear this out. No one could reasonably gain anything by shielding this criminal.

"Except himself," said Gunvald Larsson, who had a fondness for unnecessary remarks.

The only thing they could do was to work on the material they already had. Try to trace the weapon and go on interrogating all who had had any connection with the victims. These interviews were now carried out by the reinforcements—Månsson from Malmö and a detective inspector from Sundsvall by the name of Nordin. Gunnar Ahlberg could not be spared from his ordinary work. It didn't really matter; everyone was pretty sure that these interrogations would lead nowhere.

The hours dragged past and nothing happened. Day was added to day. The days formed a week, and then another week. Once again it was Monday. The date one wrote was December 4 and the nameday was Barbro. The weather was cold and windy and the Christmas rush grew more and more hectic. The reinforcements got the blues and began to feel homesick, Månsson for the mild climate of southern Sweden and Nordin for the clear, bright cold of the northern winter. Neither of them was used to a big city and they both felt miserable in Stockholm. A lot of things got on their nerves, mainly the rush and tear, the jostling crowds and the unfriendly people. And as policemen they were irritated by the rowdyism and the petty crimes that were rife everywhere.

"It beats me how you guys stand it in this town," Nordin said.

He was a stocky, bald man with bushy eyebrows and screwed-up brown eyes.

"We were born here," Kollberg said. "We've never known anything else."

"I just came in on the subway," Nordin said. "Just between Alvik and Fridhemsplan I saw at least fifteen persons the police would have nabbed on the spot if it had been at home in Sundsvall."

"We're short of people," Martin Beck said.

"Yes, I know, but . . ."

"But what?"

"Have you ever thought of something? People are scared here. Ordinary decent people. If you ask for directions or ask them for a light, they practically turn and run. They're plain scared. Feel insecure."

"Who doesn't," Kollberg said.

"I don't," Nordin replied. "At least not as a rule. But I expect I'll be the same before long. Have you anything for me just now?"

"We have a weird sort of tip here," Melander said.

"What about?"

"The unidentified man in the bus. A woman in Hägersten. She called up and said she lives next door to a garage where a lot of foreigners collect."

"Uh-hunh. And?"

"It's usually pretty rowdy there, though she didn't put it like that. 'Noisy' is what she said. One of the noisiest was a small, dark man of about thirty-five. His clothes were

107

not unlike the description in the papers, she said, and now there hasn't been any sign of him."

"There are tens of thousands of people with clothes like that," Nordin said skeptically.

"Yes," Melander agreed, "there are. And with ninety-nine percent certainty this tip is useless. The information is so vague that there's really nothing to check. Moreover, she didn't seem at all sure. But if you've nothing else to do . . ."

He left the sentence in midair, scribbled down the woman's name and address on his notepad and tore off the sheet. The telephone rang and he lifted the receiver as he handed the paper to Nordin.

"Here you are," he said.

"I can't read it," Nordin muttered.

Melander's handwriting was cramped and almost illegible, at least to outsiders. Kollberg took the slip of paper and looked at it.

"Hieroglyphics," he said. "Or maybe ancient Hebrew. It was probably Fredrik who wrote the Dead Sea Scrolls. Though he doesn't have that much of a sense of humor. I'm his chief interpreter, however."

He copied out the name and address and said, "Here it is in plain writing."

"O.K.," Nordin said. "I can take a run out there. Is there a car?"

"Yes. But with the traffic as it is, and the state of the roads, you'd better stick to the subway. Take number 13 or 23 southbound and get off at Axelsberg."

"So long," Nordin said and went out.

"He didn't seem particularly inspired today," Kollberg remarked.

"Can you blame him?" Martin Beck replied, blowing his nose.

"Hardly," Kollberg said with a sigh. "Why don't we let these guys go home?"

"Because it's not our business," said Martin Beck. "They're here to take part in the most intensive manhunt ever known in this country."

"It would be nice to—" Kollberg began, and broke off, feeling it was superfluous to go on. It certainly would be nice to know whom one was hunting and where the hunt ought to be carried on.

"I'm merely quoting the Minister of Justice," Martin Beck said innocently. " 'Our keenest brains'—he's referring of course to Månsson and Nordin—'are working at high pressure to corner and capture an insane mass murderer; it is of prime importance to both the community and the individual that he be put out of action.' "

"When did he say that?"

"For the first time seventeen days ago. For the umpteenth time yesterday. But yesterday he was given only four lines on page 22. I bet that rankles. There's an election next year."

Melander had finished his telephone conversation. He poked at the bowl of his pipe with a straightened paper clip and said quietly, "Isn't it about time we took care of the insane mass murderer, so to speak?"

Fifteen seconds passed before Kollberg replied. "Yes, it certainly is. It's also time to lock the door and shut off the telephones."

"Is Gunvald here?" Martin Beck asked.

"Yes, Mr. Larsson is sitting in there picking his teeth with the paper knife."

"Tell them to put all calls through to him," Martin Beck said.

Melander reached for the phone.

"Tell them to send up some coffee, too," Kollberg said. "Three sweet rolls and a Mazarine for me, please."

The coffee arrived after ten minutes. Kollberg locked the door.

They sat down. Kollberg slurped the coffee and started in on the sweet rolls.

"The situation is as follows," he said with his mouth full. "The crazy murderer with a lust for sensation is standing lugubriously in the police commissioner's closet. When he's needed we take him out again and dust him off. The working hypothesis is therefore this: A person armed with a Suomi submachine gun model 37 shoots nine people dead on a bus. These people have no connection with each other, they merely happen to be in the same place at the same time."

"The gunman has a motive," Martin Beck said.

"Yes," Kollberg said, reaching for the Mazarine cupcake. "That's what I've thought all along. But he can't have a motive for killing people who are together haphazardly. Therefore his real intention is to eliminate one of them."

"The murder was carefully planned," Martin Beck said.

"One of the nine," Kollberg said. "But which? Have you the list there, Fredrik?"

"Don't need it," Melander said.

"No, of course not. Didn't think what I was saying. Let's go through it."

Martin Beck nodded. The following conversation took the form of a dialogue between Kollberg and Melander.

"Gustav Bengtsson," Melander said. "The bus driver. His presence on the bus was justified, we can say."

"Undeniably."

"He seems to have led an ordinary, normal life. No marital troubles. No convictions. Conscientious at work. Liked by his colleagues. We've also questioned some friends of the family. They say he was respectable and steady-going. He was a teetotaler. Forty-eight years old. Born here in the city."

"Enemies? None. Influence? None. Money? None. Motive for killing him? None. Next."

"I'm not following Rönn's numbering now," Melander said. "Hildur Johansson, widow, sixty-eight. She was on her way home to Norra Stationsgatan from her daughter in Västmannagatan. Born at Edsbro. Daughter questioned by Larsson, Månsson and . . . ha, it doesn't matter. She led a quiet life and lived on her old-age pension. There's not much more to say about her."

"Well, just that she presumably got on at Odengatan and only went six stops. And that no one except her daughter and son-in-law knew she would ride that particular stretch at that particular time. Go on."

"Johan Källström, who was fifty-two and born in Västerås. Foreman at a garage, Gren's on Sibyllegatan. He had been working overtime and was on his way home, that's clear. He, too, happily married. His chief interests, his car and summer cottage. No convictions. Earned good money, but no more. Those who know him say he probably took the subway from Östermalmstorg to Central Station, where he changed to the bus. Should therefore have come up at the Drottninggatan exit and boarded the bus outside Åhléns department store. His boss says he was a skilled workman and a good foreman. The mechanics at the garage say that he was—"

". . . a slavedriver to those he could bully and a boot-licker to his bosses. I went and talked to them. Next."

"Alfons Schwerin was forty-three and born in Minne-apolis, in the U.S.A., of Swedish-American parents. Came to Sweden just after the war and stayed here. He had a small business that imported Carpathian spruce for sound-ing boards, but he went bankrupt ten years ago. Schwerin drank. He had two spells at Beckomberga in the alcoholic clinic and was sentenced to three months at Bogesund for drunken driving. That was three years ago. When his business went to pot he became a laborer. He was work-ing now for the local council. On the evening in question he had been at Restaurant Pilen on Bryggargatan and was on his way home. He hadn't had much to drink, presum-ably because he was broke. His lodgings were mean and shabby. He probably walked from the restaurant to the bus stop on Vasagatan. He was a bachelor and had no relations in Sweden, his fellow workers liked him. Say he was pleasant and good-tempered, could hold his liquor and hadn't an enemy in the world."

"And he saw the killer and said something unintelligible to Rönn before he died. Have we had the expert's report on the tape?"

"No. Mohammed Boussie, Algerian, worked at a res-taurant, thirty-six, born at some unpronounceable place the name of which I've forgotten."

"Tsk, how careless."

"He had lived in Sweden for six years and before that in Paris. Took no active part in politics. He had a savings account at the bank. Those who knew him say he was shy and reserved. He had finished work at ten thirty and was on his way home. Decent, but stingy and dull."

"You're sitting there describing yourself."

"Britt Danielsson, nurse, born 1940 at Eslöv. She was

sitting beside Stenström, but there's nothing to show she knew him. The doctor she was going steady with was on duty that night at Southern Hospital. She presumably got on at Odengatan together with the widow Johansson and was on her way home. There are no time margins there. She finished work and went to the bus. Of course we don't know for sure that she was not together with Stenström."

Kollberg shook his head.

"Not a chance," he said. "Why should he bother about that pale little thing? He had all he wanted at home."

Melander looked at him blankly but let the question drop.

"Then we have Assarsson. A respectable exterior but not so pretty underneath."

Melander paused and fiddled with his pipe. Then he went on:

"Rather shady figure, this Assarsson. Sentenced twice for tax evasion and also for a sexual offense at the beginning of the 1950s. Sexually exploited a fourteen-year-old errand girl. Prison all three times. Assarsson had plenty of money. He was ruthless in business and in everything else. A lot of people had reason to dislike him. Even his wife and his brother thought he was pretty nasty. But one thing is clear. His presence on the bus had a reason. He had come from some sort of club meeting on Narvavägen and was on his way to a mistress by the name of Olsson. She lives on Karlbergsvägen and works at Assarsson's office. He had called her up and told her he was coming. We have interrogated her several times."

"Who questioned her?"

"Gunvald and Månsson. On different occasions. She says that—"

"Just a moment. Why did he take the bus?"

"Presumably because he'd had a lot to drink and didn't dare to drive his own car. And he couldn't get hold of a taxi because of the rain. The company's central switchboard was overloaded and there wasn't a vacant taxi in the whole of town."

"O.K. What does the kept woman say?"

"That she thought Assarsson was a dirty old man, and almost impotent. That she did it for the money and to

112

keep her job. Gunvald got the impression that she's a bit of a slut and has other men as well, and is rather backward."

"Mr. Larsson and women. I think I'll write a novel and call it that."

"She admitted as much to Månsson that she used to oblige Assarsson's business acquaintances, as she put it. At his orders. Assarsson was born in Gothenburg and got on at Djurgårdsbron."

"Thanks, old pal. That's exactly how I'll begin my novel. 'He was born in Gothenburg and got on at Djurgårdsbron.' Brilliant."

"All the times fit," Melander said, unperturbed.

Martin Beck broke into the conversation for the first time.

"So that leaves only Stenström and the unknown man?"

"Yes," Melander said. "All we know about Stenström is that he came from Djurgården, oddly enough. And that he was armed. As regards the unidentified man, we know that he was a narcotics addict and between thirty-five and forty. Nothing more."

"And all the others had a reason for being on the bus?" Martin Beck asked.

"Yes."

"We have found out why they were there?"

"Yes."

"The moment has come for the already classic question: What was Stenström doing on the bus?" Kollberg said.

"We must talk to the girl," Martin Beck said.

Melander took his pipe out of his mouth.

"Asa Torell? You've already talked to her, both of you. And since then we've questioned her again."

"Who?" Martin Beck asked.

"Rönn, a little over a week ago."

"No, not Rönn," he murmured to himself.

"What do you mean?" said Melander.

"Rönn's right enough in his way," Martin Beck said. "But in this case he doesn't quite understand what it's all about. Besides, he had very little contact with Stenström."

Kollberg and Martin Beck looked at each other for a

long time. Neither of them said anything, and at last it was Melander who broke the silence.

"Well? What was Stenström doing on the bus?"

"He was going to meet a girl," Kollberg said unconvincingly. "Or a pal."

Kollberg's part in these discussions was always to contradict, but this time he didn't really believe in himself.

"One thing you're forgetting," Melander said. "We've been knocking at doors in that district for ten days. And not found a single person who has ever heard of Stenström."

"That proves nothing. That part of town is full of odd little hideaways and shady boarding houses. At places like that the police are not very popular."

"All the same, I think we can dismiss the girlfriend theory as far as Stenström is concerned," Martin Beck said.

"On what grounds?" Kollberg asked quickly.

"I don't believe in it."

"But you admit that it's quite possible?"

"Yes."

"O.K. Dismiss it then. For the time being."

"The key question therefore seems to be: What was Stenström doing on the bus?" Martin Beck said.

"Wait a minute," Kollberg objected. "What was the unknown man doing on the bus?"

"Never mind the unknown man at the moment."

"Why? His presence is just as remarkable as Stenström's. Besides, we don't know who he was or what business he had there."

"Maybe he was just riding the bus."

"Just riding the bus?"

"Yes. Many homeless people do. For one krona you can ride two trips. A couple of hours."

"The subway is warmer," Kollberg objected. "And there you can ride as long as you like, what's more, provided you don't pass through the gates but only change trains."

"Yes, but—"

"And you're forgetting something important. Not only did the unidentified man have crumbs of hash and pep

114

pills in his pockets. He also had more money than all the passengers put together."

"Which, incidentally, excludes the possibility of murder for the sake of robbery," Melander put in.

"Furthermore," added Martin Beck, "as you yourself said, that district is full of hide-outs and shady boarding houses. Perhaps he lived in one of those fleabags. No, back to the basic question: What was Stenström doing on the bus?"

They sat silent for at least a minute. In the next room the telephones kept ringing. Now and then they could hear voices, Gunvald Larsson's or Rönn's. At last Melander said, "What could Stenström do?"

All three knew the answer to that question. Melander nodded slowly and answered himself.

"Stenström could shadow."

"Yes," Martin Beck said. "That was his specialty. He was skillful and stubborn. He could go on shadowing a person for weeks."

Kollberg scratched his neck and said, "I remember when he drove that sex murderer from the Göta Canal boat mad four years ago."

"Baited him," said Martin Beck.

No one answered.

"He had the knack even then," said Martin Beck. "But he had learned a lot since then."

"By the way, did you ask Hammar about that?" Kollberg said suddenly. "I mean about what Stenström did last summer when we went through unsolved cases."

"Yes," Martin Beck replied. "But I drew a blank. Stenström had discussed the matter with Hammar, who made one or two suggestions—which ones he didn't remember, but they were ruled out by age. Not because the cases were too old but because Stenström was too young. He didn't want anything that had happened when he was a boy of ten running around playing cops and robbers in Hallstahammar. At last he decided to look into that disappearance case that you too were working on."

"I never heard anything from him," Kollberg said.

"I suppose he just went through what was written."

"Probably."

Silence, and Melander was again the one to break it. Getting up he said, "Hm, where have we got to?"

"Don't quite know," said Martin Beck.

"Excuse me," Melander said and went out to the toilet.

When he had closed the door, Kollberg looked at Martin Beck and said, "Who's going to see Åsa?"

"You. It's a one-man job and of us two you're best fitted for it."

Kollberg made no answer.

"Don't you want to?" Martin Beck asked.

"No, I don't. But I will all the same."

"This evening?"

"I have two matters to attend to first. One at Västberga and one at home. Call her up and say I'll be along about seven thirty."

An hour later Kollberg entered his apartment at Palandergatan. The time was five o'clock, but outside it had already been dark for a couple of hours.

His wife was busy painting the kitchen chairs in a pair of faded jeans and a checked flannel shirt. It was his, and discarded long ago. She had rolled up the sleeves and tied it carelessly around her waist. She had paint on her hands and arms and feet, and even on her forehead.

"Strip," he said.

She stood quite still with the brush raised. Gave him a searching look.

"Is it urgent?" she asked mischievously.

"Yes."

She grew serious at once.

"Must you go again?"

"Yes, I have an interrogation."

She nodded and put the brush in the paint can. Wiped her hands.

"Åsa," he said. "It's going to be tricky in every way."

"Do you need a vaccination?"

"Yes."

"Mind you don't get paint all over you," she said, unbuttoning the shirt.

116

20

Outside a house on Klubbacken in Hägersten a snowy man stood looking thoughtfully at a scrap of paper. It was sopping wet and was coming apart; he had difficulty in making out the writing in the whirling snow and the dim light from the street lamps. However, it seemed as if he had at last found the right place. He shook himself like a wet dog and went up the steps. Stamped energetically on the porch and rang the doorbell. Knocked the wet white flakes off his hat and stood with it in his hand as he waited for something to happen.

The door was opened a few inches and a middle-aged woman peeped out. She was wearing a cleaning smock and apron and had flour on her hands.

"Police," he said raucously. Clearing his throat, he went on, "Detective Inspector Nordin."

The woman eyed him anxiously.

"Can you prove it?" she said at last. "I mean . . ."

With a heavy sigh, he transferred his hat to his left hand and unbuttoned his overcoat and jacket. Took out his wallet and showed his identification card.

The woman followed the procedure with alarm, as if expecting him to take out a bomb or a machine gun or a condom.

He kept hold of the card and she peered at it shortsightedly through the crack in the door.

"I thought detectives had badges," she said doubtfully.

"Yes, madam, I have one," he said gloomily.

He kept his badge in his hip pocket and wondered how he would get at it without laying down his hat or putting it on his head.

"Oh, I suppose this will do," the woman said grudgingly. "Sundsvall? Have you come all the way from the north to talk to me?"

"I did have some other business in town as well."

"I'm sorry, but you see . . . I mean . . . ," she faltered.

"Yes, madam?"

"I mean you can't be too careful nowadays. You never know . . ."

Nordin wondered what on earth he was to do with his hat. The snow was falling thickly and the flakes were melting on his bald head. He could hardly go on standing with the identification card in one hand and his hat in the other. He might want to note something down. To replace the hat on his head seemed the most practical but might appear impolite. It would look silly putting it down on the steps. Perhaps he ought to ask if he might go inside. But then the woman would be faced with a decision. She would have to answer yes or no, and if he had judged her rightly, such a decision might take a long time.

Nordin came from a part of the country where it was customary to invite all strangers into the kitchen, offer them a cup of coffee and let them warm themselves by the stove. A nice, practical custom, he thought. Perhaps it wasn't suitable in big cities. Collecting his thoughts, he said, "When you called up you mentioned a man and a garage, didn't you?"

"I'm awfully sorry if I disturbed you . . ."

"Oh, we couldn't be more grateful."

She turned her head and looked in toward the apartment, almost closing the door as she did so. She was evidently worried about the ginger snaps in the oven.

"Delighted," Nordin muttered to himself. "Deliriously happy. It's almost unbearable."

The woman opened the door again and said, "What did you say?"

"Er, that garage—"

"It's over there."

He followed her gaze and said, "I don't see anything."

"You can see it from upstairs," the woman said.

"And this man?"

"Well, he seemed funny. And now I haven't seen him for a couple of weeks. A short, dark man."

"Do you keep a constant watch on the garage?"

"Well, I can see it from the bedroom window."

118

She flushed. What have I done wrong now, Nordin wondered.

"Some foreigner has it. All sorts of queer characters hang about there. And what I'd like to know is—"

It was impossible to know whether she broke off or went on talking in such a low voice that he couldn't catch the words.

"What was strange about this short, dark man?"

"Well . . . he laughed."

"Laughed?"

"Yes. Awfully loud."

"Do you know if there's anyone in the garage now?"

"There was a light not long ago. When I went up and had a look."

Nordin sighed and put on his hat.

"Well, I'll go and make inquiries," he said. "Thank you, madam."

"Won't you . . . come in?"

"No thanks."

She opened the door another few inches, gave him a quick glance and said graspingly, "Is there any reward?"

"For what?"

"Er . . . I don't know."

"Good-bye."

He trudged off in the direction she had indicated. It felt as if someone had put a fomentation on his head. The woman had shut the door at once and had now presumably taken up her post at the bedroom window.

The garage, a small building standing by itself, had fibrous cement walls and a corrugated iron roof. There was room for two cars at the most. Above the doors was an electric light.

He opened one half of the double doors and went in.

The car standing inside was a green Skoda Octavia, 1959 model. It might fetch 400 kronor if the engine wasn't too worn out. Thought Nordin, who had spent a great deal of his time as policeman on motor vehicles and shady car deals. It was propped up on low trestles and the hood was open. A man lay on his back under the chassis, quite still. All that could be seen of him was a pair of legs in blue overalls.

Dead, thought Nordin, going up to the car and poking the man with his right foot.

The figure under the car started as though at an electric shock, crawled out and got to his feet. Stood with the hand lamp in his right hand staring in amazement at the visitor.

"The police," Nordin said.

"My papers are in order," the man said quickly.

"I don't doubt it," Nordin retorted.

The garage owner was about thirty, a slender man with brown eyes, wavy dark hair and well-combed sideburns.

"Are you Italian?" Nordin asked. He was not much of an expert at foreign accents except Finnish.

"Swiss. From German Switzerland. The canton of Graubünden."

"You speak good Swedish."

"I've lived here for six years. What is it you want?"

"We're trying to get in touch with a pal of yours."

"Who?"

"We don't know his name."

Eyeing the man in the dungarees Nordin said, "He's not quite as tall as you but a bit fatter. Dark hair, rather long, and brown eyes. About thirty-five."

The other shook his head.

"I've no pal that looks like that. I don't meet much people."

"Many people," Nordin corrected amiably.

"Yes, of course. 'Many people.' "

"But I've heard there are usually a lot of people out here at the garage."

"Guys come with cars. They want me to fix when there is something wrong."

He thought hard, then said by way of information:

"I am a mechanic. Work at a garage in Ringweg . . . Ringvägen. Now only in the mornings. All these Germans and Austrians know that I have this garage. So they come out and want repairs free. Many I do not know at all. There are many in Stockholm."

"Well," Nordin said, "this man we want to get hold of might have been dressed in a black nylon coat and a beige suit."

"That tells me nothing. I do not remember anyone like that. That's certain."

"Who are your buddies?"

"Friends? A few Germans and Austrians."

"Have any of them been here today?"

"No. They know all I am busy. I work day and night on this."

He pointed to the car with an oily thumb and said, "I get it fixed up by Christmas, so I can drive home and see my parents."

"To Switzerland?"

"Yes."

"Some drive."

"Yes. I pay only 100 kronor for this car. But I get it ready. I good mechanic."

"What's your name?"

"Horst. Horst Dieke."

"Mine's Ulf. Ulf Nordin."

The Swiss smiled, showing perfect white teeth. He seemed a pleasant, steady-going young man.

"Well, Horst, so you don't know who I mean?"

Dieke shook his head.

"No. I'm sorry."

Nordin was in no way disappointed. He had simply drawn the blank that everyone expected. If there hadn't been such a scarcity of clues, this tip would never have been followed up at all. But he was not prepared to give in yet, and besides he didn't fancy the subway with its horde of unfriendly people in damp clothes. The Swiss was evidently trying to be helpful. He said, "There is nothing else? About that guy, I mean?"

Nordin considered. At last he said, "He laughed. Loud."

The man's face brightened at once.

"Ah, I think I know. He laughs like this."

Dieke opened his mouth and emitted a bleating sound, shrill and harsh as the cry of a snipe.

It came as an utter surprise and about ten seconds passed before Nordin could say, "Yes, perhaps."

"Yes, yes," Dieke said. "I know now who you mean. Little dark guy."

Nordin waited expectantly.

"He has been here four or five times. Maybe more. But his name, I do not know it. He came with a Spaniard who wanted to sell me spare parts. He came several times. But I did not buy."

"Why not?"

"Cheap. I think stolen."

"What was this Spaniard's name?"

Dieke shrugged.

"Don't know. Paco. Pablo. Paquito. Something like that."

"What sort of car did he have?"

"Good car. Volvo Amazon. White."

"And this man who laughed?"

"Don't know at all. He was just in the car. He'd had a few drinks, I think. But of course he didn't drive."

"Was he Spanish too?"

"I think not. I think Swedish. But I don't know."

"How long ago he came here?"

That didn't sound right. Nordin pulled himself together.

"How long since he was here last?"

"Three weeks ago. Perhaps two. Exactly I do not know."

"Have you seen this Spaniard since then? Paco or whatever his name is?"

"No. I think he was going back to Spain. Needed money, that why he wanted to sell. So he said anyway."

Nordin paused to consider.

"You said he seemed a bit drunk, this guy. Do you think he might have had a fix?"

A shrug.

"Don't know. I think he had been drinking. But—dope? Well, why not? Nearly everybody here gets high. Lie in their junkie pads when they're not out stealing. No?"

"You've no idea what his name is or what they call him?"

"No. But a couple of times a girl was in the car. With him, I think. A big girl. Long fair hair."

"What's her name?"

"I don't know. But they call her—"

"Yes? What?"

"Blonde Malin, I think."

"How do you know?"

"I have seen her before. In town."

"Whereabouts in town?"

"At a café on Tegnérgatan. Near Sveavägen. Where all foreigners go. She is Swedish."

"Blonde Malin?"

"Yes."

Nordin couldn't think of anything more to ask. He looked doubtfully at the green car and said, "I hope you get home all right."

Dieke gave his infectious smile.

"Oh yes."

"When are you coming back?"

"Never."

"Never?"

"No. Sweden bad country. Stockholm bad city. Only violence, narcotics, thieves, liquor."

Nordin said nothing. With the last he was inclined to agree.

"Misery," the Swiss said, summing up. "But easy to earn money for foreigner. Everything else hopeless. I live in a room with three others. Pay 400 kronor a month. How do you say—extortion? Dirty trick. Just because there is a housing shortage. Only rich men and criminals can afford to go to restaurants. I have saved money. I'm going home, I get my own little garage and marry."

"Haven't you met any girls here?"

"Swedish girls are not worth having. Maybe students and the like can meet nice girls. Ordinary workmen meet only one sort. Like this Blonde Malin."

"What sort?"

"Whores." He pronounced the "W."

"You mean you don't want to pay for girls?"

Horst Dieke pouted.

"Many cost nothing. Whores all the same. Free whores."

Nordin shook his head.

"You've only seen Stockholm, Horst. Pity."

"Is the rest any better?"

Nordin nodded emphatically. Then he said, "And you don't remember anything more about this guy?"

"No. Only that he laughed. Like this."

Dieke opened his mouth and again emitted the shrill, bleating cry.

Nordin nodded good-bye and left.

Under the nearest lamp post he stopped and took out his notebook.

"Blonde Malin," he murmured. "Junkie pads. Free whores. What a profession to have chosen."

It's not my fault, he thought. The old man forced me into it.

A man approached along the sidewalk. Nordin raised his Tyrolean hat, which was already covered with snow, and said, "Excuse me, can you—"

With a swift, suspicious glance at him the man hunched his shoulders and hurried on.

". . . tell me where the subway station is?" Nordin murmured to the whirling blobs of wet snow.

Shaking his head, he scribbled a few words on the open page.

Pablo or Paco. White Amazon. Café Tegnérgatan–Sveavägen. Laughter. Blonde Malin, free whore.

Then, putting pen and paper in his pocket, he sighed and trudged away out of the circle of light.

21

Kollberg stood outside the door of Åsa Torell's apartment in Tjärhovsgatan. The time was already eight o'clock in the evening and in spite of everything he felt worried and absent-minded. In his right hand he held the envelope they had found in the drawer out at Västberga.

The white card with Stenström's name was still on the door above the brass plate.

The bell didn't seem to be working and, true to habit, he pounded with his fist on the door. Åsa Torell opened it at once. Stared at him and said, "All right, all right, here I am. For God's sake don't kick the door down."

"Sorry," Kollberg mumbled.

It was dark in the apartment. He took his coat off and switched on the hall light. The old police cap was lying on the hat rack, just as before. The wire of the doorbell had been wrenched loose and was dangling from the jamb.

Asa Torell followed his gaze and muttered, "A horde of idiots kept intruding. Journalists and photographers and God knows who. The bell never stopped ringing."

Kollberg said nothing. He went into the living room and sat down in one of the safari chairs.

"Can't you put the light on so that at least we can see one another?"

"I can see quite well enough. All right, if you like, if you like, sure I'll put it on."

She switched on the light, but did not sit down. She paced restlessly to and fro, as though she were caged in and wanted to get out.

The air in the apartment was stale and stuffy. The ashtrays had not been emptied for several days. The whole room was untidy and didn't seem to have been cleaned at all, and through the open door he saw that the bedroom too was in a mess and that the bed had certainly not been made. From the hall he had also glanced into the kitchen, where dirty plates and saucepans lay piled up in the sink.

Then he looked at the young woman. She walked up to the window, swung around and walked back toward the bedroom. Stood for a few seconds staring at the bed, turned again and went back to the window. Over and over again.

He had to keep moving his head from side to side to follow her with his eyes. It was almost like watching a tennis match.

Asa Torell had changed during the nineteen days that had passed since he saw her last. She had the same thick gray skiing socks on her feet, or at any rate similar ones, and the same black slacks. But this time they were spotted with cigarette ash and her hair was uncombed and matted. Her gaze was unsteady and she had dark rings under her eyes; the skin on her lips was dry and cracked. She could not keep her hands still and the insides of the forefinger and middle finger of her left hand were stained a virulent yellow with nicotine. On the table lay five opened cigarette packets. She smoked a Danish brand—Cecil. Åke Stenström had not smoked at all.

"What do you want?" she asked gruffly.

She walked up to the table, shook a cigarette out of one of the packets, lighted it with trembling hands and dropped the burnt match on the floor. Then she said, "Nothing, of course. Just like that idiot Rönn, who sat here mumbling and rolling his head for two hours."

Kollberg didn't answer.

"I'll have the phone turned off," she announced abruptly.

"Aren't you working?"

"I'm on sick leave."

Kollberg nodded.

"Stupidly," she said. "The firm has its own doctor. He said I was to rest for a month in the country or preferably go abroad. Then he drove me home."

She drew deeply at her cigarette and tapped off the ash; most of it fell beside the ashtray.

"That was three weeks ago," she said. "It would have been much better if I could have gone on working as usual."

She swung around and went over to the window, looked down into the street and plucked at the curtain.

"As usual," she said to herself.

Kollberg squirmed in his chair, ill at ease. This was going to be worse than he expected.

"What do you want?" she asked again, without turning her head. "Answer me, for God's sake. Say something."

Somehow he must break the isolation. But how?

He got up and went over to the big carved bookcase. Looked at the books and took one out. It was rather an old one, *Manual of Crime Investigation* by Otto Wendell and Arne Svensson, printed in 1949. He turned over the title page and read:

> *This is a numbered and limited edition. This copy, No. 2080, is for Detective Lennart Kollberg. The book is intended as a guide for policemen in their often difficult and responsible work on the scene of*

the crime. The contents are of a confidential nature, and the authors therefore request everyone to see that the book does not fall into the wrong hands.

He himself had written in the words "Detective Lennart Kollberg" long ago. It was a good book and it had been very useful to him in the old days.

"This is my old book," he said.

"Take it then," she replied.

"No. I gave it to Åke a couple of years ago."

"Oh. Then he hasn't stolen it at any rate."

He dipped into it as he considered what ought to be said or done. Here and there he had underlined certain passages. In two places he noticed a stroke in the margin made with a ballpoint pen. Both were under the chapter heading *Sex Murders*.

The sex murderer (the sadist) is often impotent and his violent crime is in that case an abnormal act for the attainment of sexual satisfaction.

Someone—Stenström, without a doubt—had underlined this sentence. Beside it he had drawn an exclamation mark and written the words "or the reverse."

In the paragraph a little farther down the same page that began with the words *In cases of sex murder the victim can have been killed,* he had underlined two points:

4) *after the sex act in order to prevent accusation*

and

5) *because of the effect of shock.*

In the margin he had made the following comment:

6) to get rid of the victim, but is it then a sex murder?

"Åsa," Kollberg said.

"Yes, what is it?"

"Do you know when Åke wrote this?"

She came up to him, glanced swiftly at the book and said, "No idea."

"Åsa," he said again.

She plunged her half-smoked cigarette into the overflowing ashtray and remained standing beside the table with her hands loosely clasped over her stomach.

"Yes, what the dickens is it?" she asked irritably.

Kollberg looked at her searchingly. She looked small and wretched. Today she was wearing a shortsleeved blue overblouse instead of the knitted sweater. She had goose-flesh on her arms and although the blouse hung like a loosely draped cloth over her thin body, her large nipples showed as distinct protrusions under the material.

"Sit down," he commanded.

She shrugged, took a new cigarette and walked over to the bedroom door while she fumbled with the lighter.

"Sit down!" Kollberg roared.

She jumped, and looked at him. Her brown eyes almost glittered with hatred. Nevertheless, she went to the armchair and sat down opposite him. Stiff as a poker, with her hands on her thighs. In her right hand she held the lighter, in her left the still unlighted cigarette.

"We have to put our cards on the table," Kollberg said, stealing an embarrassed glance at the brown envelope.

"Splendid," she said in an icy, clear voice. "It's just that I haven't any cards to put."

"But I have."

"Oh?"

"When we were here last we weren't altogether frank with you."

She frowned.

"In what way?"

"In several ways. First let me ask you: Do you know what Åke was doing on that bus?"

"No, no, no and again no. I—do—not—know."

"Nor do we," said Kollberg.

He paused. Then, drawing a deep breath, he went on. "Åke lied to you."

Her reaction was violent. Her eyes flashed. She clenched her fists. The cigarette was crushed between her fingers and flakes of tobacco were strewn over her slacks.

"How *dare* you say that to me!"

"Because it's true. Åke was not on duty—either on the Monday when he was killed or on the previous Saturday. He had had an unusual amount of time off during the whole of October and the first two weeks of November."

She stared at him without saying anything.

"That is a fact," Kollberg went on. "Another thing I

would like to know: was he in the habit of carrying his pistol when he was not on duty?"

It was some time before she answered.

"Go to the devil and stop tormenting me with your interrogation tactics. Why doesn't the Great Interrogator himself come? Martin Beck?"

Kollberg bit his lower lip.

"Have you cried a lot?" he asked.

"No. I'm not made that way."

"Well then, answer for Christ's sake. We must help each other."

"What with?"

"With getting hold of the man who killed him. And the others."

"Why?"

She sat quiet for a while. Then she said, so softly that he could hardly hear it: "Revenge. Of course. To be revenged."

"Did he usually carry his pistol?"

"Yes. Often at any rate."

"Why?"

"Why not? As it turned out, he needed it. Didn't he?"

He made no reply.

"Though a lot of help it was."

Kollberg still said nothing.

"I loved Åke," she said.

The voice was clear and matter-of-fact. Her eyes were fixed on a point behind Kollberg.

"Åsa?"

"Yes?"

"He was away a lot, then. You don't know what he was up to and we don't know either. Do you think he might have been together with someone else? Some other woman, that is?"

"No."

"You don't think so?"

"I don't think anything. I know."

"How can you know?"

"That's *my* business. And I know."

She looked him suddenly in the eye and said in astonishment, "Did you get it into your heads that he had a mistress?"

"Yes. We still reckon with that possibility."

"Then you can stop doing so. It's completely out of the question."

"Why?"

"I've said it's none of your business."

Kollberg drummed his fingertips on the tabletop.

"But you know for sure?"

"Yes, I know for sure."

He took another deep breath, as though plucking up his courage.

"Was Åke interested in photography?"

"Yes. It was about his only hobby after he stopped playing soccer. He has three cameras. And there's one of those enlarging gadgets in the john. He used the bathroom as a darkroom."

She looked at Kollberg in surprise.

"Why do you ask that?"

He pushed the envelope across to her side of the table. She put down the cigarette lighter and took out the pictures with trembling hands. Looked at the one on top and went scarlet.

"Where . . . where did you get hold of these?"

"They were in his desk out at Västberga."

"What! In his desk?"

She blinked hard and asked unexpectedly, "How many have seen them? The entire police force?"

"Only three people."

"Who?"

"Martin, myself and my wife."

"Gun?"

"Yes."

"Why did you show them to her?"

"Because I was coming here. I wanted her to know what you look like."

"What I look like? And what we look like? Åke and—"

"Åke is dead," Kollberg said tonelessly.

Her face was still fiery red. So were her neck and arms. Tiny glistening beads of sweat had broken out on her forehead, just below her hairline.

"The pictures were taken in here?" he asked.

She nodded.

"When?"

Asa Torell bit her underlip nervously.

"About three months ago."

"I presume he took them himself?"

"Naturally. He has . . . had all kinds of photography gadgets. Self-timer and tripod and whatever they're called."

"Why did he take them?"

She was still flushed and perspiring but her voice was steadier.

"Because we thought it was fun."

"And why did he have them in his desk?"

Kollberg paused briefly.

"You see, he didn't have a single personal thing in his office," he said, explaining. "Apart from these photographs."

A long silence. At last she shook her head slowly and said, "No. I don't know."

Time to change the subject, Kollberg thought. Aloud he said, "Did he always go about with a pistol?"

"Nearly always."

"Why?"

"He liked to. Lately. He was interested in firearms."

She seemed to be thinking something over. Then she got up suddenly and walked quickly out of the room. Through the short passage he saw her go into the bedroom and up to the bed. Sticking her hand under one of the crumpled pillows, she said hesitantly, "I've a thing here . . . a pistol . . ."

Kollberg's relative obesity and phlegmatic appearance had deceived many in various fashions. He was in extremely good trim and his responses were amazingly quick.

Asa Torell was still bending over the bed when he stood beside her and wrenched the weapon from her hand.

"This is no pistol," he said. "It's an American revolver. A Colt .45 with a long barrel. Peacemaker it's called, absurdly enough. Besides which, it is loaded. And cocked."

"As if I didn't know that," she mumbled.

He opened the chamber and took out the cartridges.

"With cross-filed bullets, what's more," he said. "Forbidden even in America. The most dangerous small firearm imaginable. You can kill an elephant with it. If you shoot a human being at a range of five yards, the bullet makes a wound as big as a soup plate and hurls the body ten yards backward. Where the hell did you get it from?"

She shrugged bewilderedly.

"Ake. He's always had it."

"In bed?"

With a shake of her head she said quietly, "No, no. It was I who . . . now . . ."

Slipping the cartridges into his pants pocket, he pointed the revolver at the floor and pulled the trigger. The click echoed in the silent apartment.

"Moreover, the trigger has been filed," he said. "To make it quicker and more sensitive. Horribly dangerous. You'd only have had to turn over in your sleep to—"

He fell silent.

"I haven't slept much lately," she said.

"Hm," Kollberg muttered to himself. "He must have smuggled this away when he was confiscating weapons at some time. Swiped it, in fact."

He looked at the big, heavy revolver and weighed it in his hand. Then he glanced at the girl's right wrist. It was as slender as a child's.

"Well, I can understand him," he mumbled. "If you're fascinated by firearms . . ."

Suddenly he raised his voice.

"But I'm not fascinated," he shouted. "I hate this sort of thing. Do you get that? This is a foul thing that shouldn't be allowed to exist. No firearms should exist. The fact that they are still made and that all sorts of people have them lying about in drawers or carry them around in the street just shows that the whole system is perverted and crazy. Some bastard makes a fat profit by making and selling arms, just the way other people make a fat profit on factories that make narcotics and deadly pills. Do you get it?"

She looked at him with an entirely new expression; her eyes focused on him now with a clear, direct look.

"Go and sit down," he said curtly. "We're going to talk. This is serious."

Asa Torell said nothing. She went straight into the living room and sat down in the armchair.

Kollberg went out into the hall and put the revolver on the hat rack. Took off his jacket and tie. Unbuttoned his collar and rolled up his sleeves. Then he went into the kitchen, put some water on to boil and made some tea. Brought the cups in and set them on the table. Emptied the ashtrays. Opened a window. Sat down.

"First of all," he said, "I want to know what you meant by 'lately.' When you said that lately he liked to go armed."

"Quiet," said Asa.

After ten seconds she added, "Wait."

She drew up her legs so that her feet in the big gray ski socks were resting against the edge of the armchair. Then she put her arms around her shins and sat quite still.

Kollberg waited.

To be precise, he waited for fifteen minutes, and during the whole of this time she did not look at him once. Neither of them said a word. Then she looked him in the eye and said, "Well?"

"How do you feel?"

"No better. But different. Ask what you like. I promise to answer. Answer anything at all. There's only one thing I want to know first."

"Yes?"

"Have you told me everything?"

"No," Kollberg replied. "But I'm going to now. The reason why I'm here at all is that I don't believe in the official version—that Stenström merely chanced to fall a victim to a crazy mass murderer. And quite apart from your assurances that he was not unfaithful to you or whatever you like to call it, and what you base them on, I do not believe that he was on that bus for pleasure."

"Then what *do* you believe?"

"That you were right from the outset. When you said that he was working. That he was busy with something in his capacity as policeman but for one reason or another

133

didn't want to tell anybody, either you or us. One possibility, for instance, is that he had been shadowing someone for a long time, and that this someone at last grew desperate and killed him. Though I personally don't think that that theory is plausible."

He paused briefly.

"Åke was very good at shadowing. It amused him."

"Yes, I know."

"You can shadow in two ways," Kollberg went on. "Either you follow a person as invisibly as possible, to find out what he's up to. Or else you follow him quite openly, to drive him to desperation and make him do something rash and give himself away. Stenström had mastered the art of both methods better than anyone else I know."

"Does anyone else besides you believe this?" Åsa Torell asked.

"Yes. Beck and Melander at least."

He scratched his neck.

"But there are several weaknesses in the argument. We needn't go into them now."

She nodded.

"What do you want to know?"

"I'm not sure. We'll have to feel our way. I haven't quite understood you on all points. What did you mean, for instance, when you said that lately he carried a pistol because it amused him? Lately?"

"When I first met Åke over four years ago he was still a little boy," she said calmly.

"In what way?"

"He was shy and childish. When someone killed him three weeks ago he had grown up. That development took place not so much at his work together with you and Beck, but here. Here at home. The first time we were together, in that room and in that bed, the pistol was the last thing he took off."

Kollberg raised his eyebrows.

"He kept his shirt on, you see," she said. "And he laid the pistol on the bedside table. I was staggered. To tell the truth, I didn't even know he was a policeman that

134

time and I wondered what sort of madman had got into my bed."

She looked gravely at Kollberg.

"We didn't fall in love that first time, but we did the next. And then it dawned on me. Åke was twenty-five then and I had just turned twenty. But if either of us could be called grown-up and more or less mature, it was I. He went about with a pistol because he thought it made him a tough guy. He was childish, as I said, and it gave him huge pleasure to see me lying there naked, staring idiotically at a man dressed in a shirt and shoulder belt. He soon grew out of all that, but by that time it had become a habit. Besides, he was interested in firearms—"

She broke off and asked, "Are you brave? Physically brave?"

"Not especially."

"Åke was physically a coward though he did everything to try and overcome it. The pistol gave him a feeling of security."

Kollberg made an objection.

"You said that he grew up. He was a policeman, and professionally it's not very grown-up to let yourself be shot down from behind by the man you're shadowing. I said before, I find it hard to believe."

"Exactly," Åsa Torell agreed. "And I definitely don't believe it. Something doesn't add up."

Kollberg pondered this. After a while he said, "The fact remains. He was working on something and no one knows what. I don't. Nor do you. Am I right?"

"Yes."

"Did he change in any way? Before this happened?"

She didn't answer. Raised her left hand and passed her fingers through her short dark hair.

"Yes," she said at last.

"How?"

"It isn't easy to say."

"Have these pictures anything to do with the change?"

"Yes. I'll say they have."

Stretching out her hand, she turned the photographs over and looked at them.

"To talk to anyone about this calls for a degree of confidence that I'm not sure I have in you," she said. "But I'll do my best."

Kollberg's palms had begun to sweat and he wiped them against the legs of his pants. The roles had been reversed. She was calm and he was nervous.

"I loved Åke," she said. "From the start. But we didn't suit each other very well sexually. We were different as regards tempo and temperament. We didn't have the same demands."

Åsa gave him a searching look.

"But you can be happy just the same. You can learn. Did you know that?"

"No."

"We proved it. We learned. I think you understand this."

Kollberg nodded.

"Beck wouldn't understand it," she said. "And certainly not Rönn or anyone else I know."

She shrugged.

"In any case, we learned. We adjusted ourselves to each other, and we had it good."

Kollberg forgot, for a moment, to listen. This was an alternative that he had never even thought existed.

"It's difficult," she said. "I must explain this. If I don't, I can't explain in what way Åke changed. And even if I give you a lot of details belonging to my private life, it's not certain you'll grasp it. But I hope you will."

She coughed and said in a matter-of-fact tone, "I've been smoking far too much this last week or two."

Kollberg could feel that something was about to change. Suddenly he smiled. And Åsa Torell smiled back, a trifle bitterly, but still.

"Anyway, let's get this over," she said. "The quicker the better. Unfortunately, I'm rather shy. Oddly enough."

"It's not in the least odd," Kollberg replied. "I'm as shy as hell. It's part of the rest of one's emotions."

"Before I met Åke I began to think I was a nymphomaniac or something," she said swiftly. "Then we fell in love and learned to adjust to each other. I really tried hard, and so did Åke, and we succeeded. We had it good together, better than I ever dreamed of. I forgot that I was more highly sexed than he was, we talked it over once or twice at the beginning, then we never talked any more about sexuality. There was no need. We made love when he felt like it, which was once or twice a week, three times at the most, we did it very well and never needed anything else. That is, we were not unfaithful to one another, as you so wittily put it. But then . . ."

". . . suddenly last summer," Kollberg said.

She gave him a swift, approving glance.

"Exactly. Last summer we went to Mallorca on vacation. While we were away you all had a difficult and very nasty case here in town."

"Yes. The park murders."

"By the time we got home they had been cleared up. Åke got sore about it."

She paused, then went on, just as quickly and fluently, "It sounds bad, but so does a lot of what I've said and am going to say. The fact is he got sore because he had missed the investigation. Åke was ambitious, almost to a fault. I know that he always dreamed of coming upon something big that everyone else had overlooked. Moreover, he was much younger than the rest of you and in the early days, at any rate, he often felt pushed around at work. I know, too, that he thought you were one of those who bullied him most."

"He was right, I'm afraid."

"He didn't like you very much. He preferred Beck and Melander. I didn't, but that's neither here nor there. About the end of July or beginning of August he changed —suddenly, as I said, and in a way that turned the whole of our life together upside down. That's when he took these pictures. Lots more, come to that, dozens of them. We had a sort of routine in our sex life, as I said, and it was fine. Now it was upset all of a sudden, and he was the one to upset it, not I. We . . . we were together . . ."

"Made love, you mean," Kollberg said.

"O.K., we made love as many times in a day as we normally did in a month. Some days he wouldn't even let me go to work. There's no use denying that it was a pleasant surprise to me. I was amazed. You see, we'd been living together for over four years, but . . ."

"Go on," Kollberg urged.

She took a deep breath.

"Sure, I thought it was just great. That he walked me about like a wheelbarrow and woke me up at four in the morning and wouldn't let me sleep or have any clothes on or go to work. That he wouldn't leave me alone even in the kitchen and took me in the sink and in the bathtub and from in front and from behind and upside down and in every chair there was. But he himself hadn't really changed and after a while I got the idea that he was trying out some sort of experiment on me. I asked him, but he only laughed."

"Laughed?"

"Yes, he was in a very good mood all this time. Right up to . . . well, until he was killed."

"Why?"

"That's what I don't know. But one thing I did understand, as soon as I'd got over the first shock."

"And that was?"

"That he was using me as a kind of guinea pig. He knew everything about me—everything. He knew that I'd get ridiculously horny if he made the slightest effort. And I knew all about him. For instance, that basically he wasn't particularly interested, other than now and again."

"How long did this go on?"

"Until the middle of September. That's when he suddenly had so much to do and began to be away such a lot."

"Which doesn't at all fit in."

Kollberg looked steadily at her, then added, "Thanks. You're a great kid. I like you."

She gave him a surprised and rather suspicious glance.

"And he didn't tell you what he was working on?"

She shook her head.

"Didn't even hint?"

Another shake of the head.

"And you didn't notice anything special?"

"He was out a lot. I mean, out of doors. I couldn't help noticing that. He would come home wet and cold."

Kollberg nodded.

"More than once I was woken up in the small hours when he came home and got into bed, as cold as an icicle.

But the last case he talked to me about was one he had in the first half of September. A man who had killed his wife. I think his name was Birgersson."

"I remember it," Kollberg said. "A family tragedy. A very simple, ordinary story. I don't really know why we were brought into it—the case might have been taken out of the textbooks. Unhappy marriage, neuroses, quarrels, money troubles. At last the man killed his wife more or less by accident. Was going to take his own life but didn't dare to and went to the police. But you're right, Stenström did have charge of it. He did the interrogating."

"Wait—something happened during those interrogations."

"What?"

"I don't know. But one evening Åke came home very cheerful."

"Not much to be cheerful about. Dreary story. Typical welfare-state crime. A lonely man with a status-poisoned wife who kept nagging at him because he didn't earn enough. Because they couldn't afford a motorboat and a summer cottage and a car as swell as the neighbors'."

"But during the interrogations this man said something to Åke."

"What?"

"I don't know. But it was something he considered very important. I asked the same as you, of course, but he only laughed and said I'd soon see."

"Did he say exactly that?"

" 'You'll soon see, darling.' Those were his exact words. He seemed very optimistic."

"Odd."

They sat in silence for a while. Then Kollberg shook himself, picked up the open book from the table and said, "Do you understand these comments?"

Åsa Torell got up, walked round the table and put her hand on his shoulder as she looked at the book.

"Wendel and Svensson write that the sex murderer is often impotent and attains abnormal satisfaction from committing a crime of violence. And in the margin Åke has written 'or the reverse.' "

Kollberg shrugged and said, "He means, of course, that the sex murderer may also be oversexed."

She took her hand away suddenly. Looking up at her, he noticed to his surprise that she was blushing again.

"No, he doesn't mean that," she said.

"Then what does it mean?"

"The very opposite. That the woman—the victim, that is—may lose her life because *she* is oversexed."

"How do you know that?"

"Because we once discussed the matter. In connection with the American girl who was murdered on the Göta Canal."

"Roseanna," Kollberg said.

He thought for a moment, then said, "But I hadn't given him this book then. I remember that I found it when I was clearing out my drawers. When we moved from Kristineberg. That was much later."

"And that other comment of his seems rather illogical," she said.

"Yes. Aren't there any pads or diaries in which he used to write things down?"

"Didn't he have his notebook on him?"

"Yes. We've looked at it. Nothing of interest there."

"I've searched the apartment," she said.

"And what have you found?"

"Nothing much. He wasn't in the habit of hiding things. Besides, he was very tidy. He had an extra notebook, of course. It's over there on the desk."

Kollberg got up and fetched the notebook. It was of the same type as the one Stenström had had in his pocket.

"There's hardly anything in that book," Åsa Torell said.

She pulled the ski sock off her right foot and scratched herself under the instep.

Her foot was thin and slender and gracefully arched, with long straight toes. Kollberg looked at it. Then he looked inside the notebook. She was right. There was almost nothing in it. The first page was covered with jottings about the poor wretch of a man called Birgersson who had killed his wife.

At the top of the second page was a single word. A name. Morris.

Åsa Torell looked at the pad and shrugged.

"A car," she said.

"Or a literary agent in New York," Kollberg replied.

She was standing by the table. Her eye caught the much-discussed photographs. Suddenly she slammed her hand down on the table and shouted, "If at least I'd been pregnant!"

Then she lowered her voice.

"He said we had plenty of time. That we'd wait until he was promoted."

Kollberg moved hesitantly toward the hall.

"Plenty of time," she mumbled.

And then: "What's to become of me?"

Turning around, he said. "This won't do, Åsa. Come."

Whirling around, she snarled at him, "Come? Where? To bed? Oh, sure."

Kollberg looked at her.

Nine hundred and ninety-nine men out of a thousand would have seen a pale, thin, undeveloped girl who held herself badly, who had a delicate body, thin nicotine-stained fingers and a ravaged face. Unkempt and dressed in baggy, stained clothes and with one foot covered by a skiing sock many sizes too large.

Lennart Kollberg saw a physically and mentally complex young woman with blazing eyes and a promising width between her thighs, provocative and interesting and worth getting to know.

Had Stenström also seen this, or had he been one of the nine hundred and ninety-nine and merely had a stroke of luck?

Luck.

"I didn't mean that," Kollberg said. "Come home with me. We have plenty of room. You've been alone long enough."

She was hardly in the car before she started to cry.

22

A cutting wind greeted Nordin as he emerged from the subway at the corner of Sveavägen and Rådmansgatan. It was blowing from behind him and he walked briskly south along Sveavägen. When he turned into Tegnérgatan he was sheltered and slowed his steps. About 20 yards from the street corner lay a café. He stopped outside the window and peered in.

Behind the counter sat a red-haired woman in a pistachio-green uniform, talking on the phone. The café otherwise was empty.

Nordin walked on, crossed Luntmakargatan and regarded an oil painting that was hanging inside the glass door of a second-hand bookshop. While he stood puzzling as to whether the artist had meant the picture to represent two elks, two reindeer or perhaps an elk and a reindeer, he heard a voice behind him.

"Aber Mensch, bist Du doch ganz verrückt?"

Nordin turned around and saw two men crossing the street. Not until they reached the sidewalk on the other side did he see the café. When Nordin entered, the two men were on their way down a curving staircase beyond the counter. He followed them.

The place was full of young people and the music and the buzz of voices were deafening. He looked around for a vacant table, but there didn't seem to be one. For a moment he wondered whether he ought to take off his hat and coat, but decided not to risk it. You couldn't trust anyone in Stockholm, he was convinced of that.

Nordin studied the female guests. There were several blondes in the room but none who fitted the description of Blonde Malin.

German seemed to be the predominating language. Beside a thin brunette, who was obviously Swedish, there was a vacant chair. Nordin unbuttoned his coat and sat down.

Put his hat in his lap, thinking that his coat of lodencloth and his Tyrolean hat probably made him look a good deal like one of the many Germans there.

He had to wait a quarter of an hour before the waitress came to him. Meanwhile he looked about him. The brunette's girlfriend on the other side of the table eyed him guardedly from time to time.

He stirred his cup of coffee and stole a glance at the girl in the chair next to him. In the faint hope of being taken for a regular customer he took pains to utter the words in the Stockholm dialect when he turned to her and said, "Do you know where Blonde Malin is this evening?"

The brunette stared at him. Then she smiled, bent over the table and said to her girlfriend, "Eva, this guy from the north is asking after Blonde Malin. Do you know where she is?"

The friend looked at Nordin, then she called to someone at a table farther off, "There's a cop here who's asking where Blonde Malin is. Do any of you know?"

"No-o-o," came a chorus from the other table.

As Nordin sipped his coffee he wondered gloomily how they could see he was a policeman. He couldn't make these Stockholmers out.

When he had mounted the stairs to the shop floor where the pastries were sold, the waitress who had brought his coffee came up to him.

"I heard you're looking for Blonde Malin," she said. "Are you really a policeman?"

Nordin hesitated. Then he nodded lugubriously.

"If you can run that tramp in for something, I couldn't be more pleased. I think I know where she is. When she isn't here, she's usually at a café on Engelbrektsplan."

Nordin thanked her and went out into the cold.

Blonde Malin was not at the other café either; all its regular customers seemed to have deserted it. Nordin, reluctant to give in, went up to a woman who was sitting by herself and reading a thumbed and grubby magazine. She didn't know who Blonde Malin was, but suggested that he should look in at a wine restaurant on Kungsgatan.

Nordin trudged on along the odious Stockholm streets, wishing he were at home in Sundsvall again.

This time he was rewarded for his pains.

He shook his head at the cloakroom attendant who came forward to take his coat, stood in the doorway of the restaurant and looked around. He caught sight of her almost at once.

She was big-framed, but didn't seem fat. Her fair hair, bleached by the look of it, was piled up on top of her head.

Nordin didn't doubt for a moment that this was Blonde Malin.

She was sitting on a wall-seat with a wineglass in front of her. Beside her sat a much older woman, whose long black hair, hanging in unruly curls to her shoulders, didn't make her look younger. Sure to be a free whore, Nordin thought.

He observed the two women for a while. They were not talking to each other. Blonde Malin was staring at the wineglass, which she twiddled between her fingers. The black-haired woman kept looking around the room, now and then flinging her long hair aside with a coquettish toss of the head.

Nordin turned to the cloakroom attendant.

"Excuse me, but do you know the name of that blonde lady sitting over by the wall?"

The man looked across the room.

"Lady!" he snorted. "Her! No, I don't know her name, but I think they call her Malin. Fat Malin or something like that."

Nordin gave him his hat and coat.

The black-haired woman looked at him expectantly as he came up to their table.

"Pardon my intrusion," Nordin said. "I'd like a word with Miss Malin if she doesn't mind."

Blonde Malin looked at him and sipped her wine.

"What about?" she said.

"About a friend of yours," Nordin said. "Perhaps we could move to another table and have a quiet talk?"

Blonde Malin looked at her companion and he hastened to add, "If your friend doesn't mind, of course."

The black-haired woman filled her glass from the carafe on the table and got up.

144

"Don't let me disturb you," she said huffily.

Blonde Malin said nothing.

"I'll go and sit with Tora," the woman said. "So long, Malin."

She picked up her glass and went over to a table farther down the room.

Nordin drew out a chair and sat down. Blonde Malin looked at him expectantly.

"I'm Detective Inspector Ulf Nordin," he said. "It's possible that you can help us with something."

"Oh yeah?" Blonde Malin said. "And what would that be. You said it was about a friend of mine."

"Yes," Nordin replied. "We'd like some information about a man you know."

Blonde Malin looked at Ulf Nordin contemptuously.

"I'm not squealing on anybody," she said.

Nordin took out a pack of cigarettes and offered it to her. She took one and he lighted it for her.

"It's not a question of being a fink," he said. "A few weeks ago you rode with two men in a white Volvo Amazon to a garage in Hägersten. The garage is on Klubbacken and is owned by a Swiss named Horst. The man who drove the car was a Spaniard. Do you remember that occasion?"

"Supposing I do," Blonde Malin said. "What of it? Nisse and I only went with this Paco so Nisse could show him the way to the garage. Anyway, he's gone back to Spain now."

"Paco?"

"Yes."

She drained her glass and poured out the rest of the wine in the carafe.

"May I offer you something?" Nordin asked. "A little more wine?"

She nodded and Nordin beckoned to the waitress. He ordered half a carafe of wine and a stein of beer.

"Who's Nisse?" he asked.

"The guy with me in the car, of course. You said so yourself just now."

"Yes, but what's his other name besides Nisse? What does he do?"

"His name's Göransson. Nils Erik Göransson. I don't know what he does. I ain't seen him for a couple of weeks."

"Why?" Nordin asked.

"Eh?"

"Why haven't you seen him for a couple of weeks? Didn't you meet quite often before that?"

"We ain't married, are we? We're not even going steady. We just went together sometimes. Maybe he's met some gal. How do I know. I haven't seen him for a while at any rate."

The waitress brought the wine and Nordin's beer. Blonde Malin immediately filled her glass.

"Do you know where he lives?" Nordin asked.

"Nisse? No, he sort of didn't have anywhere to live. He lived with me for a time and then with a pal on the South Side, but I don't think he's there now. I don't know, really. And even if I did, I'm not so all-fired sure I'd tell a cop. I'm not going to inform on anybody."

Nordin took a draught of beer and looked amiably at the large, fair girl opposite him.

"You don't have to, Miss— Pardon me, but what's your name besides Malin?"

"My name ain't Malin at all," she said. "My name's Magdalena Rosén. People call me Blonde Malin because I'm so blonde."

She stroked her hair.

"What do you want Nisse for, anyway? Has he done something? I ain't going to sit here answering a lot of questions if I don't know what it's all about."

"No, of course not. I'll tell you what it is you can help us with," Ulf Nordin said.

He finished his beer and wiped his mouth.

"May I ask just one more question?" he said.

She nodded.

"How was Nisse usually dressed?"

She frowned and thought for a moment.

"Most of the time he wore a suit," she said. "One of them light beige-colored ones with covered buttons. And shirt and shoes and shorts, like all other guys."

"Didn't he have an overcoat?"

"Well, I'd hardly call it an overcoat. One of them thin black things—nylon, you know. Why?"

She looked inquiringly at Nordin.

"Well, Miss Rosén, it's possible that he is dead."

"Dead? Nisse? But . . . why . . . why do you say it's possible? How do you know he's dead?"

Ulf Nordin took out his handkerchief and wiped his neck. It was very warm in the restaurant and his whole body felt sticky.

"The thing is," he said, "we've a man out at the morgue we haven't been able to identify. There's reason to suspect that the dead man is Nils Erik Göransson."

"How's he supposed to have died?" Blonde Malin asked suspiciously.

"He was one of the passengers on that bus, that you've no doubt read about. He was shot in the head and must have been killed outright. Since you're the only person we've traced who knew Göransson well, we'd be grateful if you'd come out to the morgue tomorrow and see if it's him."

She stared at Nordin in horror.

"Me? Come out to the morgue? Not on your life!"

The time was nine o'clock on Wednesday morning when Nordin and Blonde Malin got out of a taxi outside the institute for forensic medicine on Tomtebodavägen. Martin Beck had been waiting for them for a quarter of an hour and together they entered the morgue.

Blonde Malin was pale under her carelessly applied makeup. Her face was bloated and her fair hair was not arranged as neatly as it was the evening before.

Nordin had had to wait in her hall while she got ready. When at last they came out into the street, he noted that she showed up considerably more to her advantage in the dimness of the restaurant than in the bleary morning light.

The staff of the morgue were prepared and the superintendent showed them into the cold-storage room.

A cloth had been laid over the corpse's bullet-shattered face, but the hair had been left free.

Blonde Malin gripped Nordin's arm and whispered, "Jesus Christ."

Nordin laid his arm around her broad back and led her closer.

"Take a good look," he said quietly. "See if you recognize him."

She put her hand to her mouth and looked at the naked body.

"What's wrong with his face?" she asked. "Can't I see his face?"

"You can be glad you're spared it," Martin Beck said. "You should be able to recognize him just the same."

Blonde Malin nodded. Then she took her hand away from her mouth and nodded again.

"Yes," she said. "Yes, that's Nisse. Them scars and . . . yes, it's him all right."

"Thank you, Miss Rosén," Martin Beck said. "Now what about a cup of coffee with us at police headquarters?"

Blonde Malin, pale and quiet, sat beside Nordin in the back of the taxi. Now and then she mumbled, "Jesus Christ, how awful."

Martin Beck and Ulf Nordin treated her to coffee and sweet rolls and after a while Kollberg and Melander and Rönn joined them.

She soon recovered and it was obvious that not only the coffee, but also the attention shown her, cheered her up. She answered their questions obligingly and before leaving she pressed their hands and said, "Imagine, I never would have thought that co— police could be such sweethearts."

When the door had closed behind her they considered this for a moment. Then Kollberg said, "Well, sweethearts? Shall we sum up?"

They summed up:

Nils Erik Göransson.

Age: 38 or 39.

Since 1965 or earlier, no permanent employment.

March 1967–August 1967, lived with Magdalena Rosén (Blonde Malin), Arbetargatan 3, Stockholm K.

Thereafter and until some time in October lived with Sune Björk on the South Side.

The weeks prior to his death whereabouts unknown.

Drug addict, smoking, swallowing and mainlining whatever he could get hold of.

Possibly also a pusher.

Had gonorrhea.

Last seen by Magdalena Rosén November 3 or 4 outside Restaurant Damberg. Then in same suit and coat as November 13.

Usually had plenty of money.

23

Of all the men who were working on the bus murders, Nordin was thus the first to show something which, with a little good will, could be called a constructive result. But even on this point, opinions were divided.

"Well," Gunvald Larsson said. "Now we know the name of that bum. So what?"

"Mmm . . . er . . . mnyaa . . . ," Melander murmured thoughtfully.

"What are you mumbling about?"

"He was never picked up for anything, that Göransson. But I seem to remember the name."

"Oh?"

"I think he cropped up in connection with an investigation at some time."

"You mean you once interrogated him?"

"No. I would remember that. I have never spoken to him and doubt if I've seen him either. But the name. Nils Erik Göransson. I've come across it at some time or other."

Melander stared abstractedly out into the room, puffing at his pipe.

Gunvald Larsson waved his big hands in front of his face. He was opposed to people using tobacco and was irritated by the smoke.

"I'm more interested in that swine Assarsson," he said.

"I expect I'll think of it," Melander said.

"Not a doubt. If you don't die of lung cancer first."

Gunvald Larsson got up and went into Martin Beck's office.

"Where did this Assarsson get his money from?" he asked.

"Don't know."

"What does the firm do?"

"Imports a lot of junk. Presumably anything that pays. From cranes to plastic Christmas trees."

"Plastic Christmas trees?"

"Yes, they sell a lot of them nowadays. Unfortunately."

"I took the trouble to find out what these gentlemen and their firm have paid in taxes during the last few years."

"And?"

"About one third of what you or I fork out. And when I think of what it looked like at the widow's apartment . . ."

"Yes?"

"I've a damn good mind to ask for permission to raid their office."

"On what grounds?"

"Don't know."

Martin Beck shrugged. Gunvald Larsson walked toward the door. Stopped in the doorway and said, "An ugly customer, that Assarsson. And his brother is probably no better."

Shortly afterward Kollberg appeared in the doorway. He looked tired and dejected, and his eyes were bloodshot.

"What are you busy at?" Martin Beck asked.

"I've been playing back the tapes from Stenström's interrogation with Birgersson. The guy who killed his wife. It took all night."

"And?"

"Nothing. Nothing at all. Unless I've overlooked something."

"It's always possible."

"Kind of you to say so," Kollberg snapped, slamming the door behind him.

Martin Beck propped his elbows on the edge of the desk and put his head in his hands.

It was already Friday and the eighth of December. Twenty-five days had passed and the investigation was getting nowhere. In fact, it showed signs of falling to pieces. Everyone was clinging to his own particular straw.

Melander was puzzling over where and when he had seen or heard the name of Nils Erik Göransson.

Gunvald Larsson was wondering how the Assarsson brothers had made their money.

Kollberg was trying to make out how a mentally unbalanced wife-killer by the name of Birgersson could conceivably have cheered up Stenström.

Nordin was trying to establish a connection between Göransson, the mass murder and the garage in Hägersten.

Ek had made such a technical study of the red double-decker bus that nowadays it was practically impossible to talk to him about anything except electric circuits and windshield-wiper controls.

Månsson had taken over Gunvald Larsson's diffuse ideas that Mohammed Boussie must have played some sort of leading role because he was Algerian; he had systematically interrogated the entire Arab colony in Stockholm.

Martin Beck himself could think only of Stenström, what had he been working on, whether he had been shadowing someone and whether this someone had shot him. The argument seemed far from convincing. Would a comparatively experienced policeman really let himself get shot by the man he was shadowing? On a bus?

Rönn could not tear his thoughts away from what Schwerin had said at the hospital during the few seconds before he died.

On this very Friday afternoon he had a talk with the sound expert at the Swedish Broadcasting Corporation who had tried to analyze what was said on the tape.

The man had taken his time, but now he seemed ready with his report.

"Not very copious material to work with," he said. "But I've come to certain conclusions. Like to hear them?"

"Yes, please," Rönn said.

He transferred the receiver to his left hand and reached for the notepad.

"You're from the North yourself, aren't you?"

"Yes."

"Well, it's not the questions that are interesting, but the answers. First of all I've tried to eliminate all the background noise like whirring and dripping and so on."

Rönn waited with his pen at the ready.

"As regards the first answer, referring to the question as to who did the shooting, one can clearly distinguish four consonants—*d, n, r,* and *k.*"

"Yes," Rönn said.

"A closer analysis reveals certain vowels and diphthongs between and after these consonants. For example, an *e* or an *i* sound between *d* and *n.*"

"Dinrk," Rönn said.

"Yes, that's more or less how it sounds to an untrained ear," the expert said. "Furthermore, I think I can hear the man say a very faint *oo* after the consonant *k.*"

"Dinrk oo," Rönn said.

"Something like that, yes. Though not such a marked *oo.*"

The expert paused. Then he went on reflectively, "This man was in pretty bad shape, wasn't he?"

"Yes."

"And he was probably in pain."

"Very likely," Rönn agreed.

"Well," the expert said lightly, "that could explain why he said *oo.*"

Rönn nodded and made notes. Poked at the tip of his nose with the pen. Listened.

"However, I'm convinced that these sounds form a sentence, composed of several words."

"And how does the sentence go?" Rönn asked, putting pen to paper.

"Very hard to say. Very hard indeed. For example 'dinner reckon' or 'dinner record, oo.' "

" 'Dinner record, oo'?" Rönn asked in astonishment.

"Well, just as an example, of course. As to the second reply—"

" 'Koleson'?"

"Oh, you thought it sounded like that? Interesting. Well, I didn't. I've reached the conclusion that there's an *l* before the *k*, and that he says two words: 'like,' repeating the last word of the question, and 'oleson.' "

" 'Oleson'? And what does that mean?"

"Well, it might be a name . . . "

" 'Like Oleson'?"

"Yes, exactly. You have the same thick *l* in the word 'Oleson' too. Perhaps a similar dialect."

The sound technician was silent for a few seconds. Then he went on: "That's about the lot then. I'll send over a written report, of course, together with the bill. But I thought I'd better call up in case it was urgent."

"Thanks very much," Rönn said.

Putting the receiver down, he regarded his notes thoughtfully.

After careful consideration he decided not to take the matter up with the investigation chiefs. At any rate not at present.

Although the time was only a quarter to three in the afternoon, it was already pitch-dark when Kollberg arrived at Långholmen. He felt cold and miserable, and the prison surroundings didn't exactly cheer him up. The bare visitors' room was shabby and bleak, and he paced gloomily up and down while waiting for the prisoner he had come to see. The man, whose name was Birgersson and who had killed his wife, had undergone a thorough mental examination at the clinic of forensic psychiatry. In due course, he would be exempted from punishment and transferred to some institution.

After about fifteen minutes the door opened and a prison guard in a dark-blue uniform admitted a small, thin-haired man of about sixty. The man stopped just inside the door, smiled and bowed politely. Kollberg went up to him. They shook hands.

"Kollberg."

"Birgersson."

The man was pleasant and easy to talk to.

"Inspector Stenström? Oh yes indeed, I remember him. Such a nice man. Please give him my kind regards."

"He's dead."

"Dead? I can't believe it . . . He was just a boy. How did it happen?"

"That's just what I want to talk to you about."

Kollberg explained in detail why he had come.

"I've played back the whole tape and listened carefully to every word. But I presume that the tape recorder was not going when you sat talking over coffee and so on."

"That's right."

"But you did talk then, too?"

"Oh yes. Most of the time, anyway."

"What about?"

"Well, everything really."

"Can you recall anything that Stenström seemed specially interested in?"

The man thought hard and shook his head.

"We just talked about things in general. On this and that. But something special? What would that have been?"

"That's exactly what I don't know."

Kollberg took out the notebook he had brought from Asa's apartment and showed it to Birgersson.

"Does this convey anything to you? Why has he written 'Morris'?"

The man's face lit up at once.

"We must have been talking about cars. I had a Morris 8, the big model, you know. And I think I mentioned it on one occasion."

"I see. Well, if you happen to think of anything else, please call me up at once. At any time."

"It was old and didn't look much, my Morris, but it went well. My . . . wife was ashamed of it. Said she was ashamed to be seen in such an old rattletrap when all the neighbors had new cars—"

He blinked rapidly and broke off.

Kollberg quickly wound up the conversation. When the guard had led the prisoner away a young doctor in a white coat entered the room.

"Well, what did you think of Birgersson?" he asked.

"He seemed nice enough."

"Yes," the doctor said. "He's O.K. All he needed was to be rid of that bitch he was married to."

Kollberg looked hard at him, put his papers into his pocket and left.

The time was eleven thirty on Saturday evening and Gunvald Larsson felt cold in spite of his heavy winter coat, his fur cap, ski pants and ski boots. He was standing in the doorway of Tegnérgatan 53, as still as only a policeman can stand. He was not there by chance, and it was not easy to see him in the dark. He had already been there for four hours and this was not the first evening, but the tenth or eleventh.

He had decided to go home as soon as the light went out in certain windows he was watching. Shortly before midnight a gray Mercedes with foreign license plates stopped outside the door of the apartment house nearly opposite across the street. A man got out, opened the trunk and lifted out a suitcase. Then he crossed the sidewalk, unlocked the door and went inside. Two minutes later a light was switched on behind lowered Venetian blinds in two windows on the ground floor.

Gunvald Larsson strode swiftly across the street. He had already tried out a suitable key to the street door two weeks ago. Once inside the entrance hall, he took off his overcoat, folded it neatly and hung it over the handrail of the marble staircase, placing his fur cap on top. Unbuttoned his jacket and gripped the pistol that he wore clipped to his waistband.

He had known for a long time that the door opened inward. Looked at it for five seconds and thought: If I break in without a valid reason, I'm overstepping my authority, and I'll probably be suspended or sacked.

Then he kicked in the door.

Ture Assarsson and the man who had alighted from the foreign car were standing one on either side of the desk. To use a hackneyed phrase, they looked thunderstruck. They had just opened the suitcase and it was lying between them.

Gunvald Larsson waved them aside with the pistol, following up the train of thought he had begun out in the hall: But it doesn't matter because I can always go to sea again.

Gunvald Larsson lifted the receiver off and dialed 90 000. With his left hand and without lowering his service pistol. He said nothing. The other two said nothing either. There was not much to say.

The suitcase contained 250,000 of a brand of dope tablets called Ritalina. On the black market they were worth about one million Swedish kronor.

Gunvald Larsson got home to his apartment at Bollmora at three o'clock on Sunday morning. He was a bachelor and lived alone. As usual he spent twenty minutes in the bathroom before putting on his pajamas and getting into bed. He picked up the novel by Övre Richter-Frich that he was reading, but after only a minute he put it down and reached for the telephone.

The phone was a white Ericofon. Turning it upside down, he dialed Martin Beck's number.

Gunvald Larsson made it a rule never to think of his work when he was at home, and he could not recall ever before having made an official call after he had gone to bed.

Martin Beck answered after only the second ring.

"Hi. Did you hear about Assarsson?"

"Yes."

"Something has just occurred to me."

"What?"

"That we might have been making a mistake. Stenström was of course shadowing Gösta Assarsson. And the murderer killed two birds with one stone—Assarsson and the man who was shadowing him."

"Yes," Martin Beck agreed. "There may be something in what you say."

Gunvald Larsson was wrong. Nevertheless, he had just put the investigation on to the right track.

24

For three evenings in succession Ulf Nordin trudged about town trying to make contact with Stockholm's underworld, going in and out of the beerhalls, coffeehouses, restaurants and dance halls that Blonde Malin had given as Göransson's haunts.

Sometimes he took the car, and on Friday evening he sat in the car staring out over Mariatorget without seeing anything of more interest than two other men sitting in a car and staring. He didn't recognize them but gathered they belonged to the district's patrol of plainclothesmen or drug squad.

These expeditions did not provide one new fact about the man whose name had been Nils Erik Göransson. In the daytime, however, he managed to supplement Blonde Malin's information by consulting the census bureau, parish registers, seamen's employment exchanges and the man's ex-wife, who lived in Borås and said she had almost forgotten her former husband. She had not seen him for nearly twenty years.

On Saturday morning he reported his lean findings to Martin Beck. Then he sat down and wrote a long, melancholy and yearning letter to his wife in Sundsvall, now and then casting a guilty look at Rönn and Kollberg, who were both hard at work at their typewriters.

He had not had time to finish the letter before Martin Beck entered the room.

"What idiot sent you out into town?" he said fretfully.

Nordin quickly slipped a copy of a report over the letter. He had just written ". . . and Martin Beck gets more peculiar and grumpy every day."

Pulling the paper out of the typewriter, Kollberg said, "You."

"What? *I* did?"

"Yes, you did. Last Wednesday after Blonde Malin had been here."

Martin Beck looked disbelievingly at Kollberg.

"Funny, I don't remember that. It's idiotic all the same to send out a northerner who can hardly find his way to Stureplan on a job like that."

Nordin looked offended, but had to admit to himself that Martin Beck was right.

"Rönn," Martin Beck said. "You'd better find out where Göransson hung out, whom he was with and what he did. And try and get hold of that guy Björk, the one he lived with."

"O.K.," Rönn said.

He was busy making a list of possible interpretations of Schwerin's last words. At the top he had written: Dinner record. At the bottom was the latest version: Didn't reckon.

Each was busier than ever with his own particular job.

Martin Beck got up at six thirty on Monday morning after a practically sleepless night. He felt slightly sick and his condition was not improved by his drinking cocoa in the kitchen with his daughter. There was no sign of any other member of the family. His wife slept like a top in the mornings, and the boy had evidently taken after her; he was nearly always late for school. But Ingrid rose at six thirty and shut the front door behind her at a quarter to eight. Invariably. Inga used to say that you could set the clock by her.

Inga had a weakness for clichés. You could make a collection of the expressions she used in daily speech and sell it as a phrasebook for budding journalists. A kind of pony. Call it, of course, *If You Can Talk, You Can Write.* Thought Martin Beck.

"What are you thinking about, Daddy?" Ingrid asked.

"Nothing," he said automatically.

"I haven't seen you laugh since last spring."

Martin Beck raised his eyes from the Christmas brownies dancing in a long line across the oilcloth tablespread, looked at his daughter and tried to smile. Ingrid was a good girl, but that wasn't much to laugh at either.

She left the table and went to get her books. By the time he had put on his hat and coat and galoshes she was standing with her hand on the doorhandle, waiting for him. He took the Lebanese leather bag from her. It was the worse for wear and had gaudy FNL labels stuck all over it.

This, too, was routine. Nine years ago he had carried Ingrid's bag on her first day at school, and he still did so. On that occasion he had taken her hand. A very small hand, which had been warm and moist and trembling with excitement and anticipation. When had he given up taking her hand? He couldn't remember.

"On Christmas Eve you're going to laugh, anyway," she said.

"Really?"

"Yes. When you get my Christmas present."

She frowned and said, "Anything else is out of the question."

"What would you like yourself, by the way?"

"A horse."

"Where would you keep it?"

"I don't know. I'd like one all the same."

"Do you know what a horse costs?"

"Yes, unfortunately."

They parted.

At Kungsholmsgatan Gunvald Larsson was waiting, and an investigation which didn't even deserve to be called a guessing game. Hammar had been kind enough to point this out only two days ago.

"How is Ture Assarsson's alibi?" Gunvald Larsson asked.

"Ture Assarsson's alibi is one of the most watertight in the history of crime," Martin Beck replied. "At the time in question he was at the City Hotel in Södertälje making an after-dinner speech to twenty-five persons."

"Hmm," Gunvald Larsson muttered darkly.

"What's more, if I may say so, it's not very logical to imagine that Gösta Assarsson would not notice his own brother getting on the bus with a submachine gun under his coat."

"Yes, the coat," said Gunvald Larsson. "It must have

159

been pretty wide if he could have an M 37 under it. If he wasn't carrying it in a case, that is."

"You're right, there," Martin Beck said.

"It does sometimes happen that I'm right."

"Lucky for you," Martin Beck retorted. "If you'd been wrong the night before last we'd have been sitting pretty now, I *don't* think."

Pointing his cigarette at the other man he said, "You're going to get it one of these days, Gunvald."

"I doubt it."

And Gunvald Larsson stumped out of the room. In the doorway he met Kollberg, who stepped aside quickly, stole a glance at the broad back and said, "What's wrong with the walking battering ram? Sore?"

Martin Beck nodded. Kollberg went over to the window and looked out.

"Jesus Christ," he growled.

"Is Åsa still staying with you?"

"Yes," Kollberg replied. "And don't say, 'Have you got yourself a harem?' because Mr. Larsson has already asked that."

Martin Beck sneezed.

"Bless you," Kollberg said. "I very nearly tossed him out of the window."

Kollberg was about the only one who could have done it, Martin Beck thought. Aloud he said, "Thanks."

"What are you thanking me for?"

"For saying 'bless you.' "

"Oh yes. Not many people nowadays have the courtesy to say thank you. I had a case once. A press photographer who beat his wife black and blue and then flung her out in the snow naked because she hadn't thanked him when he said 'bless you.' On New Year's Eve. He was drunk, of course."

He stood silent for a while, then said doubtfully, "I doubt if I can get anything more out of her. Åsa, I mean."

"Well, never mind, we know what Stenström was working on," Martin Beck said.

Kollberg gaped at him. "Do we?"

"Sure. The Teresa murder. Clear as daylight."

"The Teresa murder?"

"Yes. Hadn't you realized that?"

"No," Kollberg said. "I hadn't. And I've thought back over everything from the last ten years. Why didn't you say anything?"

Martin Beck looked at him and bit his ball-point pen thoughtfully. They both had the same thought and Kollberg put it into words.

"One can't communicate merely by telepathy."

"No," Martin Beck said. "Besides, the Teresa case is sixteen years old. And you had nothing to do with the investigation. The Stockholm police had charge of it from start to finish. I think Ek is the only one left here from that time."

"So you've already gone through all the reports?"

"By no means. Only skimmed through them. There are several thousand pages. All the papers are out at Västberga. Shall we go out and have a look?"

"Yes, let's. My memory needs refreshing."

In the car Martin Beck said, "Perhaps you remember enough to realize why Stenström took on the Teresa case?"

Kollberg nodded.

"Yes, because it was the most difficult one he could tackle."

"Exactly. The most impossible of all things impossible. He wanted to show what he was capable of, once and for all."

"And then he went and got himself shot," Kollberg said. "Christ, how stupid. And where's the connection?"

Martin made no reply and nothing more was said until, after various difficulties and delays, they had threaded their way out to Västberga and parked in the sleet outside the southern police headquarters. Then Kollberg said, "Can the Teresa case be solved? Now?"

"Shouldn't think so for a moment," Martin Beck replied.

25

Kollberg sighed unhappily, as he listlessly and irrationally turned the pages of the reports piled in front of him.

"It will take a week to wade through all this," he said.

"At least. Do you know the actual circumstances?"

"No, not even in broad outline."

"There's a résumé somewhere. Otherwise I can give you a rough idea."

Kollberg nodded. Martin Beck picked out one or two sheets and said, "The facts are clear-cut. Very simple. Therein lies the difficulty."

"Fire away," Kollberg said.

"On the morning of June 10, 1951, that's to say more than sixteen years ago, a man who was looking for his cat found a dead woman in some bushes near Stadshagen sportsground on Kungsholmen here in town. She was naked, lying on her stomach with her arms by her sides. The forensic medical examination showed that she had been strangled and that she had been dead for about five days. The body was well preserved and had evidently been lying in a cold-storage room or something similar. All available evidence pointed to a sex murder, but as such a long time had elapsed, the doctor who did the postmortem could not find any definite signs that she had been sexually assaulted."

"Which on the whole means a sex murder," Kollberg said.

"Yes. On the other hand, the examination of the scene of the crime showed that the body could not have been lying there for more than twelve hours at the most; this was also confirmed later by witnesses, who had passed the shrubbery the previous evening and who could not have helped seeing the body if it had been there then. Further, fibers and textile particles were found indicating that she had been transported there wrapped in a gray blanket. It was therefore quite clear that the crime had not been committed in the place where the body was found, and that the body had just been slung into the bushes. Little or no attempt had been made to hide it with the help of moss or branches. Well, that's about all . . . No, I was forgetting. Two more things: She had not eaten for several hours before she died. And there was no trace of the murderer in the way of footprints or anything."

Martin Beck turned over the pages and eyed through the typewritten text.

"The woman was identified the very same day as one Teresa Camarão. She was twenty-six years old and born in Portugal. She had come to Sweden in 1945 and the same year had married a fellow countryman called Henrique Camarão. He was two years older than she and had been a radio officer in the merchant marine but had gone ashore and got a job as radio technician. Teresa Camarão was born in Lisbon in 1925. According to the Portuguese police she came from a good home and a very respectable family. Upper middle class. She had come to study, rather belatedly because of the war. That's as far as her studies got. She met this Henrique Camarão and married him. They had no children. Comfortably off. Lived on Torsgatan."

"Who identified her?"

"The police. That's to say the vice squad. She was well-known there and had been for the last two years. On May 15, 1949—circumstances were such that it was in fact possible to determine the exact date—she had completely changed her way of life. She had run away from home—so it says here—and since then she had circulated in the underworld. In short, Teresa Camarão had become a whore. She was a nymphomaniac and during these two years she had gone with hundreds of men."

"Yes, I remember," Kollberg said.

"Now comes the best part of it. Within the space of three days the police found no less than three witnesses who, at half-past eleven the evening before, had seen a car parked on Kungsholmsgatan by the approach to the path beside which the body was found. All three were men. Two of them had passed in a car, one of them on foot. The two witnesses who had been driving had also seen a man standing by the car. Beside him on the ground lay an object the size of a body, wrapped in something that seemed to be a gray blanket. The third witness walked past a few minutes later and saw only the car. The descriptions of the man were vague. It was raining and the person had stood in the shadow; all that could be said for sure was that it was a man and that he was fairly tall. Pressed for what they meant by tall, they varied between 5 feet 9 and 6 feet 1 inches, which includes ninety percent of the country's male population. But . . ."

"Yes? But what?"

"But as regards the vehicle, all three witnesses were agreed. Each said that the car was French, a Renault model CV-4, which was put on the market in 1947 and which turned up year after year with no changes to speak of."

"Renault CV-4," Kollberg said. "Porsche designed it while the French kept him prisoner as a war criminal. They shut him up in the gatekeeper's house at the factory. There he sat designing. Then, I think, he was acquitted. The French made millions out of that car."

"You have a staggering knowledge of the most widely differing subjects," Martin Beck said drily. "Can you tell me now what connection there is between the Teresa case and the fact that Stenström was shot dead by a mass murderer on a bus four weeks ago?"

"Wait a bit," Kollberg said. "What happened then?"

"The police here in Stockholm carried out the most extensive murder investigation ever known in this country. It swelled to gigantic proportions. Well, you can see for yourself. Hundreds of persons were questioned who had known and been in touch with Teresa Camarão, but it could not be established who had last seen her alive. All trace of her came to an abrupt end exactly one week before she was found dead. She had spent the night with a guy in a hotel room on Nybrogatan and parted from him at twelve thirty next day outside a wine restaurant on Mäster Samuelsgatan. Period. After that every single

164

Renault CV-4 was tracked down. First in Stockholm, since the witnesses said that the car had an A license plate. Then every car in the whole country of that make and model was checked, with the idea that it might have had a false license plate. It took almost a year. And at last it could be proved, actually proved, that not one of all those cars could have stood at Stadshagen at eleven thirty on the evening of June 9, 1951."

"Hm. And at that moment . . ." Kollberg said.

"Precisely. At that moment the entire investigation was as dead as a doornail. It was completed. Wound up. The only thing wrong with it was that Teresa Camarão had been murdered and it was not known who had done it. The last twitch of life in the Teresa investigation was in 1952, when the Danish, Norwegian and Finnish police informed us that the goddam car could not have come from any of those countries. At the same time the Swedish customs confirmed that it could not have come from anywhere else abroad. As you probably remember, there were not so many cars at that time, and it involved an awful lot of red tape if you wanted to get a motor vehicle across a frontier."

"Yes, I remember. And these witnesses . . ."

"The two in the car were friends from work. One was foreman at a garage and the other a car mechanic. The third witness was also very well informed in the matter of cars. By profession he was—guess."

"Manager of the Renault factories?"

"No. Police sergeant. Specialist in traffic questions. Carlberg, his name was—he's dead now. But not even this point was overlooked—we had started trying out witness psychology even then. These three men were made to undergo a series of tests. One at a time they were asked to identify silhouettes of different types of cars, projected on slides. All three recognized every current model, and the foreman guy even knew the most exotic makes, like Hispano-Suiza and Pegaso. They couldn't even trick him when they drew a car that didn't exist. He said, 'The front is a Fiat 500, and the back is from a Dyna Panhard.' "

"What did the guys in charge of the investigation think? Privately?" Kollberg asked.

"The inside talk was something like this: The murderer is to be found among all the papers, it's one of the count-less men who have slept with Teresa Camarão and who, in a fit of whatever it is that comes over sex maniacs, has strangled her. The investigation has collapsed because someone has bungled over the checkup of all these Re-nault cars. So let's check them once again. And once again. Then they thought, quite rightly, that after all that time the scent had grown cold. They still thought that at some point or other the run-down of the cars had slipped up and that it was too late to do anything about it. I'm sure that Ek, for instance, who was in on it, thinks so to this day. And on the whole I agree. I can't see any explana-tion."

Kollberg sat silent for a while. Then he said, "What happened to Teresa on that day you mentioned? In May, 1949?"

Martin Beck studied the papers and said, "She received a kind of shock, which led to a psychological phenomenon and a mental and physical state which is comparatively rare but by no means unique. Teresa Camarão had grown up in an upper-middle-class family. Her parents were Catholics like herself. She was a virgin when she married at the age of twenty. She lived for four years together with her husband in a typical Swedish manner, although both were foreigners, and in the environment that was, and is, typical of the comfortable upper middle class. She was reserved, sensible and had a quiet disposition. Her hus-band considered the marriage a happy one. She was, a doctor says here, a pure product of these two environ-ments, strict Catholic upper class and strict Swedish bour-geoisie, with all the moral taboos inherent in each, to say nothing of the combined result. On May 15, 1949, her husband was away on a job in the north. She went to a lecture with a woman friend. There they met a man whom the friend had known for years. He accompanied them back to the Camarãos' apartment on Torsgatan, where the friend was to spend the night, as she too was a grass widow. They had tea and then sat talking about the lecture over a glass of wine. This guy was feeling a bit down because he had fallen out with a girl—whom incidentally he married not long afterward. He was at a loose end. He thought Teresa was attractive, which she was, and started making a pass at her. The woman friend, who knew that Teresa was the most moral person imaginable, went off to bed—she slept on a sofa in the hall, within earshot. The guy said about a dozen times to Teresa that they should go to bed, but she kept saying no. At last he simply lifted her out of the chair, carried her into the bedroom, undressed her and made love to her. As far as is known, Teresa Camarão had never before shown herself naked to anybody, not even to women. Teresa Camarão had never had an orgasm. That night she had about twenty. Next morning the guy said 'so long,' and off he went. She kept calling him up ten times a day for the next week, and after that he never heard from her again. He made it up with his girl and married her, and got on very well. There are a dozen different interrogations with him in this pile. He was really grilled, but he had an alibi and did not have a car; moreover, he was a good, decent guy who was happily married and was never unfaithful to his wife."

"And Teresa started running about like a bitch in heat?"

"Yes. Literally. She left home, her husband would have nothing more to do with her, and she was dropped by all her friends and acquaintances. For two years she lived for short periods with a score of different men and had sexual relations with ten times as many. She was a nymphomaniac, ready for anything. At first she did it for nothing, but toward the last she did accept money occasionally. Of course, she never met anyone who could put up with her for any length of time. She had no women friends. She tumbled right down the social ladder. Within less than six months the only people she mixed with were those who belonged to what we then called the underworld. She also started drinking. The vice squad knew of her but could never quite keep up with her. They were going to pick her up for vagrancy, but before they could do anything she was dead."

Pointing to the bundle of reports, Martin Beck went on.

"Among all these papers are a lot of interrogations with men who fell prey to her. They say she never left them alone and was impossible to satisfy. Most of them got scared to death the very first time, especially those who were married and were just out for a bit of fun on the side. She knew a large number of shady characters and semi-gangsters, thieves and con men and black market swindlers and the like. Well, you remember the clientele from that time."

"What happened to her husband?"

"Not unnaturally, he considered himself scandalized. He changed his name and became a Swedish citizen. Met a girl of good family from Stocksund, remarried, had two children and lived happily ever after in a house of his own on Lidingö. His alibi was as watertight as Captain Cassel's raft."

"As what?"

"The only thing you know nothing about is boats," Martin Beck said. "If you look through that folder you'll understand where Stenström got some of his ideas."

Kollberg looked inside it.

"Jesus Christ! That's the hairiest little broad I've ever seen. Who took these pictures?"

"A man interested in photography who had a perfect alibi and who had nothing to do with a Renault car. But unlike Stenström, he sold his pictures at a fat profit. As you remember, we didn't have the same profusion of advanced pornography then as we have now."

They sat silent for a while. At last Kollberg said, "What possible connection can this have with the fact that Stenström and eight other people are shot dead on a bus sixteen years later?"

"None at all," Martin Beck replied. "We're simply on our way back to the mentally deranged sensation murderer."

"Why did he say nothing—" Kollberg began, and broke off.

"Exactly," Martin Beck said. "All that is explained now. Stenström was going through unsolved cases. As he was very ambitious and still rather naïve he picked the most hopeless one he could find. If he solved the Teresa murder it would be a fantastic detective feat. And he said nothing to us because he knew that some of us would laugh at him. When he told Hammar he didn't want to tackle anything too old, he had already decided on this. When Teresa Camarão lay in the morgue Stenström was twelve and probably didn't even read the newspapers. He considered he could look at it in quite an unbiased way. He combed right through this investigation."

"And what did he find?"

"Nothing. Because there's nothing to find. There's not one loose thread."

"How do you know?"

Martin Beck looked gravely at Kollberg and said, "I know because I did exactly the same thing eleven years ago. I didn't find anything either. And I didn't have any Åsa Torell to carry out sexual-psychological experiments on. The minute you told me that about her, I knew what he had been working on. But I forgot that you didn't know as much about Teresa Camarão as I did. Come to that, I should have realized it when we found those pictures in his drawer."

"So he was trying out a kind of psychological method?"

"Yes. That's all there is left. Find a person who resembles Teresa in some respect and see how she reacts. There's a certain amount of sense in it, especially if you already happen to have such a person at home. The investigation as such has no gaps. Otherwise . . ."

"What?"

"I was going to say that otherwise we'd have to turn to a clairvoyant. But some bright guy has already done that. It's there somewhere in the file."

"But this doesn't tell us what he was doing on the bus."

"No. It doesn't tell us a damn thing."

"I'll check a couple of things anyway," Kollberg said.

"Yes, do," Martin Beck said.

Kollberg searched out Henrique Camarão, who now called himself Hendrik Caam, a corpulent, middle-aged man who sighed and stole an unhappy glance at his blonde upper-class wife and a thirteen-year-old son with velvet jacket and Beatles hair-do, and said, "Am I never to be left in peace? Only last summer there was a young detective here and . . ."

Kollberg also checked Caam's alibi for the evening of November 13. It was faultless.

He also tracked down the man who had taken the pictures of Teresa eighteen years earlier, and found a toothless old alcoholic in a cell in the long-term pavilion of the central prison. The man, who had been a burglar, screwed up his mouth and said, "Teresie. I'll say I remember her. She had nipples the size of beer-bottle tops. Funny thing, there was another cop here a few months ago and . . ."

Kollberg read every word of the report. It took him exactly a week. On the evening of Tuesday, December 18, 1967, he read the last page. Then he looked at his wife, who had been asleep for some hours; her head, with its dark ruffled hair, was burrowed into the pillow. She was lying on her stomach with her right knee drawn up and the quilt had slipped down to her waist. He heard the sofa creak in the living room as Åsa Torell got up and tiptoed out to the kitchen for a drink of water. She still slept badly.

There's no missing part in this, Kollberg thought. No loose ends. All the same, tomorrow I'll make a list of all the people who were interrogated or who are known to have been with Teresa Camarão. Then we'll see who all are still left and what they're doing now.

26

A month had passed since the sixty-seven shots were fired in the bus on Norra Stationsgatan, and the ninefold murderer was still at large.

The police board, the press and the general public were

not the only ones who showed their impatience. There was yet another category who were particularly anxious for the police to find the guilty man as soon as possible. This category comprised what is popularly known as the underworld.

Most of the people who usually busied themselves with crime had been forced into inactivity during the last month. So long as the police were on the alert, it was best to lie low. There was not a thief, junkie, pusher, mugger, bootlegger or pimp in the whole of Stockholm who didn't hope that the mass murderer would soon be seized so that the police could once more devote their time to Vietnam demonstrators and parking offenders and they themselves could get back to work.

One result of this was that for once they made common cause with the police, and most of them had no objections to helping in the hunt.

Rönn's work in his search for the pieces of the jigsaw puzzle called Nils Erik Göransson was also made much easier by this willingness. He was quite well aware of the motives behind the unusual good will shown to him, but he was nonetheless grateful for it.

He had spent the last few nights contacting people who had known Göransson. He had found them in condemned houses, restaurants, beer bars, billiard parlors and common rooming houses. Not all were willing to give information, but many did.

On the evening of December 13, on a barge moored at Söder Mälarstrand, he met a girl who promised to put him in touch the next evening with Sune Björk, the man who had let Göransson share his apartment for a week or two.

The next day was a Thursday and Rönn, who had snatched only a few hours in bed during the last few days, spent half the day sleeping. He got up at one o'clock and helped his wife to pack. He had persuaded her to go up to her parents at Arjeplog over the Christmas holidays, as he suspected that he himself would not have much spare time for celebrating Christmas this year.

Having seen his wife off by the train, he drove home again and sat down at the kitchen table with paper and pen. He laid Nordin's report and his own notebook in front of him, put on his glasses and began to write.

Nils Erik Göransson.
Born in the Finnish parish, Stockholm, 10.4.1929.
Parents: Algot Erik Göransson, electrician, and Benita Rantanen. Parents divorced 1935, mother moved to Helsinki and father given custody of the child.
G. lived with father at Sundbyberg till 1945.
Went to school for 7 years, thereafter 2 years at trade school learning house-painting.
1947 moved to Gothenburg, where he worked as painter's apprentice. Married Gudrun Maria Svensson in Gothenburg 12.1.1948. Divorced 5.13.1949.
From June 1949 to March 1950 deckhand on boats of the Svea Steamship Company. Baltic coastal trade. Moved in the summer of 1950 to Stockholm. Employed by the painting firm of Amandus Gustavsson until November, 1950, when he was dismissed for being drunk at work. From then on he seems to have gone downhill. He got odd jobs, as night porter, errand boy, porter, warehouseman etc., but probably made a living mainly out of petty thieving and other minor crimes. Was never apprehended, however, as suspected of any crime but on several occasions was charged with being drunk and disorderly. For a time he called himself by his mother's maiden name, Rantanen. Father died 1958 and between 1958 and 1964 he lived in father's apartment at Sundbyberg. Evicted 1964 because he was three months in arrears with rent.
He seems to have started using narcotics some time during 1964. From that year until his death he had no fixed residence. In January, 1965, he moved in with Gurli Löfgren, Skeppar Karls gränd 3, and lived with her until the spring of 1966. During this time neither he nor Löfgren had any regular work. Löfgren was registered with the vice squad but considering her age and appearance, she cannot have earned much from prostitution during this time. Löfgren too was addicted to drugs. Gurli Löfgren died of cancer at the age of 47 on Christmas Day, 1966. At the beginning of March, 1967, he met Magdalena Rosén

172

*(Blonde Malin) and lived with her at Arbetargatan 3
until 8.29.1967. From beginning of September until
middle of October this year he had a temporary
domicile with Sune Björk.*

*Was treated for venereal disease (gonorrhea) twice
during October–November at St. Göran's Hospital.*

*The mother has remarried. She still lives in Helsinki
and has been notified by letter of her son's death.*

*Rosén says that Göransson was never without money
and that she doesn't know where this money came
from. To her knowledge, he was not a pusher and
did not carry on any other form of business.*

Rönn read through what he had written. His handwriting was so microscopic that it all fitted on to less
than one sheet of legal-sized paper. Putting the paper in
his briefcase and the notebook in his pocket, he went off
to see Sune Björk.

The girl from the barge was waiting for him by the
newspaper kiosk on Mariatorget.

"I'm not coming with you," she said. "But I've talked
to Sune, so he knows you're coming. Hope I haven't done
anything stupid."

She gave him an address on Tavastgatan and made off
down toward Slussen.

Sune Björk was younger than Rönn had expected, he
couldn't have been more than twenty-five. He had a blond
beard and seemed nice enough. There was nothing about
him to indicate that he was an addict, and Rönn wondered
what he could have had in common with the much older
and seedier Göransson.

The apartment consisted of one room and kitchen and
was poorly furnished. The windows looked on to an
untidy courtyard. Rönn sat down in the only chair and
Björk sat on the bed.

"I heard you wanted to know about Nisse," Björk said.
"I must confess I don't know much about him myself,
but I thought you could perhaps take care of his things."

He bent down and fished out a shopping bag from
under the bed and gave it to Rönn.

"He left this here when he cleared out. He took some
stuff with him—that's mostly clothes. Worthless crap."

Rönn took the bag and placed it beside the chair.

"Can you tell me how long you knew Göransson, where and how you met and how you came to let him stay here with you?"

Björk settled down on the bed and crossed his legs.

"I can if you like," he said. "Can I bum a cigarette?"

Rönn took out a pack of Prince and shook out a cigarette for Björk, who lighted it after nipping off the filter.

"It was like this, see. I was down at Zum Franziskaner having a beer and Nisse was sitting at the next table. I'd never seen him before but we started talking and he stood me a glass of wine. I thought he seemed a nice guy so when they closed and he said he had no pad, I brought him back here. We got pretty loaded that night and the next day he stood me a couple of drinks and some grub at Södergård. This must have been the third or fourth of September, I don't remember exactly."

"Did you notice he was an addict?" Rönn asked.

Björk shook his head.

"No, not at once. But after a couple of days he gave himself a fix in the morning as soon as we woke up and then, of course, I realized it. He asked if I wanted one, by the way, but I don't dig that sort of thing."

Björk had rolled his sleeves up above his elbows. Rönn cast a practiced eye at the bends of his arms and noted that he was evidently telling the truth.

"You haven't much room here," he said. "Why did you let him stay here for so long? Did he pay for his keep, by the way?"

"I thought he was O.K. He didn't actually pay any rent, but he had plenty of money and always brought home grub and liquor and so on."

"Where did he get his money from?"

Björk shrugged.

"I dunno. It wasn't my business anyway. But he didn't have any job, I know that."

Rönn looked at Björk's hands, which were black with ingrained dirt.

"What's your job?"

"Cars," Björk replied. "I've got a date with a broad in

a while, so you'd better get a move on. Anything more you wanted to know?"

"What did he talk about? Did he tell you anything about himself?"

Björk rubbed his forefinger quickly to and fro under his nose and said, "He said he'd been to sea, though I think that was years ago. And he used to talk about dames. Especially one he'd been living with who had kicked the bucket not long before. She was like a mom, he said, only better."

Pause.

"You can't screw your mom, you know," Björk said gravely. "Otherwise he wasn't so keen on talking about himself."

"When did he clear out of here?"

"On the eighth of October. I remember because it was a Sunday and it was his nameday. He took his things, all except them there. He didn't have many, they all went into an ordinary bag. He said he had got himself another pad but that he'd come by and say hello in a day or two."

He paused and stubbed out his cigarette in a coffee cup that was standing on the floor.

"After that I never saw him again. And now he's dead," Sivan said. Was he really one of those on the bus?"

Rönn nodded.

"Do you know where he went to from here?"

"Haven't a clue. He never looked me up and I didn't know where he was. He met several of my mates here, but I never met any of his. So I really know goddam little about him."

Björk got up, went over to a mirror hanging on the wall and combed his hair.

"Do you know who it was?" he asked. "The guy on the bus?"

"No," Rönn replied. "Not yet."

Björk pulled off his sweater.

"I have to change now," he said. "My dame's waiting."

Rönn stood up, took the shopping bag and walked toward the door.

"So you've no idea what he did with himself after the eighth of October?" he asked.

"I said no, didn't I?"

He took a clean shirt out of the chest of drawers and tore off the laundry's paper strip.

"I only know one thing," he said.

"What?"

"He was as nervy as hell for a week or two before he cleared out. Seemed to have something on his mind."

"But you don't know what?"

"No, I don't."

When Rönn got home to his empty apartment he went out into the kitchen and emptied the contents of the shopping bag onto the table. Then he picked the objects up cautiously and studied them before dropping them back into the bag, one at a time.

A spotted, threadbare cap, a pair of undershorts that had once been white, a wrinkled tie with red and green stripes, an artificial leather belt with a yellow brass buckle, a pipe with a chewed stem, a wool-lined pigskin glove, a pair of yellow crepe nylon socks, two dirty handkerchiefs and a crumpled light-blue poplin shirt.

Rönn held the shirt up and was just going to put it back in the bag when he noticed a scrap of paper sticking out of the breast pocket. Putting the shirt down, he unfolded the paper. It was a bill for Kr. 78:25 from Restaurant Pilen. It was dated October 7 and according to the sums stamped by the cash register, one was for food, six were for liquor and three for soda water.

Rönn turned the bill over. In the margin on the back someone had written with a ball-point pen:

10.8 bf	3 000
Morph	500
Owe ga	100
Owe mb	50
Dr P	650
	1 700
Bal	1 300

Rönn thought he recognized Göransson's handwriting, of which he had seen several examples at Blonde Malin's. He took the jottings to mean that Göransson, on the eighth of October—the same day he left Sune Björk—was to get 3,000 kronor from somewhere, perhaps from a person with the initials B.F. Out of this money he would buy morphine for 500, pay 150 in debts and give a Dr. P 650, for drugs or something else. That would leave him 1,700. When he was found dead in the bus over a month later he had had over 1,800 kronor in his pocket. So he must have received more money after the eighth of October. Rönn wondered whether this, too, had come from the same source, *bf* or B.F. It needn't be a person, it could just as well be an abbreviation for something else.

Brought forward? Göransson didn't seem the type that would have a bank account. The most likely thing after all was that *bf* was a person. Rönn looked at his notebook, but none of those he had talked to or heard about in connection with Göransson had the initials B.F.

Rönn picked up the bag and went out into the hall. He put the bill in his briefcase and placed bag and briefcase on the hall table. Then he went to bed.

He lay wondering where Göransson had got his money from.

27

On the morning of Thursday, December 21, it was no fun being a policeman. The evening before, in the midst of the Christmas hysteria downtown, an army of police in uniform and plainclothes had got caught up in a spectacular and utterly chaotic fight with a large number of workmen and intellectuals who were streaming out from a Vietnam meeting in the Trades Union Hall.

Opinions as to what really happened were divided and would probably remain so, but there were very few laughing policemen on this dismal and chilly morning.

The only one to have derived any profit from the incident was Månsson. He had unsuspectingly said that he had nothing to do and had immediately been sent out to help keep order. At first he had hidden in the shadows around Adolf Fredrik's Church on Sveavägen in the hope that disturbances, if any, would not spread in that direction. But the police pressed in on all sides, unsystematically, and the demonstrators, who had to go somewhere, began also to force their way toward Sveavägen. Månsson retired swiftly northward and came at last to a restaurant. He went in to warm himself and do a little investigating. On his way out he took a toothpick from the cruet stand on one of the tables. It was wrapped in paper and tasted of menthol.

Presumably he was the only one in the entire police force who was happy on this miserable morning. He had already called up the stock-keeper of the restaurant and got the address of the supplier.

Einar Rönn was not happy. He stood in the wind on Ringvägen, gazing at a hole in the ground and a tarpaulin; some of the highway department's trestles had been placed around about them. The hole was quite uninhabited. Not so the service truck which was parked over 50 yards away. Rönn knew the four men who sat inside fiddling with their thermos flasks and merely said, "Hello, there."

"Hello. Shut the door. But if you were the one who clubbed my boy on the head on Barnhusgatan last night, then I'm not talking to you."

"No," Rönn said. "It wasn't me. I was at home looking at TV. The wife has gone up north."

"Sit down, then. Like some coffee?"

"Thanks, I don't mind if I do."

After a while one of the men said, "Want anything special?"

"Yes . . . A man named Schwerin—he was born in America. Was it noticeable when he talked?"

"Was it! He had an accent just like Anita Ekberg's. And when he was drunk he spoke English."

"When he was drunk?"

"Yes. And when he lost his temper. Or forgot himself."

Rönn took No. 54 back to Kungsholmen. It was a red doubledecker Leyland Atlantean model bus with a cream-colored top and a gray-lacquered roof. Despite Ek's assertion that the doubledeckers took only seated passengers, the bus was packed with people who stood clutching for support with one hand and grasping packages and shopping bags with the other.

He thought hard all the way. Then he sat down at his desk for a while. Went into the next room and said, "He didn't recognize him," and went out again.

"Now he's gone crazy too," Gunvald Larsson growled.

"Wait a second," Martin Beck said. "I think he's got something there."

He got up and went after Rönn. The room was empty. Hat and coat were gone.

Half an hour later Rönn once again opened the door of the truck on Ringvägen. The men who had been Schwerin's co-workers were sitting in exactly the same place as before. The hole in the road looked untouched by human hands.

"Christ, you scared me," one of them said. "I thought it was Olsson."

"Olsson?"

"Yes. Or 'Oleson,' as Alf used to say."

Rönn did not produce his results until the next morning, two days before Christmas Eve.

Martin Beck stopped the tape recorder and said, "So you think it should go like this: You say, 'Who did the shooting?' And he answered in English, 'Didn't recognize him.' "

"Yes."

"And then you say, 'What did he look like?' And Schwerin answers, 'Like Olsson.' "

"Yes. And then he died."

"Splendid, Einar," Martin Beck said.

"Who the hell is Olsson?" Gunvald Larsson asked.

"A sort of inspector. He goes around between the different working sites and checks that the men aren't loafing."

"And what the hell *does* he look like?"

"He's next door in my office," Rönn said modestly.

Martin Beck and Gunvald Larsson went in and stared at Olsson. Gunvald Larsson for only ten seconds, then he said, "Un-huh."

And went out. Olsson stared after him, mouth agape.

Martin Beck stayed for thirty seconds while he said, "I gather you've taken all the particulars, Einar?"

"Yes," Rönn said.

"Thank you, Mr. Olsson."

Martin Beck went out. Olsson looked more puzzled than ever.

When Martin Beck returned from lunch, having managed to get down only a glass of milk, two pieces of cheese and a cup of coffee, Rönn had put a sheet of paper on his desk. It bore the brief title: Olsson.

Olsson is 46 years old and is an inspector for the highway department.

He is 6 feet tall and weighs 170 pounds stripped.

He has ash-blond wavy hair and gray eyes. He is lankily built.

His face is long and lean with distinct features, prominent nose, rather crooked, wide mouth, thin lips and good teeth.

Shoe size: 9.

Rather dark complexion, which he says is due to his work, which forces him to be so often out of doors. Clothing, neat: gray suit, white shirt with tie and black shoes. Out-of-doors while at work, wears a waterproofed, knee-length raincoat, wide and loose-fitting. Color, gray. He has two such coats and always wears one of them in winter. On his head he has a black leather hat with narrow brim. He has heavy black shoes with deep-ribbed rubber soles on his feet. In rain or snow, however, he usually wears black rubber boots with reflex tape.

Olsson has an alibi for the evening of November 13. At the time in question, from 10 P.M. to midnight, he was at premises belonging to a bridge club of which he is a member. He took part in a competition and his presence is confirmed by the competition score card and the testimonies of the three other players.

Regarding Alfons (Alf) Schwerin, Olsson says that he was easy to get on with but lazy and given to strong drink.

"Do you think Rönn stripped him and weighed him?" Gunvald Larsson said.

Martin Beck did not answer.

"Nice logical conclusions," Gunvald Larsson went on. "He had the hat on his head and the shoes on his feet. He wore only one overcoat at a time. And is it his nose or his mouth that's rather crooked? What are you going to do with that?"

"Don't know. It's a sort of description."

"Yes, of Olsson."

"What about Assarsson?"

"I was talking to Jacobsson just now," Gunvald Larsson said. "An ugly customer."

"Jacobsson?"

"Yes, him too," Gunvald Larsson replied. "I suppose he's sore because they can't pull off their own goddam dope hauls and we have to do their job for them."

"Not 'we.' You."

"Even Jacobsson admits, of course, that Assarsson was the biggest wholesale dealer in dope they've ever laid hands on. They must have made money by the sackful, those brothers."

"And that other shady type? The foreigner?"

"He was just a courier. Greek. The bastard had a diplomatic passport. He was an addict himself. Assarsson thinks he was the one who squealed. Says it's very dangerous to confide anything to heads. He's not at all pleased. Probably because he didn't get rid of the courier long ago in some suitable way."

He paused briefly.

"That Göransson on the bus was also an addict. I wonder . . ."

Gunvald Larsson did not finish the sentence, but he had given Martin Beck something to think about.

Kollberg plodded away with his lists but preferred not to show them to anyone. He began more and more to understand how Stenström had felt while he was working on this old case. As Martin Beck had rightly pointed out, the Teresa investigation was unassailable. Some incorrigible stickler for form had even made the comment that "technically the case was solved and the investigation was a model of perfectly carried out police work."

The consequences of this should be the much talked-of perfect crime.

The work with the list of men who had associated with Teresa Camarão was by no means easy. It was amazing how many people managed to die, emigrate or change their names in sixteen years. Others had become incurably insane and awaited the end in some institution. Still others were in prison or in homes for chronic alcoholics. A number had simply disappeared, either at sea or in some other way. Many had long since moved to distant parts of the country, made a new life for themselves and their families and could in most cases be written off after a quick routine checkup. By this time Kollberg had twenty-nine names on his list. Persons who were at large and still lived in Stockholm or at any rate in the vicinity of the city. Up to now he had collected only summary information about these people. Present age, profession, postal address and civil status. At the moment the list was as follows, numbered from one to twenty-nine and arranged in alphabetical order:

   1. *Sven Ahlgren, 41, shop assistant, Stockholm NO, married*
   2. *Karl Andersson, 63, ?, Stockholm SV (Högalid institution), unmarried*
   3. *Ingvar Bengtsson, 43, journalist, Stockholm Va, divorced*
   4. *Rune Bengtsson, 56, businessman, Stocksund, married*
   5. *Jan Carlsson, 46, junk dealer, Upplands Väsby, unmarried*

182

6. *Rune Carlsson, 32, engineer, Nacka 5, married*

7. *Stig Ekberg, 83, former laborer, Stockholm SV (Rosenlund Home for the Aged), widower*

8. *Ove Eriksson, 47, car mechanic, Bandhagen, married*

9. *Valter Eriksson, 69, former stevedore, Stockholm SV (Högalid institution), widower*

10. *Stig Ferm, 31, housepainter, Sollentuna, married*

11. *Björn Forsberg, 48, businessman, Stocksund, married*

12. *Bengt Fredriksson, 56, artist, Stockholm C, divorced*

13. *Bo Frostensson, 66, actor, Stockholm Ö, divorced*

14. *Johan Gran, 52, former waiter, Solna, unmarried*

15. *Jan-Åke Karlsson, 38, clerk, Enköping, married*

16. *Kenneth Karlsson, 33, truck driver, Skälby, unmarried*

17. *Lennart Lindgren, 81, former bank manager, Lidingö 1, married*

18. *Sven Lundström, 37, warehouseman, Stockholm K, divorced*

19. *Tage Nilsson, 61, lawyer, Stockholm SÖ, unmarried*

20. *Carl-Gustaf Nilsson, 51, former mechanic, Johanneshov, divorced*

21. *Heinz Ollendorf, 46, artist, Stockholm K, unmarried*

22. *Kurt Olsson, 59, civil servant, Saltsjöbaden, married*

23. *Bernhard Peters, 39, commercial artist, Bromma, married (Negro)*

24. *Vilhelm Rosberg, 71, ?, Stockholm SV, widower*

25. *Bernt Turesson, 42, mechanic, Gustavsberg divorced*

26. *Ragnar Viklund, 60, major, Vaxholm, married*

27. *Bengt Wahlberg, 38, buyer (?), Stockholm K, unmarried*

28. *Hans Wennström, 76, former assistant fish-*
monger, Solna, unmarried
29. *Lennart Öberg, 35, civil engineer, Enskede,*
married

Kollberg sighed and looked at the list. Teresa Camarão
had included all social groups in her activities. She had
also operated within different generations. When she died
the youngest of these men had been fifteen and the eldest
sixty-seven. On this list alone there was everything from
bank managers in Stocksund to alcoholic old burglars at
the Högalid institution.

"What are you going to do with that?" Martin Beck
asked.

"Don't know," Kollberg replied despondently but truth-
fully.

Then he went in and laid the papers on Melander's
desk.

"You remember everything. When you have a moment
to spare, will you see if you recall anything extraordinary
about any of these men?"

Melander cast a blank look at the list and nodded.

On the twenty-third Månsson and Nordin flew home,
missed by nobody. They were to return immediately after
Christmas.

Outside, the weather was cold and horrible.

The consumer society creaked at the joints. On this
particular day everything could be sold, at any price. Very
often upon presentation of credit cards and dud checks.

On his way home that evening, Martin Beck thought
that Sweden now had, not only its first mass murder, but
also its first unsolved police murder.

The investigation had stuck fast. And technically—unlike the Teresa investigation—it looked like a pile of
rubbish.

28

Christmas Eve arrived.

Martin Beck got a Christmas present which, despite all speculations to the contrary, did not make him laugh.

Lennart Kollberg got a Christmas present which made his wife cry.

Both had resolved not to give a thought either to Åke Stenström or Teresa Camarão, and both failed in their intention.

Martin Beck woke up early but stayed in bed reading the book about the *Graf Spee* until the rest of the family began to show signs of life. Then he got up, put away the suit he had worn the day before and pulled on a pair of jeans and a sweater. His wife, who thought people ought to be dressed up on Christmas Eve, frowned as she eyed his clothes but for once said nothing.

While she paid her traditional visit to her parents' grave, Martin Beck decorated the tree together with Rolf and Ingrid. The children were noisy and excited, and he did his best not to dampen their spirits. His wife returned from her ritual call on the dead and he gamely joined in a custom that he didn't care for—dipping bread into the pot in which the ham had been cooked.

Before long the dull pain in his stomach made itself felt. Martin Beck was so used to these attacks that he paid no attention to them any more, but he had an idea that they had been occurring more frequently and more violently of late. Nowadays he never told Inga that he was in pain. At one time he had done so, and she had nearly been the death of him with her herbal potions and incessant fussing. For her, illness was an event on a par with life itself.

The Christmas dinner was colossal, seeing that it was meant for only four persons, of whom one very seldom managed to get down a normal portion of cooked food, one was dieting and one was too exhausted by the work of preparing it, to eat. That left Rolf, who, on the other hand, ate all the more. He was twelve years old and Martin Beck never ceased to be amazed that his son's spindly body was able to dispose of as much food in a day as he himself forced himself to eat in a week.

They all lent a hand with the washing-up, this too something that happened only on Christmas Eve.

Then Martin Beck lighted the candles on the tree, thinking of the Assarsson brothers who imported plastic Christmas trees as a cloak for their drugs traffic. Then came the hot punch and the gingerbread biscuits and Ingrid who said, "Now I think it's time to lead in the horse."

As usual they had all promised to give only one present to each and as usual they had all bought a lot more.

Martin Beck had not bought a horse for Ingrid, but as a substitute he gave her some riding breeches and paid for her riding lessons for the next six months.

His own presents included a model construction kit of the clipper ship *Cutty Sark* and a scarf two yards long, knitted by Ingrid.

She also gave him a flat package, watching him expectantly as he unwrapped the paper. Inside was a 45 r.p.m. EP record. On the sleeve was a photograph representing a fat man in the familiar uniform and helmet of the London bobby. He had a large, curling mustache and knitted mittens on his hands, which he held spread out over his stomach. He was standing in front of an old-fashioned microphone and to judge from his expression he was roaring with laughter. His name was apparently Charles Penrose and the record was called *The Adventures of the Laughing Policeman*.

Ingrid fetched the record player and put it on the floor beside Martin Beck's chair.

"Just wait till you hear it," she said. "It'll kill you."

She took the record out of the sleeve and looked at the label.

"The first song is called *The Laughing Policeman*. Pretty appropriate, eh?"

Martin Beck knew very little about music, but he heard at once that the recording must have been made in the twenties or even earlier. Each verse was followed by long bursts of laughter, which were evidently infectious, as Inga and Rolf and Ingrid howled with mirth.

Martin Beck was left utterly cold. He couldn't even manage a smile. So as not to disappoint the others too much he got up and turned his back, pretending to adjust the candles on the tree.

When the record was finished he went back to his chair. Ingrid wiped the tears from her eyes and looked at him.

"Why, Daddy, you didn't laugh," she said reproachfully.

"I thought it was awfully amusing," he said as convincingly as he could.

"Listen to this, then," Ingrid said, turning the record over. *"Jolly Coppers on Parade."*

Ingrid had evidently played the record many times and she joined in the song as though she had done nothing else but sing duets with the laughing policeman:

> There's a tramp, tramp, tramp
> At the end of the street.
> It's the jolly coppers walking on parade.
> And their uniforms are blue
> And the brass is shining too.
> A finer lot of men were never made . . .

The candles burned with a steady flame, the fir tree gave out its scent in the warm room, the children sang and Inga curled up in her new dressing gown and nibbled the head off a marzipan pig. Martin Beck sat leaning forward, his elbows propped on his knees and his chin in his hands, staring at the laughing policeman on the record sleeve.

He thought of Stenström.

And the telephone rang.

Somewhere inside him Kollberg felt far from content and least of all off duty. But as it was hard to say exactly what he was neglecting, there was no reason to spoil his Christmas Eve with unnecessary brooding.

He therefore mixed the punch with care, tasting it

several times before he was satisfied, sat down at the table and regarded the deceptively idyllic scene surrounding him. Bodil lying on her stomach beside the Christmas tree, making gurgling noises. Åsa Torell sitting with crossed legs on the floor, playfully poking at the baby. Gun sauntering about the apartment with a soft, indolent nonchalance, barefoot and dressed in some mysterious garment which was a cross between pajamas and a tracksuit.

He helped himself to a serving of fish, prepared especially for Christmas Eve. Sighed happily at the thought of the large, well-deserved meal he was about to gobble up. Tucked the napkin into his shirt and draped it over his chest. Poured out a big drink of akvavit. Raised the glass. Looked dreamily at the clear, ice-cold liquid and the mist forming on the glass. And at that moment the phone rang.

He hesitated a moment, then drained the glass at one gulp, went into the bedroom and lifted the receiver.

"Good evening, my name is Fröjd, from Långholmen prison."

"Well, that's cheering."

Said Kollberg in the secure knowledge that he was not on the emergency list and that not even a new mass murder could drive him out into the snow. Capable men were detailed for such things, for example Gunvald Larsson, who was in fact on call, and Martin Beck, who had to take the consequences of his higher rank.

"I work at the mental clinic here," the man said. "And we have a patient who insists on talking to you. His name's Birgersson. Says he has promised and that it's urgent and—"

Kollberg frowned.

"Can he come to the phone?"

"Sorry, no. It's against the rules. He's undergoing . . ."

Kollberg's face took on a sorrowful expression. The A-1 team was obviously not on duty on Christmas Eve.

"O.K., I'll come," he said and put down the phone.

His wife had heard these last words and stared at him wide-eyed.

"Have to go to Långholmen," he said wearily. "How

the hell do you get a taxi at this hour on Christmas Eve?"

"I can drive you," Åsa said. "I haven't drunk anything."

They did not talk on the way. The guard at the entrance peered suspiciously at Åsa Torell.

"She's my secretary," Kollberg said.

"Your what? Just a moment, I must take another look at your identification card."

Birgersson had not changed. If possible he seemed even more gentle and polite than he had been two weeks earlier.

"What do you want to tell me?" Kollberg said gruffly.

Birgersson smiled.

"It seems silly," he said. "But I just remembered something this evening. You were asking about the car, my Morris. And—"

"Yes? And?"

"Once when Inspector Stenström and I had a break and sat having something to eat, I told him a story. I remember we had boiled pickled pork and mashed turnips. It's my favorite dish, and today when we had Christmas dishes . . ."

Kollberg regarded the man with massive disapproval.

"A story?" he asked.

"A story about myself, really. From the time we lived on Roslagsgatan, my—"

He broke off and looked doubtfully at Åsa Torell. The prison guard over by the door yawned.

"Well, go on," Kollberg growled.

"My wife and I, that is. We had only one room and when I was at home I always used to feel nervous and shut-in and restless. I also slept badly."

"Un-huh," Kollberg grunted.

He felt hot and slightly dizzy. He was very thirsty and above all hungry. Moreover, his surroundings depressed him and he longed for home. Birgersson went on talking, quietly but long-windedly.

". . . so I used to go out of an evening, just so as to get away from home. This was nearly twenty years ago. I walked and walked the streets for hours, sometimes all

189

night. Never spoke to anyone, just wandered about so as to be left in peace. After a while I'd calm down, it usually took an hour or so. But I had to occupy my thoughts with something, you see, in order to keep from worrying about everything else. Being at home and my wife and all that. So I used to find things to do. To divert myself, you might say, take my mind off my troubles and keep myself from brooding."

Kollberg looked at his watch.

"Yes, yes, I see," he said impatiently. "What did you do?"

"I used to look at cars."

"Cars?"

"Yes. I used to walk along the street and through parking lots, looking at the cars that stood there. Actually I wasn't at all interested in cars, but in that way I got to know all the makes and models there were. After a time I became quite an expert. It was satisfying, somehow. I could do something. I could recognize all cars 40 or 50 yards away, from whichever side I saw them. If I could have taken part in one of those quiz programs on TV, you know when they ask you questions on one special subject, I'd have won first prize. From in front or from behind or from the side, it made no difference."

"What about if you saw them from above?" Asa Torell asked.

Kollberg looked at her in astonishment. Birgersson's face darkened slightly.

"Well, I never got much practice in that. I mightn't have been so good at that."

He pondered for a while. Kollberg shrugged resignedly.

"But you can get a lot of pleasure out of a simple occupation like that," Birgersson went on. "And excitement. Sometimes I saw very rare cars like a Lagonda or Zim or EMW. That cheered me up."

"And you told Inspector Stenström about this?"

"Yes, I'd never told anyone else."

"And what did he say?"

"He said he thought it was interesting."

"I see. And this is what you brought me here to say? At nine thirty in the evening? On Christmas Eve?"

Birgersson looked hurt.

"Yes," he replied. "You did say I was to tell you anything I remembered . . ."

"Yes, sure," Kollberg said wearily. "Thank you."

He stood up.

"But I haven't told you the most important yet," the man murmured. "It was something that interested Inspector Stenström very much. It occurred to me since we'd been talking about a Morris."

Kollberg sat down again.

"Yes? What?"

"Well, it had its problems, this hobby, if I may call it that. It was very hard to distinguish certain models when it was dark or if they were a long way off. For instance, Moskvitch and Opel Kadett or DKW and IFA."

He paused, and then said emphatically, "Very, very hard. Just small details."

"What has this to do with Stenström and your Morris 8?"

"No, not my Morris," Birgersson replied. "What interested the Inspector so much was when I told him that the hardest of all was to see the difference between a Morris Minor and a Renault CV-4 from in front. Not from the side or the back, that was easy. But from straight in front or obliquely in front—that was very difficult indeed. Though I learned in time and seldom made a mistake. It did happen of course."

"Wait a moment," Kollberg said. "Did you say Morris Minor and Renault CV-4?"

"Yes. And I remember that Inspector Stenström gave quite a jump when I told him. All the time I was talking he had just sat there nodding, and I didn't think he was listening. But when I said that he was terribly interested. Asked me about it several times."

"From in front, you said?"

"Yes. He asked that too, several times. From in front or obliquely in front. Very difficult."

When they were sitting in the car again, Asa Torell asked, "What's this all about?"

"I don't quite know yet. But it might mean quite a lot."

"About the man who killed Åke?"

"Don't know. At any rate it explains why he wrote down the name of that car in his book."

"I've also remembered something," she said. "Something Åke said a couple of weeks before he was killed. He said that as soon as he could take two days off he'd go down to Småland and investigate something. To Eksjö, I think. Does that tell you anything?"

"Not a thing," Kollberg replied.

The city lay deserted. The only signs of life were two ambulances, a police car, and a few Santa Clauses staggering about, delayed in the exercise of their profession and handicapped by far too many glasses in far too many hospitable homes. After a while Kollberg said, "Gun told me you're leaving us in the new year."

"Yes. I've exchanged the apartment for a smaller one at Kungsholms Strand. I'm selling the furniture, lock, stock and barrel, and buying new stuff. I'm going to get a new job, too."

"Where?"

"I haven't quite decided. But I've been thinking it over."

She was silent for a few seconds. Then she said, "What about the police force? Are there any vacancies?"

"I'll say there are," Kollberg replied absently.

Then he started and said, "What! Are you serious?"

"Yes," she replied. "I am serious."

Asa Torell concentrated on her driving. She frowned and peered out into the whirling snow.

When they got back to Palandergatan, Bodil had fallen asleep, and Gun was curled up in an armchair reading. There were tears in her eyes.

"What's wrong?" he asked.

"That goddam dinner," she said. "It's ruined."

"Not at all. With your appearance and my appetite you could put a dead cat on the table and make me overjoyed."

"And that hopeless Martin called up. Half an hour ago."

"O.K.," Kollberg said jovially. "I'll give him a buzz while you're getting the grub."

He took off his jacket and tie and went to the phone.

"Hello. Beck."

"Who's doing all that howling?" Kollberg asked suspiciously.

"The laughing policeman."

"What?"

"A phonograph record."

"Oh yes, now I recognize it. An old music hall tune. Charles Penrose, isn't it? Goes back to before the First World War."

A roar of laughter was heard in the background.

"It makes no difference," Martin Beck said joylessly. "I called you because Melander called me."

"What did he want?"

"He said that at last he had remembered where he had seen the name Nils Erik Göransson."

"Where?"

"In the investigation concerning Teresa Camarão."

Kollberg unlaced his shoes. Thought for a moment. Then said, "Then you can tell him from me that he's wrong for once. I've just read the whole pile, every damn word. And I'm not so dumb that I wouldn't have noticed a thing like that."

"Have you the papers at home?"

"No. They're at Västberga. But I'm sure. Dead sure."

"O.K. I believe you. What did you do at Långholmen?"

"Got some information. Too vague and complicated for me to explain now, but if it's right—"

"Yes?"

"Then you can use every single sheet of the Teresa investigation as toilet paper. Merry Christmas."

He put down the phone.

"Are you going out again?" his wife asked suspiciously.

"Yes. But not until Wednesday. Where's the akvavit?"

29

It took a lot to depress Melander, but on the morning of the twenty-seventh he looked so miserable and puzzled that even Gunvald Larsson brought himself to ask, "What's with you?"

"It's just that I don't usually make a mistake."

"There's always a first time," Rönn said consolingly.

"Yes. But I don't understand, all the same."

Martin Beck had knocked on the door and before anyone had time to react he was in the room, standing there tall and grave, coughing slightly.

"What is it you don't understand?"

"About Göransson. That I could make a mistake."

"I've just been out at Västberga," said Martin Beck. "And I know something that might cheer you up."

"What is that?"

"There's a page missing from the Teresa investigation. Page 1244, to be exact."

At three o'clock in the afternoon Kollberg was standing outside an automobile firm in Södertälje. He had already got through a lot this day. For one thing, he had made sure that the three witnesses, who had observed a car at Stadshagen sportsground sixteen and a half years earlier, must have seen the vehicle from in front or possibly from obliquely in front. For another, he had supervised some photographic work, and rolled up in his inside pocket he had a dark-toned, slightly retouched advertising picture of a Morris Minor 1950 model. Of the three witnesses two were dead, the police sergeant and the mechanic. But the real expert, the workshop foreman, was still hale and hearty. And he worked here in Södertälje. He was not a foreman any more but something grander and sat in an office with glass walls, talking on the phone. When the call was finished Kollberg went in to him, without knocking and without in any way saying who he was. He merely laid the photograph on the desk in front of the man and said, "What make of car is this?"

"A Renault CV-4. An old job."

"Are you sure?"

"Bet your life, I'm sure. I'm never wrong."

"Positive?"

The man glanced again at the picture.

"Yes," he said. "It's a CV-4. Old model."

"Thanks," Kollberg said, reaching for the photograph.

The man gave him a puzzled look and said, "Wait a sec. Are you trying to trick me?"

He examined the picture thoroughly. After a good fifteen seconds he said slowly, "No. This isn't a Renault. It's a Morris. A Morris Minor model '50 or '51. And there's something wrong with the picture."

"Yes," Kollberg said. "It has been touched up and made to look as if it were taken in a bad light and in the rain, for instance on a summer evening."

The man stared at him.

"Look here, who are you anyway?"

"Police," Kollberg replied.

"I might have known it," the man said. "There was a policeman here early last fall who . . ."

Shortly before five thirty the same afternoon Martin Beck had assembled his immediate colleagues for a briefing at investigation headquarters. Nordin and Månsson had returned from Christmas leave, and the force was complete. The only one missing was Hammar, who had gone away for the vacation. He knew how little had happened during forty-four intensive days of investigation and thought it unlikely that there would be any new development between Christmas and New Year's, a time when both hunters and hunted mostly sit at home belching and wondering how to make ends meet until January.

"Oh, so a page was missing," Melander said with satisfaction. "Who can have taken it?"

Martin Beck and Kollberg exchanged a quick glance.

"Does anyone consider himself a specialist in house-searching?" Martin Beck asked.

"I'm good at searching," Månsson said listlessly from his seat over by the window. "If there's anything to be found, I'll find it."

"Good," Martin Beck said. "I want you to comb through Åke Stenström's apartment on Tjärhovsgatan."

"What shall I look for?"

"A page out of a police report," Kollberg said. "It should be numbered 1244 and it's possible that the name Nils Erik Göransson occurs in the text."

"Tomorrow," Månsson said. "It's always easier in daylight."

"O.K., that's fine," Martin Beck said.

"I'll give you the keys in the morning," Kollberg informed him.

He already had them in his pocket but wanted to remove one or two traces of Stenström's photography before Månsson set to work.

At two o'clock the next afternoon the phone on Martin Beck's desk rang.

"Greetings. It's Per."

"Per who?"

"Månsson."

"Oh, it's you. Well?"

"I'm in Stenström's apartment. The sheet of paper isn't here."

"Are you sure?"

"Sure?"

Månsson sounded deeply offended.

"Of course, I'm goddam sure. But are *you* sure he's the one who took that page?"

"We think so, anyway."

"Oh well, I'd better go on looking somewhere else."

Martin Beck massaged his scalp.

"What do you mean by somewhere else?" he asked.

But Månsson had already put the phone down.

"There must be a copy in the central files, for Christ's sake," Gunvald Larsson growled.

"Yes," Martin Beck said, pressing a button on the telephone and dialing an inter-office number.

In the room next door, Kollberg and Melander were discussing the situation.

"I've been looking through your list."

"Did you find anything?"

"Yes, a lot. But I don't know whether it's of any use."

"I'll soon tell you."

"Several of those guys are recidivists. For example, Karl Andersson, Vilhelm Rosberg and Bengt Wahlberg. Thieves all three. Sentenced dozens of times. They're too old to work now."

"Go on."

"Johan Gran was a fence then and no doubt still is. That waiter business is sheer bluff. He did time only a year ago. And this Valter Eriksson—do you know how he became a widower?"

"No."

"He killed his wife with a kitchen chair during a drunken brawl. Was convicted of manslaughter and got five years."

"Well, I'll be damned."

"There are other troublemakers besides him in this collection. Both Ove Eriksson and Bengt Fredriksson have been sentenced for assault and battery. Fredriksson no less than six times. A couple of the charges should have been for attempted manslaughter, if you ask me. And the junk dealer, Jan Carlsson, is a shady figure. He has never been caught, but it was a close shave a couple of times. I remember Björn Forsberg, too. He was up to quite a few crooked dealings at one time and was fairly well known in the underworld in the last half of the forties. Then he turned over a new leaf and made a nice career for himself. Married a wealthy woman and became a respected businessman. He has only one old sentence for swindling from 1947. Hans Wennström also has a first-rate list of crimes, everything from shoplifting to safecracking. Boy, what a title."

"Former assistant fishmonger," Kollberg said, looking at the list.

"I think he had a stall in the marketplace at Sundby-berg twenty-five years ago. Well, he's another one of the real old-timers. Ingvar Bengtsson calls himself a journalist nowadays. He was one of the pioneers in check forging. He was a pimp too, come to that. Bo Frostensson is a third-rate actor and a notorious junkie."

"Didn't this girl ever take it into her head to sleep with any decent guys?" Kollberg said plaintively.

"Oh yes, sure. You have several on this list. For example, Rune Bengtsson, Lennart Lindgren, Kurt Olsson and Ragnar Viklund. Upper class, the whole bunch. Not a shadow on them."

Kollberg had a good grasp of the investigation.

"No," he said. "They were married too, all four of them. Had a hell of a time, I expect, explaining this to their wives."

"On that point the police were pretty discreet. When it comes to these youngsters, who were about twenty or even younger, there was nothing much wrong with them. Out of six of that age on your list there's only one, actually, that hasn't made the grade. Kenneth Karlsson, he's been picked up once or twice. Reform school and so on. Though that's some time ago and nothing very serious. Do you want me to start rooting seriously in these people's past?"

"Yes, please. You can weed out the old 'uns, for instance those who are over sixty now. Likewise the youngest, from thirty-eight downward."

"That makes eight plus seven. Fifteen. That leaves fourteen. The field is shrinking."

"What field?"

"Hm," said Melander. "All these men, of course, have an alibi for the Teresa murder."

"Bet your goddam life they have," Kollberg said. "At least for the time when the body was placed at Stadshagen."

The search for copies of the report of the Teresa investigation had been started on December 28, but New Year's Eve and 1968 arrived before it showed any result.

Not until the morning of January 5 was there a dusty pile of papers lying on Martin Beck's desk. He didn't need to be a detective to see that it had come from the

innermost recesses of the files and that several years had
passed since it had last been opened by human hand.

Martin Beck turned over quickly until he came to page
1244. The text was brief. Kollberg leaned over his
shoulder and they read:

*Interrogation of salesman Nils Erik Göransson,
August 7, 1951.*

*Regarding himself, Göransson states that he was
born in the Finnish parish in Stockholm on Oct. 4,
1939, son of electrician Algot Erik Göransson and
Benita Göransson, née Rantanen. He is at present
employed as salesman by the firm of Allimport, Holländaregatan 10, Stockholm.*

*Göransson owns to having known Teresa Camarão,
who periodically moved in the same circles as he did,
though not during the months immediately prior to
her death. Göransson owns further that on two occasions he had intimate sexual relations (intercourse)
with Teresa Camarão. On the first occasion in an
apartment in Svartmansgatan here in town, when several other persons were also present. Of these he says
he remembers only one Karl Åke Birger Svensson-
Rask. On the second occasion the meeting took place
in a cellar at Holländaregatan here in town. On this
occasion too Svensson-Rask was present and he also
had intimate sex relations (intercourse) with Mrs.
Camarão. Göransson says he does not remember the
exact dates but thinks the events must have taken
place at an interval of several days at the end
of November and/or beginning of December the
previous year, i.e. 1950. Göransson says he knows
nothing of Mrs. Camarão's acquaintances otherwise.*

*From June 2–13 Göransson was in Eksjö, to which
he drove in an automobile with registration number
A 6310 for the purpose of the sale of clothes for the
firm where he is employed. Göransson is the owner
of automobile A 6310, a 1949 model Morris Minor.
This statement read out and approved.*

                                        (Signed)

*It can be added that the abovementioned Karl Åke
Birger Svensson-Rask is identical with the man who
first informed the police that Göransson had had*

intimate sexual relations (intercourse) with Mrs. Camarão. Göransson's account of his visit to Eksjö is confirmed by the staff of the City Hotel at that place. Questioned in detail about Göransson's movements on the evening of June 10, Sverker Johnsson, waiter at the said hotel, states that Göransson sat the whole evening in the hotel dining room, until this was closed at 11:30 P.M. Göransson was then the worse for liquor. Sverker Johnsson's statements should be credited, the more so as they are confirmed by items on Göransson's hotel bill.

"Well, that's that," Kollberg said. "So far."

"What are you going to do now?"

"What Stenström didn't have time for. Go down to Eksjö."

"The pieces of the puzzle are beginning to fit together," Martin Beck said.

"Yes," Kollberg agreed. "By the way, where's Månsson?"

"At Hallstahammar, I think, looking for that piece of paper. At Stenström's mother's place."

"He's not one to give up easily," Kollberg said. "Pity. I was going to borrow his car. Mine has something wrong with the ignition."

Kollberg arrived in Eksjö on the morning of January 8. He had driven down during the night, 208 miles in a snowstorm and on icy roads, but did not feel particularly tired even so. The City Hotel was in the main square and was a handsome, old-fashioned building which blended perfectly into the idyllic setting of this little Swedish country town. The waiter called Sverker Johnsson had died ten years ago, but a copy of Nils Erik Göransson's hotel bill still existed. It took several hours to fish it out of a dusty cardboard box in the loft.

The bill seemed to confirm that Göransson had stayed at the hotel for eleven days. He had had all his meals and done all his drinking in the hotel dining room, and signed the bills, after which the amounts had been transferred to his hotel bill. There were also a number of other expenses, including telephone calls, but the numbers Göransson had called up were not recorded. Another item, however, caught Kollberg's eye.

On June 6, 1951, the hotel had paid out 52 kronor and 25 öre to a garage on the guest's behalf. The amount was for "towing and repairs."

"Does this garage still exist?" Kollberg asked the hotel owner.

"Oh, sure it does, and the same owner the last twenty-five years. Just follow the road out toward Långanäs and . . ."

Actually the man had had the garage for twenty-seven years. He stared incredulously at Kollberg and said, "Sixteen and a half years ago? How the hell can I remember that?"

"Don't you keep books?"

"You bet I do," the man said indignantly. "This is a properly run place."

It took him an hour and a half to find the old ledger. He wouldn't let it out of his hands but turned the pages slowly and carefully until he came to the day in question.

"The sixth of June," he murmured. "Here it is. Picked up from hotel, that's right. The throttle cable had gone haywire. It cost 52:25, the whole business. With towing and all."

Kollberg waited.

"Towing," muttered the man. "What an idiot. Why didn't he hook up the throttle cable with something and drive here himself?"

"Have you any particulars about the car?" Kollberg asked.

"Yes. Registration number A . . . A . . . something. I can't read it. Someone's put an oily thumb over the figures. Evidently a Stockholmer, anyway."

"You don't know what sort of car it was?"

"Sure I do. A Ford Vedette."

"Not a Morris Minor?"

"If it says Ford Vedette here, then a Ford Vedette it damn well was," the garage owner said testily. "Morris Minor? There's a slight difference, isn't there."

Kollberg took the ledger with him, after a good half

hour's threats and persuasions. When finally he was on his way, the workshop owner said, "Well, anyway, that explains why he wasted money on towing."

"Really. Why?"

"He was a Stockholmer, wasn't he?"

When Kollberg got back to the City Hotel in Eksjö it was already evening. He was hungry, cold and tired, and instead of starting the long drive north he took a room at the hotel. Had a bath and ordered dinner. While he was waiting for the food to be prepared he made two phone calls. First to Melander.

"Will you please find out which of the guys on the list had a car in June, 1951? And what makes?"

"Sure. Tomorrow morning."

"And the color of Göransson's Morris?"

"Yes."

Then Martin Beck.

"Göransson didn't bring his Morris here. He was driving another car."

"So Stenström was right."

"Can you put someone on to finding out who owned that firm in Holländaregatan where Göransson was employed, and what it did?"

"Sure."

"I should be back in town about midday tomorrow."

He went down into the dining room and had dinner. As he sat there it suddenly dawned on him that he had in fact stayed at this hotel exactly sixteen years ago. He had been working on a taxi murder. They had cleared it up in three or four days. If he had known then what he knew now he could probably have solved the Teresa case in ten minutes.

Rönn was thinking about Olsson and about the restaurant bill he had found among the rubbish in Göransson's paper shopping bag. On Tuesday morning he got an idea and as usual when something was weighing on his mind he went to Gunvald Larsson. Despite the far from cordial attitude they adopted toward each other at work, Rönn and Gunvald Larsson were friends. Very few outsiders knew this, and they would have been even more surprised had they known that the two had in fact spent both Christmas and New Year's Eve together.

"I've been thinking about the bit of paper with the initials B.F.," Rönn said. "On that list that Melander and Kollberg are messing about with are three persons with those initials. Bo Frostensson, Bengt Fredriksson and Björn Forsberg."

"Well?"

"We could take a cautious look at them and see if any of them resembles Olsson."

"Can you track them down?"

"I expect Melander can."

Melander could. It took him only twenty minutes to find out that Forsberg was at home and would be at his office downtown after lunch. At twelve o'clock he was to have lunch with a client at the Ambassadör. Frostensson was in a film studio out at Solna, playing a small part in a film by Arne Mattsson.

"And Fredriksson is presumably drinking beer at the Café Ten Spot. He's usually to be found there at this hour of day."

"I'll come with you," Martin Beck said surprisingly. "We'll take Månsson's car. I've given him one of ours instead."

Sure enough Bengt Fredriksson, artist and brawler, was hard at it drinking beer in the beer hall in the Old Town. He was very fat, had a bushy, unkempt red beard and lank gray hair. He was already drunk.

Out at Solna the production manager piloted them through long, winding corridors to a corner of the big film studio.

"Frostensson is to play a scene in five minutes," he said. "It's the only line he has in the film."

They stood at a safe distance but in the mercilessly strong spotlights they clearly saw the set behind a jumble of cables and shifted scenery. It was evidently meant to be the interior of a little grocery store.

"Stand by!" the director shouted. "Silence! Camera! Action!"

A man in a white cap and coat came into the stream of light and said, "Good morning, madam. May I help you?"

"Cut!"

There was a retake, and another. Frostensson had to say the line five times. He was a lean, bald little man with a stammer and a nervous twitch around his mouth and the corners of his eyes.

Half an hour later Gunvald Larsson braked the car twenty-five yards from the gates of Björn Forsberg's house at Stocksund. Martin Beck and Rönn crouched in the back. Through the open garage doors they could see a black Mercedes of the largest type.

"He should be leaving now," Gunvald Larsson said. "If he doesn't want to be late for his lunch appointment."

They had to wait fifteen minutes before the front door opened and a man appeared on the steps together with a blonde woman, a dog and a little girl of about seven. He kissed the woman on the cheek, lifted the child up and kissed her. Then he strode down to the garage, got into the car and drove off. The little girl blew him a kiss, laughed and shouted something.

Björn Forsberg was tall and slim. His face, with regular features and candid expression, was strikingly handsome, as though drawn from the illustration for a short story in a woman's magazine. He was suntanned and his bearing was relaxed and sporty. He was bareheaded and was wearing a loose-fitting, gray overcoat. His hair was wavy and brushed back. He looked younger than his forty-eight years.

"Like Olsson," Rönn said. "Especially his build and clothes. The overcoat, that is."

"Hm," Gunvald Larsson murmured. "The difference being that Olsson paid 300 kronor for his coat at a sale three years ago. This guy has probably shelled out 5,000 for his. But someone like Schwerin wouldn't notice that."

"Nor would I, to tell the truth," Rönn said.

"But I notice it," Gunvald Larsson said. "Luckily there are people who have an eye for quality. Otherwise they might as well build whorehouses all along Savile Row."

"Where?" Rönn asked in astonishment.

Kollberg's schedule broke down completely. Not only did he oversleep, but the weather was worse than ever. By one thirty he had still only got as far as a motel just north of Linköping. He had a cup of coffee and called up Stockholm.

"Well?"

"Only nine of them had a car in the summer of '51," Melander replied. "Ingvar Bengtsson a new Volkswagen, Rune Bengtsson a '49 Packard, Kent Carlsson a '38 DKW, Ove Eriksson an old Opel Kapitän, prewar model, Björn Forsberg a '49 Ford Vedette and—"

"Stop. Did anyone else have one?"

"A Vedette? No."

"Then that'll do."

"The original paintwork on Göransson's Morris was pale green. The car can of course have been repainted while he had it."

"Fine. Can you switch me over to Martin?"

"One more detail. Göransson sent his car to the scrapyard in the summer of '51. It was removed from the car registry on August 15, only one week after Göransson had been questioned by the police."

Kollberg put another krona piece into the phone and thought impatiently of the 127 miles still ahead of him. In this weather the drive would take several hours. He regretted not having sent the ledger up by train the evening before.

"Hello, this is Superintendent Beck."

"Hi. What did that firm do?"

"Sold stolen goods, I should think. But it could never be proved. They had a couple of traveling salesmen who went around the provinces peddling clothes and the like."

"And who owned it?"

"Björn Forsberg."

Kollberg thought for a moment, and then said, "Tell Melander to concentrate entirely on Forsberg. And ask Hjelm if either he himself or someone else will stay at the lab until I get up to town. I've something that must be analyzed."

At five o'clock Kollberg had still not returned. Melander tapped at Martin Beck's door and went in, pipe in one hand and some papers in the other. He began speaking at once.

"Björn Forsberg was married on June 17, 1951, to a woman called Elsa Beatrice Håkansson. She was the only child of a businessman called Magnus Håkansson. He dealt in building materials and was the sole owner of his firm. He was considered very wealthy. Forsberg immediately wound up all his former commitments like the firm on Holländaregatan. He worked hard, studied economics and developed into an energetic businessman. When Håkansson died nine years ago his daughter inherited both his fortune and his firm, but Forsberg had already become its managing director in the middle of the fifties. He bought the house at Stocksund in '59. It probably cost about half a million then."

Martin Beck blew his nose.

"How long had he known the girl before he married her?"

"They seem to have met up at Åre in March, '51," Melander replied. "Forsberg was a winter sports enthusiast. Still is, for that matter. His wife too. It seems to have been so-called love at first sight. They kept on meeting right up to the wedding, and he was a frequent guest in her parents' home. He was then thirty-two and Elsa Håkansson, twenty-five."

Melander changed papers.

"The marriage seems to have been a happy one. They have three children, two boys who are thirteen and twelve and a girl of seven. He sold his Ford Vedette soon after the wedding and bought a Lincoln. He's had dozens of cars since then."

Melander was silent and lighted his pipe.

"Is this what you have found out?"

"One more thing. Important, I should think. Björn Forsberg was a volunteer in the Finnish Winter War in 1940. He was twenty-one and went off to the front straight after he'd done his military service here at home. His father was a warrant officer in the Wende artillery regiment in Kristianstad. He came from a respectable, middle-class family and was considered promising until things started to go wrong for him soon after the war."

"O.K., it seems to be him."

"Looks like it," Melander said.

"Which men are still here?"

"Gunvald, Rönn, Nordin and Ek. Shall we look at his alibis?"

"Exactly," Martin Beck said.

Kollberg didn't reach Stockholm until seven o'clock. He drove first to the laboratory and handed in the garage ledger.

"We have regular working hours," Hjelm said sourly. "Finish at five."

"Then it would be awfully good of you to—"

"O.K., O.K. I'll call you before long. Is it only the car number you want?"

"Yes. I'll be at Kungsholmsgatan."

Kollberg and Martin Beck hardly had time to begin talking when the call came through.

"A 6708," Hjelm said laconically.

"Excellent."

"Easy. You should almost have been able to see it yourself."

Kollberg put down the phone. Martin Beck gave him an inquiring look.

"Yes. It was Forsberg's car that Göransson used at Eksjö. No doubt of that. What are Forsberg's alibis like?"

"Weak. In June, '51, he had a bachelor apartment on Holländaregatan, in the same building as that mysterious firm. At the interrogation he said that he had been in Norrtälje on the evening of the tenth. Evidently he had been, too. Met some person there at seven o'clock. Then, still according to his own statement, he took the last train back to Stockholm, arriving at eleven thirty in the evening. He also said that he had lent his car to one of his salesmen, who confirmed this."

"But he was goddam careful not to say that he had exchanged cars with Göransson."

"Yes," Martin Beck said. "So he had Göransson's Morris, and this puts a different complexion on things. He made his way comfortably back to Stockholm by car in an hour and a half. The cars were parked in the rear courtyard at Holländaregatan, and no one could see in from the street. There was, however, a cold-storage room in the yard. It was used for fur coats, which officially had been left for storage over the summer but which in all probability were stolen. Why do you think they exchanged cars?"

"I expect the explanation is very simple," Kollberg said. "Göransson was a salesman and had a lot of clothes and junk with him. He could pack three times as much into Forsberg's Vedette as into his own Morris."

He sat in silence for half a minute, then said, "I don't suppose Göransson was aware of it until afterward. When he got back he realized what had happened and that the car might be dangerous. That's why he had it scrapped immediately after the interrogation."

"What did Forsberg say about his relations with Teresa?" Martin Beck asked.

"That he met her at a dance hall in the fall of 1950 and slept with her several times, how often he didn't remember. Then he met his future wife in the winter and lost interest in nymphomaniacs."

"Did he say that?"

"More or less in those words. Why do you think he killed her? To get rid of the victim, as Stenström wrote in the margin of Wendel's book?"

"Presumably. They all said they couldn't shake her off. And of course it wasn't a sex murder."

"No, but he wanted it to look like one. And then he had the unbelievable stroke of luck that the witnesses got the cars mixed up. He must have been tickled pink. That meant he could feel pretty well safe. Göransson was the only worry."

"Göransson and Forsberg were pals," Martin Beck said.

"And then nothing happened until Stenström started rooting in the Teresa case and got that strange tip from Birgersson. He found out that Göransson was the only one who had had a Morris Minor. The right color, what's more. He questioned a lot of people of his own accord and started shadowing Göransson. He soon noticed, of course, that Göransson was getting money from someone and assumed that it came from whoever had murdered

Teresa Camarão. Göransson got more and more jittery . . . By the way, do we know where he was between October 8 and November 13?"

"Yes. In a boat down at Klara Strand. Nordin found the spot this morning."

Kollberg nodded.

"Stenström figured out that sooner or later Göransson would lead him to the murderer, and so he went on shadowing him day after day, and presumably quite openly. It turned out that he was right. Though the result for his own part was not a success. If he had hurried up with that trip to Småland instead . . ."

Kollberg was silent. Martin Beck thoughtfully rubbed the root of his nose between thumb and forefinger of his right hand.

"Yes, it seems to fit," he said. "Psychologically as well. There were still nine years before the Teresa murder would have lapsed and the period of prosecution expired. And a murder is the only crime which is sufficiently grave for a more or less normal person to go to such lengths in order to avoid discovery. Besides, Forsberg has unusually much to lose."

"Do we know what he did on the evening of November 13?"

"Yes. He butchered all those people in the bus, including Stenström and Göransson, both of whom were extremely dangerous for him by this time. But the only thing we know at present is that he had an opportunity of committing the murders."

"How do we know that?"

"Gunvald managed to kidnap Forsberg's German maid. She has the evening off every Monday. And according to a pocket diary she had in her handbag, she spent the night with her boyfriend between the thirteenth and fourteenth. We also know, still from the same source, that Mrs. Forsberg was out at a ladies' dinner that evening. Consequently, Forsberg himself was presumed to be at home. On principle, they never leave the children alone."

"Where is she now? The maid?"

"Here. And we're keeping her overnight."

"What do you think about his mental condition?" Kollberg asked.

"Probably very bad. On the verge of collapse."

"The question is, do we have enough evidence to take him in?" Kollberg said.

"Not for the bus," Martin Beck replied. "That would be a blunder. But we can arrest him as a suspect for the murder of Teresa Camarão. We have a key witness, whose opinion has changed, and a number of new facts."

"When?"

"Tomorrow morning."

"Where?"

"At his office. The minute he arrives. No need to drag his wife and children into it, especially if he's desperate."

"How?"

"As quietly as possible. No shooting and no kicked-in doors."

Kollberg thought for a moment before asking his last question.

"Who?"

"Myself and Melander."

30

The blonde at the switchboard behind the marble counter put down her nail file when Martin Beck and Melander entered the reception room.

Björn Forsberg's office was on the sixth floor of a building on Kungsgatan near Stureplan. The fourth and fifth floors were also occupied by the firm.

The time was only five minutes past nine and they knew that Forsberg did not usually come until about nine thirty.

"But his secretary will be here soon," the girl at the switchboard said. "If you care to sit down and wait."

On the other side of the room, out of sight of the receptionist, some armchairs were grouped around a low glass table. The two men hung up their overcoats and sat down.

The six doors leading out of the reception room had no name plates. One of them was ajar.

Martin Beck got up, peeped in the door and vanished inside the room. Melander took out his pipe and tobacco pouch, filled his pipe and struck a match. Martin Beck came back and sat down.

They sat in silence, waiting. Now and then the telephone operator's voice was heard, and the buzz from the switchboard as she put the calls through. Otherwise the only sound was the faint noise of the traffic. Martin Beck turned the pages of a year-old number of *Industria,* Melander leaned back with the pipe in his mouth and his eyes half-closed.

At twenty past nine the outer door was pulled open and a woman came in. She was dressed in a fur coat and high leather boots and had a large handbag over her arm.

She nodded to the girl at the switchboard and walked quickly toward the half-open door. Without slowing her steps she cast an expressionless glance at the men in the armchairs. Then she banged the door behind her.

After another twenty minutes Forsberg arrived.

He was dressed in the same way as the day before and his movements were brisk and energetic. He was just about to hang up his overcoat when he caught sight of Martin Beck and Melander. He checked himself in the middle of the movement, for a fraction of a second. Recovered himself quickly, hung the coat on a hanger and went toward them.

Martin Beck and Melander stood up together. Björn Forsberg raised his eyebrows questioningly. He opened his mouth to say something, and Martin Beck put out his hand and said, "Superintendent Beck. This is Detective Inspector Melander. We'd like a word with you."

Björn Forsberg shook hands with them.

"Why, certainly," he said. "Please come in."

The man appeared quite calm and almost gay as he held open the door for them. He nodded to his secretary and said, "Good morning, Miss Sköld. I'll see you later. I'll be engaged with these gentlemen for a little while."

He preceded them into his office, which was large and light and tastefully furnished. The floor was covered from wall to wall with a deep-pile gray-blue carpet, and the big desk was shining and empty. Two telephones, a dictaphone and an intercom stood on a small table beside the swivel chair covered in black leather. On the wide windowsill stood four photographs in pewter frames. His wife and three children. On the wall between the windows hung a portrait in oils, presumably of his father-in-law. The room also contained a cocktail cabinet, a conference table with water carafe and glasses on a tray, a sofa and two easy-chairs, some books and china figures in a case with sliding glass doors, and a safe discreetly set into the wall.

All this Martin Beck saw as he closed the door behind him and as Björn Forsberg walked toward his desk with deliberate steps.

Laying his left hand on the top of the desk, Forsberg leaned forward, pulled out the drawer on the right and put his hand into it. When his hand reappeared, the fingers were closed around the butt of a pistol.

Still supporting himself against the desk with his left hand, he raised the barrel of the pistol toward his open mouth, pushed it in as far as he could, closed his lips round the shiny, blue-back steel and pulled the trigger. He looked steadily at Martin Beck the whole time. His eyes were still almost cheery.

All this happened so quickly that Martin Beck and Melander were only halfway across the room when Björn Forsberg collapsed sprawling over the desk.

The pistol had been cocked and a sharp click had been heard as the hammer fell against the chamber. But the bullet that was to have rotated through the bore, shattered the roof of Björn Forsberg's mouth and flung most of his brains out through the back of his head, never left the barrel. It was still in its brass casing inside the cartridge that lay in Martin Beck's right pants pocket, together with the other five that had been in the magazine.

Martin Beck took out one of the cartridges, rolled it between his fingers and read the text punched around the copper envelope of the percussion cap: METALLVERKEN 38 SPL. The cartridge was Swedish but the pistol,

American, a Smith and Wesson 38 Special, made in Springfield, Massachusetts.

Björn Forsberg lay with his face pressed against the smooth desktop. His body was shaking. After a few seconds he slipped to the floor and began to scream.

"We'd better call an ambulance," Melander said.

So Rönn was sitting once more with his tape recorder in an isolation ward at Karolinska Hospital. This time not in the surgical department but at the mental clinic, and in his company he had Gunvald Larsson instead of the detested Ullholm.

Björn Forsberg had been given various treatments with tranquilizing injections and a lot of other things, and the doctor concerned with his mental recovery had already been in the room for several hours. But the only thing the patient seemed able to say was, "Why didn't you let me die?"

He had repeated this over and over again and now he said it once more, "Why didn't you let me die?"

"Yes, why didn't we?" Gunvald Larsson mumbled, and the doctor gave him a stern look.

They would not have been here at all if the doctors had not said that there was a certain risk that Forsberg really would die. They had explained that he had been subjected to a shock of enormous intensity, that his heart was weak and his nerves had gone to pieces; they rounded off the diagnosis by saying that his general condition was not so bad. Except that a heart attack might make an end of him at any moment.

Rönn pondered over this remark about his general condition.

"Why didn't you let me die?" Forsberg repeated.

"Why didn't you let Teresa Camarão live?" Gunvald Larsson retorted.

"Because I couldn't. I had to get rid of her."

"Oh," Rönn said patiently. "Why did you have to?"

"I had no choice. She would have ruined my life."

"It seems to be pretty well ruined in any case," Gunvald Larsson said.

The doctor gave him another stern look.

"You don't understand," Forsberg complained. "I had told her never to come back. I'd even given her money though I was badly off. And still—"

"What are you trying to say?" Rönn said kindly.

"Still she pursued me. When I got home that evening she was lying in my bed. Naked. She knew where I used to keep my spare key and had let herself in. And my wife . . . my fiancée was coming in fifteen minutes. There was no other way."

"And then?"

"I carried her down into the cold-storage room where the furs were."

"Weren't you afraid that someone might find her there?"

"There were only two keys to it. I had one and Nisse Göransson the other. And Nisse was away."

"How long did you let her lie there?" Rönn asked.

"For five days. I wanted to wait for rain."

"Yes, you like rain," Gunvald Larsson put in.

"Don't you understand? She was crazy. In one minute she could have ruined my whole life. Everything I had planned."

Rönn nodded to himself. This was going well.

"Where did you get the submachine gun from?" Gunvald Larsson asked out of the blue.

"I brought it home from the war."

Forsberg lay silent for a moment. Then he added proudly, "I killed three bolsheviks with it."

"Was it Swedish?" Gunvald Larsson asked.

"No, Finnish. Suomi model 37."

"And where is it now?"

"Where no one will ever find it."

"In the water?"

Forsberg nodded. Seemed to be deep in thought.

"Did you like Nils Erik Göransson?" Rönn asked after a while.

"Nisse was fine. A good kid. I was like a father to him."

"Yet you killed him?"

"He was threatening my existence. My family. Everything I live for. Everything I had to live for. He couldn't help it. But I gave him a quick and painless end. I didn't torment him as you're tormenting me."

"Did Nisse know that it was you who murdered Teresa?" Rönn asked. He spoke quietly and kindly the whole time.

"He figured it out," Forsberg replied. "Nisse wasn't stupid. And he was a good pal. I gave him 10,000 kronor and a new car after I was married. Then we parted for ever."

"For ever?"

"Yes. I never heard from him again, not until last fall. He called up and said that someone was shadowing him day and night. He was scared and he needed money. I gave him money. I tried to get him to go abroad."

"But he didn't?"

"No. He was too down. And scared stiff. Thought it would look suspicious."

"And so you killed him?"

"I had to. The situation gave me no choice. Otherwise he would have ruined my existence. My children's future. My business. Everything. Not deliberately, but he was weak and unreliable and scared. I knew that sooner or later he would come to me for protection. And thereby ruin me. Or else the police would get him and force him to talk. He was a drug addict, weak and unreliable. The police would torture him till he told everything he knew."

"The police are not in the habit of torturing people," Rönn said gently.

For the first time, Forsberg turned his head. His wrists and ankles were strapped down. He looked at Rönn and said, "What do you call this?"

Rönn dropped his eyes.

"Where did you board the bus?" Gunvald Larsson asked.

"On Klarabergsgatan. Outside Åhléns."

"How did you get there?"

"By car. I parked at my office. I have a special place there."

"How did you know which bus Göransson would take?"

"He called up and was given instructions."

"In other words, you told him what he was to do in order to be murdered," Gunvald Larsson said.

"Don't you understand that he gave me no choice? Anyway, I did it humanely, he never knew a thing."

"Humanely? How do you make that out?"

"Can't you leave me in peace now?"

"Not just yet. Explain about the bus first."

"Very well. Will you go then? Promise?"

Rönn glanced at Gunvald Larsson, then said, "Yes. We will."

"Nisse called me up at the office on Monday morning. He was desperate and said that that man was following him wherever he went. I realized he couldn't hold out much longer. I knew that my wife and the maid would be out in the evening. And the weather was suitable. And the children always go to sleep early, so I . . ."

"Yes?"

"So I said to Nisse that I wanted to have a look myself at the man who was shadowing him. That he was to entice him out to Djurgården and wait until a double-decker bus came and to take it from there about ten o'clock and ride to the end of the line. Fifteen minutes before he left he was to call my direct number to the office. I left home soon after nine, parked the car, went up to the office and waited. I did not put the light on. He called up as agreed and I went down and waited for the bus."

"Had you decided on the place beforehand?"

"I picked it out earlier in the day when I rode the whole way on the bus. It was a good spot—I didn't think there would be anyone in the vicinity, especially if the rain kept up. And I figured out that only very few passengers would go all the way to the last stop. It would have been best if only Nisse and the man who was shadowing him and the driver and one more sat in the bus."

"One more?" Gunvald Larsson remarked. "Who would that be?"

"Anybody. Just for the sake of appearances."

Rönn looked at Gunvald Larsson and shook his head.

216

Then, turning to the man on the stretcher, he said, "How did it feel?"

"Making difficult decisions is always a trial. But when I've once made up my mind to carry something out—"

He broke off.

"Didn't you promise to go now?" he asked.

"What we promise and what we do are two different things," Gunvald Larsson said.

Forsberg looked at him and said bitterly, "All you do is torture me and tell lies."

"I'm not the only one in this room telling lies," Gunvald Larsson retorted. "You had decided to kill Göransson and Inspector Stenström weeks before, hadn't you?"

"Yes."

"How did you know that Stenström was a policeman?"

"I had observed him earlier. Without Nisse's noticing."

"How did you know he was working alone?"

"Because he was never relieved. I took it for granted that he was working on his own account. To make a career for himself."

Gunvald Larsson was silent for half a minute.

"Had you told Göransson not to have any identification papers on him?" he said at last.

"Yes. I gave him orders about that the very first time he called up."

"How did you learn to operate the bus doors?"

"I had watched carefully what the drivers did. Even so, there was nearly a hitch. It was the wrong sort of bus."

"Whereabouts in the bus did you sit? Upstairs or down below?"

"Upstairs. I was soon the only one there "

"And then you went down the stairs with the submachine gun at the ready?"

"Yes. I kept it behind my back so that Nisse and the others sitting at the rear wouldn't see it. Even so, one of them managed to stand up. You have to be prepared for things like that."

"Supposing it had jammed? In my day those old things often misfired."

"I knew it was in working order. I was familiar with

my weapon and I had checked it carefully before taking it to the office."

"When did you take the submachine gun to the office?"

"About a week beforehand."

"Weren't you afraid that someone might find it there?"

"No one would dare go to my drawers," Forsberg said haughtily. "Besides, I had locked it up."

"Where did you keep it previously?"

"In a locked suitcase in the attic. Together with my other trophies."

"Which way did you go after you had killed all those people?"

"I walked eastward along Norra Stationsgatan, took a taxi at Haga air terminal, fetched my car outside the office and drove home to Stocksund."

"And chucked the submachine gun away en route," Gunvald Larsson said. "Don't worry. We'll find it."

Forsberg didn't answer.

"How did it feel?" Rönn repeated gently. "When you fired?"

"I was defending myself and my family and my home and my firm. Have you ever stood with a gun in your hands, knowing that in fifteen seconds you will charge down into a trench full of the enemy?"

"No," Rönn replied. "I haven't."

"Then you don't know anything!" Forsberg shouted. "You've no right to speak! How could an idiot like you understand me!"

"This won't do," the doctor said. "He must be given treatment now."

He pressed the bell. A couple of orderlies came in. Forsberg went on raving as the bed was rolled out of the room.

Rönn started packing up the tape recorder.

"How I loathe that bastard," Gunvald Larsson muttered suddenly.

"What?"

"I'll tell you something I've never said to anyone else," Gunvald Larsson confided. "I feel sorry for nearly everyone we meet in this job. They're just a lot of scum who
218

wish they'd never been born. It's not their fault that everything goes to hell and they don't understand why. It's types like this one who wreck their lives. Smug swine who think only of their money and their houses and their families and their so-called status. Who think they can order others about merely because they happen to be better off. There are thousands of such people and most of them are not so stupid that they strangle Portuguese whores. And that's why we never get at them. We only see their victims. This guy's an exception."

"Hm, maybe you're right," Rönn said.

They left the room. Outside a door farther down the corridor stood two police patrolmen in uniform, legs apart and arms folded.

"Huh, so it's you two," Gunvald Larsson said morosely. "Oh yes, of course, this hospital is in Solna."

"You got him in the end, anyway," Kvant said.

"Yes," Kristiansson chimed in.

"We didn't," Gunvald Larsson said. "It was really Stenström himself who fixed it."

About an hour later Martin Beck and Kollberg sat drinking coffee in one of the rooms at Kungsholmsgatan.

"It was really Stenström who cleared up the Teresa murder," Martin Beck said.

"Yes," Kollberg said. "But he went about it in a silly way all the same. Working on his own like that. And not leaving so much as a piece of paper behind him. Funny, that kid never grew up."

The phone rang. Martin Beck answered.

"Hello, it's Månsson."

"Where are you?"

"I'm out at Västberga at the moment. I've found that sheet of paper."

"Where?"

"On Stenström's desk. Under the blotter."

Martin Beck said nothing.

"I thought you said you'd looked here," Månsson said reproachfully. "And—"

"Yes?"

"He's made a couple of notes on it in pencil. In the

top right-hand corner it says: 'To be replaced in the Teresa file.' And at the bottom of the page he has written a name. Björn Forsberg. And then a question mark. Does that tell us anything?"

Martin Beck made no reply. He just sat there with the receiver in his hand. Then he began to laugh.

About the Authors

PER WAHLÖÖ and MAJ SJÖWALL, his wife and co-author, wrote ten Martin Beck mysteries. Mr. Wahlöö, who died in 1975, was a reporter for several Swedish newspapers and magazines and wrote numerous radio and television plays, film scripts, short stories and novels. Maj Sjöwall is also a poet.